REMOTE CONTROL

The second time Kiondili came to, a robo med-assistant was beside her, watching her with its unblinking eyes. It extended its arm and projected a needle from within its hollow palm. "This will relax you so that you can rest."

"Get that thing away from me." She did not even try to reach out, but the robo froze, its appendage paralyzed as Kiondili unconsciously killed its fields. She waited for it to withdraw its arm. And waited. Becoming frightened, she tapped the robo and felt for its energy pack.

"I couldn't have—I don't have the power to turn a robo off," she whispered. She shuddered and fumbled for the on switch. Her panic rose as she sent the energies surging through the medast's circuits before her fingers actually touched it.

She had turned it on without touching it!

By Tara K. Harper
Published by Ballantine Books:

WOLFWALKER

SHADOW LEADER

LIGHTWING

LIGHTWING

Tara K. Harper

A Del Rey Book

BALLANTINE BOOKS • NEW YORK

A Del Rey Book
Published by Ballantine Books

Copyright © 1992 by Tara K. Harper

All rights reserved under International and Pan-American Copyright Conventions. Published in the United States of America by Ballantine Books, a division of Random House, Inc., New York, and simultaneously in Canada by Random House of Canada Limited, Toronto.

Library of Congress Catalog Card Number: 91-92392

ISBN 0-345-37161-5

Manufactured in the United States of America

First Edition: July 1992

Cover Art by Edwin Herder

To Dr. Ernest V. Curto,
who spoke in his rich brown-toned voice
to the stars in my eyes.
It is like the pillowfight
when he walked me home
the first time.

CHAPTER 1

She was late. Her shift had ended half an hour earlier, but Kiondili was just now getting rid of the last bit of interference in the ship's primary drive field. By now her class at the institute would have started, but until this field was finished, she did not dare leave. The care she took in tuning the drives might make the difference between being called back to work tomorrow and being turned away with a shrug. There were hundreds of people vying for every opening on the space-docks. Kiondili Wae could not afford to jeopardize her position, no matter how temporary it was. For the privilege of paying her rent, she could live with being late to her morning class. If she was lucky, she would not even lose her turn in the lab.

Tuning out the last field interference, she checked her results against the model in the holotank. They were good. Now she could hurry. She hauled herself up from the floor, staggering as her cramped legs refused to hold her weight, then shut the system down quickly. She turned the holotank off. Then she tore the temple jacks from her head, stuffing them in one of her pockets. She was at least ten minutes late. Two more minutes to check out with the ship's controller, one minute to the nearest free-boost chute, two minutes to the lab—she might just make it before the professor took her name off the access list and let someone else into the lab.

She barely waited for the controller to hand her credit chit back before jumping off the ramps and sprinting to a boost chute. Level-three pay . . . For a nonguild sensor, this kind of credit opportunity came along only once a year, and with her credit chit as thin as her regulation jumper, Kiondili had not hesitated to work a double night shift. Her scholarship had barely paid her tuition to the end of the year. Without the few jobs she had found this year, she would not have been able to afford even her meager rent. The first two days on this job had paid the rent for the last month, including the late fine, and the last two days would pay it up for the next six weeks. And she was still set for meals—the ten credits she had earned in the spring for robo servicing had bought enough high-pro C rations to last eight months. The thought of the tasteless wafers brought a humorless smile to her face. They were nourishing, but they left an emptiness in her gut that would not be satisfied with anything less than a real meal from a fully programmed dispenser. Not only had this job paid her rent, but as of this morning it would allow her to buy the first real meal she had had in more than five months.

She dodged a group of humans and human-mutants—or H'Mu, as the Federation classed them—and triggered the proximity light on the boost chute before she arrived. Being a sensor with esper skills had its advantages. Where other sensors had to manipulate fields by using their temple jacks, Kiondili could mentally focus her biofields to activate a small particle field. She could even control the strength of such a field—as long as it was a local adjustment. Now, as she dove toward the edge-lit hole in one of the dock's transport cylinders, she flexed the chute fields briefly. The boost chute's gravity field went to zero; the boost field went to high. She passed the chute opening and shot into free-grav, her black hair streaming out behind her as she hit the first acceleration pad hard. Rolling off her shoulder, she twisted her body into a long, straight line and slammed, hands first, into the re-direction pad at the next intersection. A roll and double thrust with her feet and a small flexing of the boost-chute fields, and she was already near top speed. Luckily, there were few others in the chutes. As fast as she was going, she had to watch the proximity IDs carefully. She could augment the boost-chute fields only so much before the chute guards were alerted. A quick twist, and she was past the two aliens who floated leisurely along in the same direction. An inline tumble, and she hit the next redirection pad just before that other H'Mu—with her esper, she sensed him coming down the opposite tunnel long before his arrival triggered a light on the proximity grid. And then she was shooting up into the exit passage, flashing through the graduated grav field, and slowing abruptly as she stepped out on the corridor floor of the institute. By the time her stomach settled back in place, her hair was smoothed and she could check her lab access. She let her breath out in relief. She was not yet late enough to be kicked off the lists.

As she slipped into the lab, the professor stared coldly at her with one of his three pairs of eyes. He did not stop speaking—that was something, at least. Last time she had been late, he had reprimanded her in front of the entire class. She pulled her flashbook out of her pocket and expanded it, ignoring her lab partner's raised eyebrow. She would have to hurry to catch up with the rest of the students, she thought, slipping one of her wafer meals into her mouth and chewing it mechanically as she jammed her temple jacks on. Her lab partner, noting the circles under her eyes, powered up her holotank for her. At least she got along better with her lab partner than with the other students, she reflected. He was not as status-conscious as the Federation students and, being esper himself, was not envious of her E-level either. She had helped him with his assignments more than once. Now, as she tried to figure out how far behind she was, he silently sent the base program to her on her flashbook.

Surprised, she returned her gratefulness. Even if he was again concentrating on his own holotank, he would pick up that esper message easily.

Imaging through her temple jacks, she created a series of beams in her holotank like the ones on which the other students were working. The projected space in front of her filled with white lines. Automatically, Kiondili separated them into colors, then added the focal lens through which all transmissions had to pass. With her attention split between the assignment and her worries, it took a minute to get the simulated lens in place. Six weeks, she thought. Six weeks and she would no longer be able to stay at the institute. She could not petition for another scholarship—she had already studied for the maximum of six years on Federation funds—and she had no sponsor to help her find permanent work on this world. With her background, she thought with a sudden surge of bitterness, she was not likely to find one. She tightened the beams abruptly. Unless she started blocking her emotions better, they were going to leak through her temple jacks and affect every transmission in this assignment. The fine lines tuned in tighter as she concentrated, but they were still fuzzy compared to the images in the other students' holotanks. At least, with the work she was doing at the spacedock, she understood this beam-tuning assignment better than she would have a week earlier.

The professor rolled his middle pair of eyes toward one student's flashscreen, then up to that student's holotank. "Riun," he said sharply, "you are focusing the transitional beams before they go through the lens. You should be tuning the beams so that the lens does that work for you. Reset your tank and show me the primary and secondary beam trajectories for a ship with a twin hull . . ."

Kiondili's fingers tapped her temple jacks absently. Two of the professor's scaly arms scrawled on the flashscreen. Beside him, the images in the main holotank shifted in response. Kiondili ignored the floating images. Instead, she picked up the answer to his question from his careless projection—the professor rarely remembered to damp his thoughts when he lectured in a lab. Even after two years P-Cryss had not realized that she could pick up his mental images as easily as if he were describing them to her. As far as she knew, he did not suspect her of being higher than an E-4 on the esper scales, and she had tested low on purpose for the last three years. As a scholarship student—and a human-mutant one at that—she was treated with less than respect by all the professors. If nothing else, this one's disdain for her low social status had made his projections stronger and even easier for her to read.

She smiled sardonically. If she had had properly trained reader's skills, P-Cryss would have had to tighten his blocks on all three of his brains—and Kiondili would not have had to jump at double-shift night jobs on the docks. A sensor with reader skills could have almost any job she wanted, on almost any kind of ship. Any job, as long as she was willing to rejoin the Trade Guild to get a faster-than-light work rating. Last month, the guild's offer had included both high-level training and an FTL rating. Even with her grudge, Kiondili had had a hard time turning that one down. But it was rejoin the guild or work temporary positions on graveyard shifts, the kind of work done under conditions that any guild worker would turn his or her nose up at. Ayara alone knew how much Kiondili hated the thought of rejoining the guild.

Traders, she spit in her mind. As the rancor leaked out her temple jacks, the beams in her holotank flared up, and she glared at them for a moment before upping the damp on her persona adjust. Even with the damp, it took a few seconds for the beams to fade back to normal. Traders, she cursed more calmly. Murderers. The guild had blacklisted her parents and then blown them and half their F-class trade ship to dust before bothering to read the ship's log. A mistake, the guild said to the fifteen-year-old girl they had left stranded on Jovani. They were terribly sorry. The apology meant little. Without her parents, without a sponsor on this world, Kiondili Wae had a Federation status little better than that of a slave. The blacklisting had been cleared, but it remained in the logs—and that history had destroyed any chance for her to find a sponsor outside the guild. Even with the education she had now, seven years later, she stood a better chance of solar surfing in deep space than landing a job on an FTL ship.

A Moal, one of those skittish aliens that looked like a bipedal avian, sang its question from the back of the lab, and its clear tones caught at Kiondili's ears. The frequencies reminded her of her transmission work, and she stared down at her flashbook. Doodles. That was all she had entered for the last three days. She scowled, and the professor turned his watery yellow gaze on her. Kiondili, still struggling with the sloppy images in her holotank, accidentally let one of the navigation fields collapse. The beam bounced in the air, its edges no longer sharp. Femtorads, she swore silently. Working that double night shift for the last four days had exhausted her. If she did not start concentrating soon, she would waste this entire lab period. If she had gotten to class on time, she would have had this problem set up properly before she had to focus the beam. Growling, she snapped images and commands through the jacks clinging to her temples. But the generator remained obstinately jammed. The edges of the beam frayed more each second. With a sudden flare, the tiny beam began to disperse. Kiondili ground her teeth. If the professor had not been watching, she could have reset the fields without touching the generator. But the teacher's second set of eyes continued to observe her holotank while he answered the Moal's question. Finally he glanced away. Quickly, Kiondili reached mentally beyond the headset. It took only a second to damp the generator's nearly useless fields until she had control of the beam herself. Now she could manipulate the fields properly. P-Cryss would not even know. She hid a humorless grin. The beam in the holotank, fuzzy and thick at first, sharpened at her directions until a hair-thin light shot like a spear through the floating tank that simulated space.

The professor had moved up beside her as she worked, and now his middle set of eyes rolled, four lids blinking down over each eye in succession. Of his six flexible arms, all but two were wrapped tightly around his body. He regarded her for a long moment. "Interesting recovery, H'Mu Wae."

Kiondili's face became expressionless. The professor moved on to the next holotank, but his words hung in the air behind him. She stared at her beam without seeing it. The formal use of the term *H'Mu* was meant to put her in her place as a human-mutant, she knew. The use of only her last name was the professor's reminder to her that she was not even a full-paying student—not worth the designation of more than one name. At least he had not called her a Mu in front of the others. Coming from P-Cryss, the slang term for mutant was almost always an insult.

Mu. Kiondili rolled the word around her tongue as she stared at her holotank. H'Mu mutant. For nine hundred years H'Mu had been engineering themselves to fit the environs of their colonies. It was cheaper than trying to change an entire planet's biosphere for a few colonists. Among the H'Mu, Kiondili Wae was not unusual. P-Cryss used the term *H'Mu* in that tone only because he knew it irked her.

Engineered mutation had given Kiondili silver-gray skin— and a sensitivity to particle fields that made her a natural for sensor jobs. When she was a child, first learning to use her biofields, she had adjusted only tiny fields, like those of her persona adapt: strengthening the repeller fields when aliens came too close, increasing the range of the persona damp when local, untuned fields irritated her skin and hair. As she sat now in the lab, the short, fine gray hair that covered her body realigned with an uneven shift of the holotank generator. She compensated absently, and the floating curves smoothed out again. With her on-the-job experience, she could use her biofields to set her navigation beams on perfect trajectories, something the other students, working through the cheap beamers the lab supplied, could not do. If she could do this kind of focus with a cheap beamer, she wondered how it would be to work with a fine-tuned beamer on a hyperlight ship?

She glanced toward the back of the class where two strangers, recruiters from one of the Federation outposts, were observing the students silently. She almost wished she did not know why the two were at the lab. The opening they were looking to fill was a research posting, one for an assistant with skills similar to her own. But there were tests to pass before one could qualify for the posting, and the first test alone cost 120 credits. Other students could afford to take this and every other test . . .

Kiondili swallowed her resentment with difficulty. It was a few minutes before she could focus enough to freeze the holotank, log her solution, kill the beams, and begin the next problem. Behind her, she sensed little interest from the recruiters. The smaller stranger was an alien—a feline with the short, speckled hair of a Dyan. The other one, a male, was H'Mu. He was tall and thin, his skin seemed strangely blurred, and his eyes were so black that they seemed to absorb what little light dared flash across them. It was as if his edges were unfocused to hide a different shape—something only a strong esper could do. If his shape was true, Kiondili could not read it. She shrugged mentally. She did not have the training to probe his blocks to see what he really was. Anyway, it did not matter to her. Once the two strangers tested the students they wanted for the outpost opening, they would be gone. And how much chance did Kiondili have to qualify for such a position? Even for a research job, she would have to pay for the screening tests herself. With her current job status of nonguild-temporary, she could hope to save the number of credits she would need in about—five years? Maybe six? They could recruit for a decade, but Kiondili Wae would not be among their prospects.

As if drawn by her unguarded attention, the H'Mu turned his gaze toward her, and she met his eyes with a resentful challenge. Then her eyes widened as she felt him read her as clearly as if she were a flashbook. The distance between them closed dizzyingly—as if he were sucking her consciousness to him—and she wrenched her mental blocks up. Then she sat frozen, unable to keep from shuddering.

That glacial touch—that H'Mu—a Ruvian? And here as a recruiter for the Federation? Most of the students would never get up the nerve to apply for the job if they knew their examiner was a Ruvian, one of those mutants so far removed from the base human stock that even other mutants treated them as alien. Did they need such a high esper for recruitment? Or had the Federation sent him because of his skills as a sensor? Ruvians were three times more sensitive to fields than Kiondili would ever be. Their field-generated mass allowed them to become a part of a system, whereas other H'Mu bodies would interfere. No wonder he seemed out of focus. His mass would be fluctuating with every change in the systems around him. Kiondili could barely sense him within the normal fields even now that she knew what to look for. She forced her gaze away. Every E-sensitive student in the lab must have felt the threat—the fields surging from the H'Mu, the terrifying wrench of his esper power . . .

Her lab partner cleared his throat and tapped his foot twice, contradicting that idea.

Kiondili looked up. Her lab partner tapped his foot more subtly, and this time she did not miss his warning look. Ayara's eyes, Kiondili swore silently. While she had been lost in the Ruvian's probe, the professor had asked another question. Now all four of his eyelids were flipping up on his first set of eyes, a measure of the curious intensity of his gaze. But what had he said? Kiondili stared at the flashscreen. It was filled with new equations—and the main holotank was empty, waiting for new imagery. She racked her brains for some memory of the question he must have asked. More about the tachyon flux? No, that set of equations looked like something out of the recombination family. But the professor was not going to cover that topic till next term.

Defeated, Kiondili met those watery eyes and—

Knew. "Delta-h-squared by ro-n3," she answered confidently. "The imaginary mass acquired during a broaxion recombination at hyperlight speeds."

There was a murmur in the lab, and Kiondili wondered what she had said. It was the answer the professor had expected, she knew. The flash of approval she had caught from him told her that. But her lab partner was staring, too. Suddenly realizing what she had done, Kiondili swore slowly, silently. Her answer had been from the third book in the hyperlight series. She had supposedly read only the first two. The professor had been testing her again, and this time she had fallen for it like a rim miner for an unknown ore. One more slip and P-Cryss was going to figure out how much she picked his brains and how much she actually studied. She used her finger to touch-flip quickly through her flashbook, searching for a reference that would justify her answer.

"I read ahead about recombinations," she said quietly. The search parameters flashed by under her fingers. Sensing the surge of antagonism from the rest of the class, she stiffened. "I stored the information by mistake," she added defensively. "It should be here somewhere."

The professor nodded, folding his tentacled arms into his body until they wrapped neatly around him. One limb snaked out and shuffled flashbooks before him as he chose his assignments. "Sections fifty-one and fifty-two tonight. For assignment, make up a problem dealing with hyperlight transmission theory that can be discussed in your work groups. Class dismissed."

Kiondili collapsed her flashbooks in disgust and put them away in the pouches on her institute jumper. Her lab partner nodded at her and tossed his own lab work down the tubemail chute. She tried not to watch in envy—even tubemail was a

luxury these days. As the other students filtered out, she
slowly made her way with them toward the door until the
professor's voice stopped her. "Kiondili Wae, remain after
class, please."

A stocky man, passing her, threw her a glance. "Old
P-Cryss is on to you now." His whisper grated on her
nerves. "You've been picking lab answers from his head
every day lately."

She gave him an irritated look. "My scores are twice what
yours are, Houghton, even without the lab work."

He jerked his head to indicate the instructor. "I bet he
found out what your real E-rating is. You tested low last time
on purpose. Don't think I don't know."

"I tested below reader level, as usual."

"As usual?" He grinned nastily. "When he finds out
you've been manipulating fields in the lab like most readers
do emotions, your score validity is going to drop like an
asteroid hitting atmosphere."

"Boost it, Houghton," she returned shortly.

"Like you did in the chute race last week?"

She shot him a sharp look.

"You were going over two hundred clicks, according to
the chute guard. Don't even try to tell me you did that without
augmenting the boost fields." He gave her a tight little smile.
"Oh, you might be able to pass that kind of speed off as a
simple sensor's trick to the others, but I know better. You
always win by a few clicks. Never more."

"Maybe I can judge the others' speeds better than
someone who has never raced himself."

He quirked his eyebrow. "And maybe you can read everyone's ratings from the chute guards as they pass the checkpoints. It would be impossible for an E-4, but it would be
no great trick for an esper-6. And you never bet, either," he
added. "Why not, Wae? Would it draw too much attention
to your race pattern? It would make an interesting study for
the guild recruiters, wouldn't it? You don't even sweat now
when you race." He was watching her sharply. "The chute

races are only once every six months, Wae. You might at least make a pretense of checking the list of challengers now and again."

Kiondili glanced significantly at the professor, who was waiting at the front of the class for the rest of the students to leave.

The man who had blocked her way followed her eyes. He grinned again at her impassive face, then sauntered away.

Kicking the man mentally, Kiondili moved slowly toward the front of the lab and waited while the professor cleared the flashboard of his writing. She waited further while he disabled the holotanks in the room. Finally, he let his third set of eyes roll in her direction.

"You are a promising student, Kiondili Wae," P-Cryss said when the room was nearly empty. "But three times now you have been both tardy and inattentive. I cannot condone faulty studies." His rightmost eye batted briefly as if something were stuck in it, and his middle brain pulsed.

"My assignments are correct," she responded automatically. "I know the material."

"Do you?" he asked frankly. "Or do you know *my* material?"

She had trouble meeting his gaze. The alien's eye was still bothering him. All four lids blinked up and down in rapid succession, and she had an urge to grab them and tack them down so they could not fly up under his eyebone and get lost.

"You know more than I teach here, Kiondili Wae. You are also using field skills in the labs that other students cannot duplicate. This has come to my attention more than once. I was at first concerned, but you do not have advanced E-training and so far have tested only E-4 on our esper scales."

One of his tentacles rubbed his head above the flickering right eye. "I suspect that you are quite esper, Kiondili Wae, and have been picking all three of my brains since you came into this class." He waved a tentacle at her to cut off her automatic protest. "I'm not offended, Mu. Rather, I am flattered that you desired to remain in this field of study instead of becoming a guild esper as so many do. Your actual talent in physics is not outstanding," he went on, "but with the ability to absorb the knowledge that you have already shown, you could be an asset to any team of researchers."

Kiondili set her jaw at the use of the term *Mu*. And then the sense of his words sank in. "What are you saying, P-Cryss?"

He regarded her for a moment. "Field manipulation is not a skill that can be denied, Mu. Nor is esper a sense that can be ignored. I do not usually take an interest in students, but, Kiondili Wae, you can no longer hide in my classes. Your skills are in demand in many places, some of which," he added, quickly forestalling her protest, "are not controlled by the Trade Guild." He acknowledged her look. "I am aware of your background. I am also aware that I might be able to further my own field by giving you an opportunity you do not now have." Two tentacles twitched in agitation. He paused, his middle set of eyes blinking down hard. "Like most H'Mu, you dream of defining your future in your own way. Setting a course for the stars, taking a scout posting, or working in a glamorous field of some sort." He absently ran a tentacle over the scale pattern on his head. "Dreams are pleasant things, Mu, but they are hardly practical. Those that become real require a great deal of work. And glamour itself is rarely part of any job." He nodded significantly. "You have talked to guild recruiters before; you know what they offer. However, there are other prospects you should consider." He waved his snakey arm toward the back of the lab, and Kiondili realized that the two recruiters had not left. "I have suggested," P-Cryss continued, "that you test for the research position open on the Corson outpost."

Kiondili stared. Test for the opening? Her heart jumped, then sank. How, by either of Ayara's eyes, was she supposed to do that? As of last night's work on the docks, she had fourteen credits to her name. "I have no credits for the test," she said flatly, trying to keep the bitterness out of her voice.

The instructor brought his two front sets of eyes to bear

on her. "This is a chance to jump beyond the job pool, Kiondili Wae. A chance that will come to you only once. Consider your decision carefully." He abruptly folded most of his arms around his body. The other limbs picked up his flashbook and flashwriters, collapsed them, and tossed them into the tubemail before he left.

Kiondili stared at the blank flashscreen, refusing to turn and face the recruiters. Why had P-Cryss picked on her? He knew she did not have the funds for the test. He even knew that in a few weeks she would no longer be able to stay at the institute. In six weeks she would be in the job pool, fighting for a two-credit chit while the other students talked with the recruiters and casually tested for every posting that came along. Damn him. She clenched her jaw. Hope was a weapon she had not expected him to use against her.

She heard a throat being cleared behind her, and, her hands clenched like her jaw, she turned slowly to face the two recruiters. The feline gestured for her to join them.

Kiondili approached reluctantly.

"Kiondili Wae." The soft voice of the alien grated against Kiondili's ear.

Kiondili felt strangely naked. She acknowledged the two politely, then regarded them with an intensity that startled even herself as her fingers dug into the back of a Soft in which no one was sitting. The fabric scratched her skin, and, impatiently, her attention still on the alien and the Ruvian, she reset the Soft to dissolve the reptilian scale pattern and style itself in a firmer, smoother texture.

"We would speak with you about your studies." The alien's voice betrayed a lisp through the translator she wore, but Kiondili barely registered that fact. The Ruvian had moved closer to the alien, and Kiondili stared, fascinated, as the feline's fine, pale hair began to stand out on end from her face.

"I have no credits to apply for the test," she repeated flatly.

"This is not a test," the feline returned calmly, softly. Her persona adapt whirred almost silently, adjusting her projected biofields and sound each time her translator kicked on. Kiondili read the projected race rating from the persona adapt absently—the Federation would not send a recruiter who would have a hard time adjusting to the species being recruited. Even so, the feline's esper rating startled Kiondili: The rating was zero. No esper? Then what was the prickling sense of watchfulness that Kiondili sensed from her? Some kind of sixth-sense awareness, such as the Ixia had for their prey? Whatever it was, it gave the feline an aura that clung to her like a shroud.

The feline regarded the Mu thoughtfully. "Kiondili Wae," she said carefully, "what will you do when you leave the institute?"

What was so disturbing about that soft voice? Its tones sent shivers down Kiondili's back, and she found herself unwilling to look into the feline's eyes. The recruiters waited, and Kiondili pulled her attention away from the alien aura to the questions she had been asked.

What did she want to do? She had asked herself that too often lately. As a fourth-class citizen, she had few choices among the inner planets of Jovani's solar system. "I'll get a job," she said finally.

"Doing what?"

"Whatever there is to do." She tried again to meet the feline's gaze but failed.

"Your scores indicate high aptitudes in field manipulation, piloting, and xenotolerance," the soft voice went on.

"Those skills won't keep me out of the job pool."

"Xenotolerance is an unusual aptitude in H'Mu, yet you have not pursued it. Many jobs require skills in that field."

"Not the ones I want," she flashed. The Ruvian smiled. So, she thought, they wanted to see how she would react.

The female recruiter regarded her for a moment. "Do you want to be a trader as your parents were?"

"My parents are dead. My life moves on beyond them," she responded automatically, noting the wider smile on the

Ruvian's face as she hid behind the ritual words. Why were they questioning her? She sensed no opportunities with them, no real hope of a job outside the pool, no threat of having done something wrong. In fact, she felt—nothing. Her probe was as blank as if it had been directed at a wall, not a person. And that disturbed her even more than that pleasantly grating voice.

"You also have considerable esper talents that you do not develop at all."

"I—" She hesitated. "I developed them as far as is useful to me."

"Useful in a shortsighted way," the feline said sharply. "You develop your blocks beyond your talent yet leave the searcher's skills immature. You develop your field manipulation skills for sensor work at the docks and practically ignore beam control and theory. You improve your probing skills and then reject all training for becoming a reader." The female paused, and Kiondili could almost sense the mental notes she made. "If you could have more schooling," the feline continued as if she had never stopped, "what would you study?"

"I already petitioned six years of schooling from the Board of Studies," Kiondili said instead. "I haven't got credits to pay for advanced studies."

"If you could?" the feline repeated.

Something about her eyes compelled Kiondili to answer. "Field physics," she said slowly. "Hyperlight mass transmission." She shifted uneasily from one foot to the other as the two aliens regarded her silently. A sudden tensing of thought brought her attention sharply back.

"Ilos," the female said, pronouncing the name with a whirring sound, "will test you now."

Kiondili had no time to protest. A thought lanced through her head and seemed to sear her mind. She blanketed its power instantly, but the Ruvian was speaking.

"Resist this pull," he commanded suddenly. It was the first time she had heard him speak, she realized. The voice she thought had been his was only the murmur he had been making in her subconscious for some time. But even as she wondered, a bubble of silence surrounded the three of them. A wave of blackness swept her mind. She was suddenly afraid—the force of the Ruvian's energy reached out to her as if to suck her down into some invisible bog, and the feline watched with the hunter gaze that made Kiondili's neck hair stand up. She tried to crouch into a fighting stance but found herself unable to move.

Not with your body. The irritable thought cracked like a whip across her consciousness. *With your mind. Center yourself and resist this with your will.* The blackness flooded in. Frightened, she fought the darkness instinctively, building a flame of light in her head that turned into a molten, red-pulsing star as the darkness spread out and became the infinity of space, painfully cold, reaching into her mind with icy fingers. Still it pressed in, forcing her to discard unused portions of her mind and concentrate only on her identity lest she lose it in this weird struggle. Depression, morbidity, death, despair. Dark emotions sucked at her mind like sinking mud. The star image grew yellow, then white-hot as its heat increased. And then the darkness became heavy, pressing down, washing in, smothering her in memory: her mother's voice echoing in the trade ship's corridors, her father's touch as he taught her to ease the ship between, not into, the space debris. Grief, which caught in her throat, changed subtly and stirred a tremor in her chest. For it was lust she felt now. She hardly noticed the yellow tinge to her white-hot star image as she felt the intoxicating power of guiding others, controlling life and death itself, the instant thoughts of cruel sadism hidden in all humans, flashes of exhilaration, broken inhibitions . . . It was wrong, a small thought said behind her—and suddenly she heard herself as she repeated the thought, and she thrust back. This was wrong. Her star image steadied, pulsing with the effort of clearing her mind. Power—it drew her down. No—she was not like that. She was herself . . . The dark tide surged. In a sudden panic she flung her focus into the star. It went nova, and the burst flooded her mind with light and air.

And then she was back in the room, sagging against the pale brown Soft with the alien and the Ruvian in front of her. The bubble of silence faded, leaving her to straighten up weakly and stare at them. Her thoughts—this test—what had it done to her? Her mind felt clear as it never had before, as if cobwebs had been blasted away and shadows had been scattered by light.

The Ruvian made a whirring, clicking noise.

"Esper-7," the feline translated, her soft voice coming abruptly to Kiondili's physical ears. She stared as the feline categorized her as casually as Kiondili might distinguish one field from another. "Potential E-8, possibly even E-9. Excellent field sensitivity and xenotolerance. Background training in basic astrosciences; some natural aptitude for piloting based on field sensitivity." The female paused for a moment. "Will you commit to a project for a span of several years? Perhaps for your human-Mu lifetime?"

Kiondili clamped her mouth shut. What right had they had to invade her like that? She opened her mouth to retort. She stopped. Astrosciences? Field sensitivity? All skills required by the research posting. She closed her mouth again. High-esper potential, and xenotolerance. She had the talents the recruiter listed. Did this mean they had tested her for free? That the E-7 rating was going on record? These recruiters were not from the guild—any rating they gave out would be authorized by the H'Mu Guardians themselves. And there must have been pressure on the Guardians by other sublight species, or the feline would not be recruiting with the Ruvian. Kiondili's stomach twisted. A rating authorized by the Guardians for a nonguild research posting . . . She could not believe they were offering her a job. But they were waiting for her answer.

She looked beyond the feline to the Ruvian. "What kind of project?"

A flash of what she took to be irritation crossed the Ruvian's face, but the feline said, "It is ever the H'Mu way to answer question with question until curiosity is satisfied before an answer is given. The project is one of research. The outpost is nineteen light-years from here. There is no guarantee of contact or travel to other worlds, though you will be working with life of different kinds and scientists from different planets."

Nineteen light-years? The Corson outpost was the only research post within that distance. Nineteen light-years. And no guarantee of getting back on-planet if she went, she realized soberly. She could be as stranded there as she had been when the trade guild had killed her parents and left her here on Jovani. But, she admitted, what future did she have if she stayed here? In six weeks she would be out in the pool with the rest of this world. Just one more mutant in a pool where thousands vied for what only a few could have. And Corson was doing FTL drive research.

"You will leave midweek," the female continued. "That allows you three days to prepare for stasis. The material you would have studied in your last six weeks here will be continued in stasis, along with other subjects you choose. It is recommended that you continue in-stasis physics with emphasis on barrier theory, field theory, and particle recombination. You are allowed one cubic zen, weight not to exceed five kil. The ship is the *Mul Hunter*, Dock fourteen."

Kiondili's mind raced. It was as if the recruiters expected her to agree right now. She could sense their impatience as she clutched the Soft. But what, she asked herself rationally, did she have to lose by taking this offer? What she had, what she was, she carried with her, inside her mind. She could not lose that. She took a breath. "Yes."

The feline extended her fingers, and Kiondili hesitated, then reached out to them without touching, the brush of mental contact, an esper respect she did not know quite how to receive. The energy of the feline seeped through her fingertips, and then the recruiters moved away. Behind them, the memory of the feline's eyes burned deep into Kiondili's mind with a promise she could not read.

CHAPTER 2

"Kiondili Wae, wake."

The voice commanded attention, and Kiondili stirred out of the cold sleep that burned in her still-frozen muscles. "Wake," the voice echoed. Unwillingly, she opened her eyes and cringed before she could help it. Two long needles seemed to pierce her brain with the light that slammed into her eyes. Her vision blurred instantly. Finally her sight cleared enough for her to see the shadows in her cabin and the shape of the medic who was standing beside her.

Medic? She raised her arm to wipe away the involuntary tears that ran from her watering eyes down into her ears. She winced at the stiffness of the motion. So she was out of stasis. They must be near the research outpost. "How close are we?" she asked. She hardly recognized the hoarse, rusty voice as her own. She remembered now how it felt to come out of stasis: Her voice would be scratchy for days; while she recovered, her body would ache and twinge as if she had been beaten.

"We are two light-weeks from Corson," the medic answered. "You have access to the gyms, so begin working out within the half hour. Start lightly. Work out a half hour every other hour until you can exercise an hour at a time with regular breaks."

She nodded stiffly.

Noticing her movement as he packed his meditube back in his bag, he added, "The stiffness will go away in a few days. Your dispenser is programmed with the necessary nutrients."

Kiondili nodded again, making a note of the drink combos listed on the flashpad by the cabin dispenser. Her stomach was already knotting up in hunger. Two light-weeks from Corson. If the outpost was that close, she could probably find it on the high-beam scanners.

She lay back, closing her eyes and tightening her blocks, then relaxing them deliberately. Her esper sense followed the medic out and into the corridor until his thin projections merged with the distant emotional din that spoke of other traders. She was E-7 now, she remembered. She no longer had to hide behind her blocks. The recruiters had even upped her sensor rating to level four—a favor they had not had to add. And she held no debt for the testing, either. The guild, she realized with a retaliatory smugness, must be livid. A rating from the H'Mu Guardians themselves was worth even more than a guild rating, and it usually cost twice as much—and Kiondili had been rated for free. The guild would not even have found out until she was booked for transit to Corson, a trade contract for transport that the guild could not break by its own laws.

She knew the traders would not have cared if she left Jovani as a low-skilled or middle-range esper. Low-esper skills were the hunches and dreams, the premonitions that could not be otherwise explained, the sense that a friend was in trouble—had Kiondili been a low-esper, she would have been smiled at but mostly ignored. Stress and natural worries, which could lead esper skills astray, too often sabotaged the truth of those talents. Those with stronger esper talent were trained in projecting, probing, and blocking as soon as the skills began to show up in the general testing. No one had to pay for that basic training. There was too great a need for espers to charge for that, and the subsidy of the H'Mu Guardians more than compensated the guild. The only problem was that middle-range espers could not be used as readers: It was really the strongest espers that the guild hoped to discover with their classes. Offer a strong esper the choice of jobs the guild held out, and that esper would pay almost anything for high-level training.

To the guild, it was worth the trouble of sorting out the weaker espers. By selling the services of high-level esper sensors and readers, the Trade Guild gave the H'Mu Guardians the bargaining strength with which to lease FTL drives from the rest of the Federation. So the guild made a profit, while the H'Mu Guardians made advances in copying the FTL technology. The Guardians did not care what kind of profit the guild made. FTL research had an even higher priority with them than establishing colonies and trade routes. Their subsidies for esper training were hardly trivial, which meant that the guild traders must have gnashed their teeth once they realized that Kiondili's actual ratings were high enough to qualify her for training as a guild reader. She almost wished she could have seen the looks on their faces when the record of her testing went out on the comnet. She grinned again.

She was not grinning ten seconds later when she tried to sit up. She expected stiffness, but she had forgotten how agonizing it was to come out of that half-frozen state. Her nerves and muscles screamed at their now-unaccustomed use, and the light stretching she did to get her blood circulating only made her groan. She made her way to the gym slowly, swearing under her breath with each twinge and stab.

But the feel of the ship's walls under her hands and feet was reassuring. She had not been on a spaceship for a long time. Seven years. She paused to let the vibration of the engines sink into her consciousness and soothe her nerves.

Moving through the corridors of the passenger-class ship now brought back memories. Too many memories, she realized, as she caught herself listening almost unconsciously for the sound of her father's footsteps on the deck ladder. She thrust the images back in her mind and examined the ship's map instead. The gym was one deck up, along the main corridor. With luck, she would sweat the memories from her mind while she worked the stiffness from her muscles.

There was only one other person in the gym when she got there, but that did not surprise her. As far as she knew, she was the only one getting off at the Corson outpost. Everyone else was traveling farther. Wincing at the too-bright light, she nodded stiffly to the trader who was working out on one of the machines.

"Just up?" he asked unnecessarily.

She nodded again.

"Name's Bardon," he offered. "Junior navigator."

"Kiondili Wae," she returned automatically. Lucky Mu, she thought without rancor. If he was crew, he was probably one of those space-engineered mutants who spent their lives among stars rather than crops. And to land a position on a multirace trader—he had to have a powerful family or powerful friends. Resentment colored her mood, and she had to remind herself that it was the guild she hated, not the traders themselves. She dropped to the floor and began stretching her legs with the techniques embedded by the hypnotapes.

He looked at her curiously. "You're for the research outpost, then."

She grunted. Having her head tucked under one knee made it awkward to reply.

"This your first posting?"

She winced again as she twisted into a new position. "I've been six years at the institute," she explained briefly.

"Six years." He whistled in admiration. "I had four and managed to swing a good post on a PC ship with that. Passenger/Cargo isn't bad, but it would have been nice to land a multirun posting. With the troubles with the colonies, there is a decent amount of excitement building up on out on the Red Border."

She nodded noncommittally.

"What did you study?"

Kiondili had switched to a series of back exercises, so she managed her reply between stretches. "FTL physics," she grunted.

Bardon grinned. "Same species, same dreams. Care to split some Core Nectar after hours and talk? It's been cycles since I've heard a real voice outside of regular crew," he added persuasively.

Kiondili smiled involuntarily. Cycles in real time; months on-planet, and nineteen years in light. Stasis voices still echoed in her head; her ears felt as if they were new to her body. This man's tone was friendly. It was not just her sudden loneliness, outside the familiar walls of the institute, that prompted her to ask, "Where did you stop off before Corson?"

He watched her, pleased that he had gotten her to speak and intrigued by her voice, still husky from disuse. It would go away soon, he knew, but while it was there, it made the Mu, with her black hair and silvery skin, seem even more exotic. "We swung by Relinde and then had to stop at Perseus. The next question, of course, is, What do you do with all that time between stars?" he joked.

Kiondili shook her head, having groaned her way to the stomach exercises. "I grew up on a trader."

"C-class? D-class?"

"F-class."

Bardon whistled. "Xenoexotics. It's hard to make it trading goods like that, though you can buck a fortune if you get the right cargo. You must have worked the Red Border yourself."

Kiondili shrugged. The image of the red suns that marked that end of H'Mu space had never left her; it was the last space memory she had taken with her to Jovani. The fact that she had had to go to the institute told him something about her family's success—or lack of it. "We managed a few good cargoes," she agreed. "Dithwood, Dnusia bells, Perseus ginseng, Earth saffron and silks. Once," she said, pausing in the middle of a stretch and smiling reminiscently, "we took a whole shipment of Li perfumes."

"Now there's a cargo to tempt a Mu to murder," the trader said with a grin.

"They've an unholy reputation," she agreed.

"Unholy," he snorted. "They ought to be banned from the H'Mu quadrants. Hells, those scents can drive any human or mutant to almost any mood—like when the first H'Mu ambassadors came in contact with the Li."

"It's more funny to me that the original ambassadors were that sensitive about mixed sex."

He shrugged. "Who would want sex with a Li, anyway? They are about as ugly as you can get with all those open cysts on their limbs."

"They can't help the way they ovulate," she protested.

He quirked an eyebrow.

"Okay, okay, they're last on my list for explorative activities, too." Kiondili twisted herself into a knot over one of the flexible stretching machines. She thanked Ayara under her breath that the ship had set gravity control to something she was used to. Stretching exercises in zero-grav were a pain in the neck figuratively and literally. A careless movement in zero-grav could send a body shooting off across the room in any of a dozen unpredictable directions, and she was out of practice. She wondered if her sensor skills were up to manipulating the gravitational fields in the gym. It would be different from a boost chute, but she wanted only a bit, right around the machines. She would have to experiment later.

"Getting back to the beer," the trader continued, watching her stretch, "I get off shift at second bell. Want to meet in the Hub?"

Kiondili nodded, agreeing, but was relieved when he left. She hated feeling like an exhibitionist.

Several hours later she found herself wandering the decks.

It felt good to be in space again, she admitted, recognizing her longing for the feel on her feet of meta-plas boots and the ring in her ears of a hatch closing nearby. She almost grinned at the alien who emerged from the opening to her right.

But his voice snapped her daydream brusquely. "What are you doing here, Mu?" he demanded.

Her aura solidified abruptly. Kiondili braced herself for an argument as she felt his blocks and hers snap into place. "I was looking for the scanner deck," she returned steadily. "I wanted to see Corson if it's in sight."

Looking her up and down as if to find fault in the way she wore the ship's regulation jumper, the trader nodded curtly. "Two decks up, right passage." He made a rude whistling noise through his reptilian nose and slipped past her in the metal corridor.

"I'm Kiondili Wae," she said deliberately, forcing him to turn back to her.

The reptilian stared at her, giving her the sensation of touching her though he stood several meters away, and nodded again, less curtly. "Kilu," he introduced himself. His jumper identified him as the cargomaster. The ruffled scale pattern on his skin was less noticeable as his agitation decreased.

"Citizen T'se," she acknowledged politely.

The cargomaster met her eyes, sensing her blocks and widening his lizard-slit eyes in sudden interest as he saw that she did not draw back from him. "Citizen H'Mu," he said deliberately. He turned away then and moved soundlessly to the next deck ladder, climbing effortlessly out of sight.

Kiondili followed him slowly, waiting for him to disappear before starting up the rung ladder. She felt suddenly drained. She hated having to work her blocks like that while she fought to control her reactions. The cargomaster's arrogance was irritating, and the fact that he held no regard for her was also hard to ignore. Where did he get off being such a snob? After all, she had been raised trader, too.

But as she climbed the rungs more slowly, Kiondili knew that it would not have made any difference to Kilu if she were on the trade board itself. She was no more welcome here than she would have been had she been carrying parasites. She sighed and swung up onto the next deck. To have her own ship . . .

The decks were neatly marked, so she had no trouble finding the scanner room. After she pressed her palm against the ID lock, the door slid open easily so that she caught a glimpse of a room lined with screens before the two people inside looked around.

"Citizen H'Mu," acknowledged the captain. Kiondili had met him at the institute before signing into stasis on the *Mul Hunter*, but he looked different in his ship—larger, and more stern, and somehow unapproachable. He motioned at the woman next to him, saying, "This is Cari Newonton, astrogator."

"Call me Cari," the woman said, smiling. "Everyone else does."

Kiondili was relieved. The captain might be somber, but this woman was at least polite, if not friendly. "I'm Kiondili Wae," she returned. "I was hoping to get a look at Corson if it's in range."

The captain turned to the astrogator. "If you would, Cari. I'll be in my cabin later."

Kiondili blushed, realizing that she had interrupted them. "Sorry," she said to the woman as he left.

Cari, noticing the long look Kiondili gave the captain, laughed. "Don't worry about it. The whole ship knew about it light-years ago. Let's get down to business. Corson is just barely in view now—you knew Corson was above and not actually in the plane of the star system, didn't you? Good. Sometimes we get such dillies to cart around, I wonder why we don't just space them. Their heads are so empty that a little more vacuum wouldn't hurt. Besides, it would save us a lot of air recycling."

Kiondili smiled. Cari continued to chatter absently while

focusing the view through her temple jacks and adjusting the slides of one of the big screens. A fuzzy image began to take shape in the main holotank.

"Damned by the toes of Totillion," the astrogator swore easily. "Ah, wait—there it is. How's that? Clear enough?" She paused, regarding the image critically.

Kiondili nodded, staring at the screen. The outpost was different from what she had expected. She had seen holos of other research stations, but they had been spheroid or blockily built into asteroids themselves. Corson was, well, *scattered* seemed to be the only word to describe it. The outpost looked like a cylinder with three unorthodox pincushions spinning away from it, attached to the main docks by long threads. Within the clusters there were flattened spheres, angular boxes, pyramids, rounded rectangles, and combinations of different architectures looking as if they had been tossed haphazardly into space and then tacked in place with a web of circling silver metal.

"Different from most," the woman commented, noticing Kiondili's expression. "You had not seen it before you left?"

"There wasn't time. Besides, I figured I could wait."

"Anticipation." The astrogator nodded with understanding. "How long will you be there?"

"As long as I can," Kiondili answered without turning her head from the screen.

Cari grunted. "Corson is popular with the Federation right now. They are still getting a lot of pressure from H'Mu and other sublight species to acknowledge the results of the H'Mu research, so Corson's getting a lot of traffic. Traders must blast in every quarter cycle—that's a week, to you." Kiondili, watching the scan, did not bother to tell Cari that she knew the traders' time system as well as the astrogator did. The stocky woman let the scan rotate on the screen to show the outpost from different angles. "I've never heard anything bad come out of Corson. You'll enjoy it there."

Kiondili stayed in the scanner room for an hour until she sensed the woman tiring of her company. She left the astrogator to close down the scanners and went off to explore the ship. Surprisingly, she found that she had normal access to all decks except engines and control, and full access to the ship's library, from which she had scheduled most of her hypnotapes. As the second bell rang, signifying the end of the second shift, Kiondili made her way to the Hub.

Bardon was already waiting when she arrived. "Kiondili," he said, introducing her to the man sitting beside him, "meet Fisc Hirson. Fisc is assistant cargo."

"Pleased, Mu." Fisc used the slang like a comfortable greeting. His tanned skin almost hid the scalelike pattern beneath his freckles, but the double-lidded eyes gave her no doubt.

"Likewise, Mu," she returned easily.

"So," Fisc started as Bardon punched out the request for Core Nectar on the dispenser, "when you go FTL, who gets first digs on the drive? The H'Mu Guardians? The guild?" He gestured around expansively. "Leasing this old tub is getting to be a maintenance nightmare."

Kiondili smiled wryly, though the mention of the guild left her smile stiff. She supposed that since she was not classified, the information about her was already in the ship's library. "I would not know. I'm only going to be the gofer, not the chief researcher."

The older trader shrugged, though his eyes twinkled behind those double lids as he followed her subtle change of subject. She looked away uncomfortably.

"If I had my druthers," he said easily, "I'd rather be the gofer than the chief."

She glanced back at him, grateful for his tact. "Why?"

"The pressure in some of those places is pretty heavy. Last time we docked at Corson, we took off three Mu and a pair of aliens who could not handle the load. One of the aliens had gone E-blind—lost his esper from some sort of burnout. I guess the deadlines are getting tight."

Bardon noticed Kiondili's expression. "She's newly rated, Fisc. She doesn't need to hear your horror stories."

Kiondili shook her head a little too quickly. "It doesn't bother me. I've been waiting a long time for a chance at this post, anyway."

"Well, if you don't like Corson," Bardon offered, "there are four other outposts in this quadrant researching the drives. And there are H'Mu on every staff."

"Token researchers," Fisc snorted. "Or curiosities. There aren't many species willing to share the limelight with H'Mu. Corson is the only post where there is Federation funding of real work."

Bardon agreed, punching the combination for another nectar. He did the same for Kiondili. "No one takes a sublight race seriously."

Kiondili glanced up. "Corson isn't all human-Mu, is it?"

"Not all." Fisc shook his head, the one long lock of hair scraping along his otherwise bald head and dangling over his left ear. "There's a fair number of Einain, Greggors, Tinlig, and Robul. Might be a couple of predators, too, if what I heard was right. But the majority is H'Mu."

Bardon nodded. "It's the Federation's rule—'only compatible species'—and all that."

Fisc snorted. "Yes, but what is their definition of compatible? Would you want to share a holotank with a couple of Greggors? Two minutes with them, and their subsonics would drive you nuts. And how comfortable would you be working with a predator looking over your shoulder, even if it promised not to sharpen its claws on you?"

"Walk softly at Corson, Kiondili Wae," Bardon nudged her with a stage whisper. "The Federation won't notice if you become an Ixia's snack."

She shrugged him off and sipped at her nectar.

Fisc considered her. "It is true that once you get there, you had better plan on staying. Even if you got on-planet again, you could not be guaranteed a landing on a H'Mu colony. Of the twenty-six H'Mu planets, only two are in this quadrant."

Kiondili raised her eyebrows. "There are at least sixty

H'Mu colonies," she protested. "And I know of six in this quadrant."

Fisc regarded her with amusement. "How many of them would you want to live on?"

"I see your point," she said with a slow smile.

"I don't envy the colonists these days," Bardon remarked, swinging the conversation away from Fisc as he noted Kiondili's response to the older trader's smile. "H'Mu are only allowed to bid for backwater planets now, and the colonies have to struggle just to survive, let alone turn a profit and join mainstream trade."

Kiondili raised her eyebrows. "It's the lack of FTL ships, not colonization, that's the problem. After all, our genetic engineering and our planetary sciences are far ahead of our stellar technology. We can buy as many backwater planets as we want; within two generations, every one will be habitable. What we need," she said seriously, "are more FTL ships to get us to the planets in the first place and then keep the colonies productive and in touch with the rest of H'Mu space."

Fisc laughed at her intensity. "That's an old argument around here, Wae. Do you think we'd be blasting in this old bucket if we had a working FTL drive for human-Mus? It's bad enough we have to give up fifty percent of our cargo to the Tore just to keep the drives serviced, but even at that, we can't afford to lease a trade ship from them, just this junked passenger ship."

She grinned slyly, refraining from pointing out the pride with which the trader disparaged his ship.

By the time she left the Hub, she was surprised and pleased at the warm feeling that filled her.

She studied, worked out, slept, ate. The routine was an old one she knew well; after all, she had been a trader herself from birth until she had landed on Jovani. But within two days she was bored. She did not want to study; she did not want to sleep. She stared at library flashscreens and holotanks for hours without even seeing what passed through her temple jacks. Even the gym lost its attraction. She began prowling the decks, her restlessness undefined, even to herself.

On the fifth day she had become irked enough with the tediousness of her routine to take herself to the lower levels. There she began bouncing off the corridor walls and practicing zero-grav flips. It took her a couple of hours, but she finally worked out how to use her sensor's skills with her persona adapt to cancel the corridor gravity at will. She was fine-tuning her technique near the engine rooms when a field oscillation twinged.

Kiondili let herself fall back to the floor softly. An oscillation like that should not have been present that close to the engine drive fields. She canceled her tiny zero-grav and reached out mentally. The background field shifted again, weaker to her senses now that the gravity fields of the corridor were back in place. Slowing down, she tried to pinpoint the dissension. Secondary drives? Drive support fields? It had not been a large blip. She debated calling the captain, then decided to contact Kramer, the engine master, instead. After all, they were his engines and his responsibility first.

The engine master answered the com on the third try. "Kramer," he said impatiently. "What is it?"

"Kiondili Wae," she said. She paused, then plunged ahead. The engine master might not appreciate her butting in, but he might not have noticed the discrepancy. "One of the drive support fields has a fluctuation in it," she said shortly.

The trader's voice was irritated. "Drive fields? How would you know?"

"I worked two years as a field sensor at ISA's docks on Jovani."

Kramer hesitated. "What level?"

"Sensor-3," she returned, "though I'm level four now. My experience is mostly with class C through G traders," she added, "but I did work on a few Federation ships and one Dhirrnu scout."

"You say it's one of the drive support fields?"

"I could identify it better if I was closer to the field," she said carefully.

"Hold on a minute." The engine master cut her off abruptly.

After a few minutes she realized that Kramer had forgotten about her, which was typical of a trader, she told herself with irritation. But as she turned to leave the deck, the com flashed again.

"Wae?" It was Kramer again. "The captain has authorized me to hire you to locate the oscillation. Guild fees. Level four, with in-flight hazard."

In-flight hazard? What hazard on a Tore ship? She frowned until she pulled the engine information from her hypno-fed memory. Tore ships never quite shut down. Their drive fields were maintained in a large but weak form when there was maintenance to do. No wonder Kramer did not want to touch it. Having an unbonded sensor work was three times better than risking his own E-skills on a pulsing engine. She smiled sardonically. The Tore prided themselves on having tamper-proof ships. She could not harm their engines. The worst she could do was get herself killed. Guild fees, she thought, touching her thin credit chit through her jumper pocket. And level four, at that. "Accepted," she said shortly.

"Access open," he said, signing off.

She trotted down the corridor to the next deck ladder, which was sealed to the engine deck, and slid her palm across the ID blank. The field flickered, a light flashed, the seal slid open, and she dropped easily down to see the engine master waiting for her between two engine casings. Now that she was in the unshielded engine compartment, the slight field oscillation was even more obvious. "If you'll call up the engine map," she stated without preamble, "I can locate the area better."

Nodding, he touched a flat screen and called up the diagram for one of the primary engines.

"Not that one." She shook her head and pointed to one of the thruster supports. "That one."

The engine master obligingly called up the support diagram, and they studied it together.

"It feels like the fourth support," she said slowly, tuning into the fields and letting herself sensitize to their flux. The hairs on her arms began to stand out from her skin, tingling with the touch of the fields.

Kramer frowned. "We just had that series serviced at Perseus."

"General maintenance, or was there a problem?" she asked absently. Even without her temple jacks, she could almost identify the field by the way its fluctuation interfaced with the fields around it.

"Maintenance. I run a tight ship here, Wae."

"No offense intended, Engine Master." She ran her hands over the thruster casing. "The casing needs to come off, and I'll have to get my sensors unless you have some down here."

"There are a couple pairs in the for'ard locker," he grunted, turning off the engines in the casing before opening it. Vibrations dulled. After flooding the compartment with radiation-soak, he lifted the casing and peered inside. "I can move the number three thruster out of the way, but you'll have to reach in to number four."

"No need." She put the sensors over her ears, attached one set of nodes to her temples, and ran the other set of wires down to her hands, where the second pair were attached. "I can sense it from here if you'll turn them up one at a time."

With Kramer stimulating the fields one at a time and then in combination, it took only a couple hours to pinpoint the cause of the variation. Kiondili sat back and removed the sensors. "The thruster support field is the effect, not the cause," she said to the engine master. "The problem is that one of the velocity sensors is out, and the backup sensor is not reading the next adjust valve properly. The surge is sending the support field into oscillation.''

The engine master grunted and called up a holo of the sensor system. He muttered, ''Diagnostics should have caught that.'' He zoomed into the holo, examining the adjusters more closely. ''Call Donoway for me, will you, Wae? Should be somewhere between Hub and cabin by now.''

''Just a moment.'' She stored the sensors back in the locker and washed her hands carefully in radiation-soak. Even though the compartment had been flushed, it was better not to take chances with the possibility of a burn. She located the engine assistant and passed the message on. ''Off duty,'' she said ritually to Kramer, signifying the completion of her work.

''Duty done,'' Kramer replied, his voice muffled under the hulk of the thrusters. ''That was a fast job, Wae. Well done.''

She left, a pleasant feeling in her gut as she squeezed by Donoway in the corridor and returned to her cabin. She had not realized how much she missed being a part of a ship's crew. Belonging. The field sensor work she had done at the planetside docks had not been the same, with all the ships silent and cold in their cradles. Not that she belonged here, she reminded herself realistically. Traders were cold as a dead ship to strangers who wanted to join them. But she had once been one of them. She understood their independence well.

She hummed tunelessly as she walked. To work on a living ship again, feel the thrum of the engines in her bones . . . Piloting between asteroid fields on an incoming orbit, the exhilaration of blasting off, the controlled excitement of slamming on a deep-grav brake for a stop-second landing at a spaceport . . . She missed the long hours of studying with her father and memorizing star routes with her mother, watching the galaxy rainbow into a black cylinder with colored ends in the ports as they flashed up to lightspeed, then transferred to hyperlight space. She rubbed her hands together in wonder, relishing the cool feel of radiation-soak on her skin.

On impulse, she called up the scanner's image of Corson. It looked the same, a little more clear as the distance lessened between ship and outpost but still as haphazardly built as it had first seemed. Running her hands down the wall of her cabin and feeling the vibration of the ship's engines reach into her bones, Kiondili stared at the scan and wondered again why she had accepted the posting. There would still have been a chance at a berth on a spaceship, she admitted, or even reader training once she admitted to being a higher-level esper. She looked again, trying to see some sign of life in the scan, but the outpost seemed isolated and cold in the blackness of space. Turning off the scan and staring at the blank walls of her cabin, Kiondili found herself more uncertain of her future now than when she had been looking to the hazards of the pool.

CHAPTER 3

Kiondili went down the ship's ramp with forced confidence. Around the fuel holds, the traders were servicing their ship quickly, efficiently, and with the uninterested assurance of those who have done the job too many times before. The bins of isotopes had already been set out by the robos. The tanks waited now. Robos would not load the topes; traders never allowed a dock robo to set the fuel ratios for their ships. Kiondili watched them for a moment, but none of them spared her a glance. Maybe she should have waited longer for instructions? But no one at the outpost had sent word over the viscom. After waiting an hour, Kiondili had shrugged, gotten her pack from cargo, and left the traders behind.

Down on the docks she spotted the ship's captain and two of the crew. She hurried to catch them as the they threaded their way between ship cradles. "Excuse me, Captain," she said respectfully, catching his attention. "Do you know where I should go—or if someone is to meet me?"

"Afraid not, Citizen H'Mu." He barely glanced at her.

Kiondili opened her mouth to ask a second question, but

as he strode away, the force of his disinterest hit her, and she stopped, acutely reminded of her fourth-class status. She flushed slowly, staring after him. The captain, like the other traders, did not look back.

At a loss, she shifted her pack from one hand to the other. She supposed she would have to go to Central Control. They ought to have a record of her posting there, no matter how impersonal it would be. At least it would get her into the outpost interior. But she did not move yet. The docks fascinated her, and she looked around, memorizing each detail. The docks were open—more so than at any other outpost she had landed in. Space seemed to pour in through gaping holes through which ships were maneuvered with tractor beams, the vacuum of the void held back by an invisible shield across the openings and the visual reflection of the ships shimmering as they passed through that shield. Overhead, air jets boosted tiny figures around the structure of the dock. Flashes of light caught their movements and made them dance. Squinting, Kiondili tried to make out the shapes that worked on one of the gates. Some were far from human.

From where she stood, the racks of ships and empty cradles looked more like missiles in an armory than ships in a spacedock. There were at least six D-class traders in dock, one C-class, and two M-class. Under one of the large space holes on that side, twin Tore vessels hung suspended as if stacked on top of each other. A flash of light caught her eye, and she looked past the spacecraft to see a tractor beam flare white as it tightened on a tiny sliver of a ship. The lines of brilliance shifted in a dance of light as the dock's reflection stations routed the slim ship around other activity. Silently a group of Mu trotted by. As her gaze traveled around the dock, she almost missed the flat black of the Federation scout ship tucked behind one of the other structures.

"A scout," she breathed. Then she forced her excitement to quell. A scout posting was as far from her future now as the next century. She was there to take a research job, not to dream about someone else's ship. She shook herself from her reverie, but as she started toward the outpost center, she halted again, glancing toward the access doors and questioning the nervousness in her gut. What was she doing here, anyway? No one seemed to have noticed that she had arrived. She was nineteen light-years from the institute, but only four months had passed since she had been offered this post. Did they know she was supposed to be there? What if the recruiters had not sent word of her arrival? What if there was no longer a job waiting for her? She could not help the instinctive motion toward her credit chit.

She stiffened her resolution. Even if there was no job for her here, she could make it in this port's job pool. She had done it before, when she had had only half the skills she had now. But she needed this chance. Needed it badly. Besides, she told herself deliberately, she was not going back to Jovani. There were no memories there, only ghosts.

She deliberately closed her mind to her past and started once more toward Central Control, but a nervous shiver clung to her shoulders. Even though the colors of cargo and ships and corridors filled the docking port thickly, the impression of cold meta-plas remained to chill the air. From behind her, a sudden chittering made her jump. She turned and saw a tall, four-legged alien stalking to a stack of boxes; he clicked his teeth together angrily as he shifted one, then another. One of his hooves tapped the dock impatiently as he ran his eyes over the boxes. When he caught sight of Kiondili, he turned a toothy face to her and snapped his translator on.

"You," he ordered without preamble, his translation high and stilted. "Find that box of Johanson tubes and get it to my lab immediately."

Kiondili looked around to make sure he was speaking to her. "I'm new at the outpost, Citizen," she said slowly. "I don't know where anything is."

"Then get a cargo map and find out," the alien snapped. He ducked his head suddenly to his chest, then speared her with his gaze. "Bring the tubes to the design lab, second level, Chute Thirty-four, outer triad. Hurry. We are in the middle of a launch.'' Before she could respond, he turned and galloped off.

She stared after him. Was that all the welcome she would get here? She set her meager pack next to a crate. With her luck, that alien was going to be her new adviser. She had to remind herself that it was an assistant's position she had been hired into. Her job description did not include a requirement that she like her boss.

She examined the labels on the boxes first, but none listed the tubes the alien wanted. Realizing that, she stretched her fingers out to catch the slight field characteristic of tube cores. The field was faint, as it should have been, damped by the shielding the tubes were packed in. But she found them almost instantly; they were in a box mismarked as supplies for another lab. Pulling the crate from the pile, she found it light enough to carry, so, tossing her pack over her shoulder, she hefted the package to her other shoulder and started off in the direction the alien had taken.

The chute map was straightforward; it took only a moment to memorize the alien's route as he had directed. She would have loved trying out the free-boost chutes. She wondered if they allowed chute racing in this place? But, not knowing yet what her access was, she took the corridor route instead.

Several minutes later she found herself in one of the outer hubs of the Corson pincushion. She hoped she remembered the lab's location correctly. The corridors were empty, and there was no one to ask. She slowed, looking for the right lab designation, then looked up when three H'Mu—two men and a woman—turned a corner in the hall. She waited for them to come close enough to ask for directions, but it was one of the H'Mu who spoke first.

''What are you doing in this triad, Mu?'' the first man demanded.

Kiondili's blocks hardened instantly at his implied accusation.

The woman who was with the two men frowned, her blue

skin tightening over the tiny water bags that hung under her chin. "You're new, aren't you?" she asked slowly, giving Kiondili a long look as she probed her blocks gently.

Kiondili, her blocks still stiff from the force of emotion from the first man, was not given time to nod.

"New or not," he said sharply, "she should not be here."

The blue-skinned woman gave him a disgusted look. "She could be Stilman's new assistant, Argon—"

He cut her off with a rude gesture. "She still would not be in this triad if she were." But he gave Kiondili a considering look, and the tone of his projection changed subtly so that she did now know whether to protest his words or challenge him back.

The other man peered at the box still on her shoulder. "That isn't equipment for any of these labs."

"Then she's probably stealing," Argon suggested nastily. "Call the chute guards. They will take care of this faster than we can."

Kiondili stared at them. Had the alien she was helping set her up? "I'm not stealing anything," she said in protest, finding her voice at last. "I'm taking this to an Einian's lab. He needs these tubes for a launch."

Argon glanced at the box. "That's a box of Septian boards, not tubes, and it probably belongs over in engineering. This is definitely a security matter. What's your ID number, Mu?" he demanded.

Kiondili eyes narrowed. "The box belongs here," she returned sharply. "An Einian told me to find a box of Johanson tubes and take them to his lab. Second level, Chute Thirty-four, outer triad. I am in the right place, aren't I?"

"It's the right chute, all right, but you picked the wrong equipment to steal, Mu."

"Watch your mouth," she flashed back, adding with acid sarcasm, *"Mu.* The box has been mislabeled."

"How do you know? Did you open it to make sure you had the right goods?" he asked derisively.

"I didn't have to."

"Esper . . ." He spoke the word as if it were a curse, and Kiondili sensed an envy behind the words.

The woman with the bluish skin gave him an unreadable look as she blew bubbles softly into her water bags. She looked at Kiondili with new regard. "You must be new. I know all the espers in the complex."

Kiondili opened her mouth, but the other man spoke first. "Another lab assistant was coming in this week, Argon," he said quietly. "And she seems sincere."

"If she were a lab assistant, she would have her authorization already," Argon said derisively. "Imagine, trying to take equipment in broad hall light. You say you have Johanson tubes in there? Then we'll just open the crate now and have a look."

Kiondili took a step back. "Keep your hands off, Argon-*Mu*. This is the Einian's property, not yours, and he gave me charge of it. Till it reaches his lab, it is no concern of yours."

"Give it over or you'll find yourself spaced without a suit by the chute guards," he threatened.

Kiondili tensed as Argon reached greedily for the box, and then the door beside them shimmered open abruptly and the Einian thrust his head out, glaring from one assistant to the next.

"What is going on here, Mu?" The translator of the Einian was on an even higher pitch now than before. "Where is my box of tubes?" He stamped into the hall, one of his hind feet pawing irritably at the floor. "Argon, if you're delaying my equipment—"

"Citizen," Kiondili cut in. "The Mu has not touched the tubes, which are in this box. They were mislabeled, but I believe they are what you were looking for."

The alien took the crate gently from her. As he turned, his mate, another spindly, yellowing, four-legged alien, strode out and exchanged trace elements with him before taking the box from his hands. Her hand-held laser blade flicking out, she opened the end quickly, then chittered and hurried back into the lab, the box held carefully in her hands. The other

Einian abruptly turned his back on the four people in the hall and strode after his mate, leaving Kiondili to face the three lab assistants.

"If you were trying to ingratiate yourself," Argon snarled, "it doesn't work with aliens like that."

"I was not trying to do anything," Kiondili said shortly. "I just got off ship, and before I could tell him I didn't even know where to report, he pulled me off to look for this box of tubes."

"If you have not reported yet," the other woman said slowly, "you will have to get to the director's office before they realize you are missing. I'm assuming you are the new lab assistant. They'll give you your assignment, access, and ID card there. It's two columns over, Chute Sixty-one, center triad. The signs are posted."

"Thanks," Kiondili said shortly. She turned and walked away, aware of the stares of the other assistants boring into her back. She forced herself to walk calmly, but she was so relieved when distance dimmed their emotions that she sagged against the wall for a moment. Why had Argon picked that fight with her? It was as if he had done it on purpose. Ayara's eyes, if everyone was even half as hostile as he was, she might as well have stayed at the institute.

If Kiondili thought that the three Mu had given her an uncomfortable welcome, she was not reassured by the director of the outpost. The man let her wait in the outer office for an hour before calling her in. Then he shuffled papers for several more minutes before motioning for her to sit.

"Kiondili Wae, human-mu xeno-2, E-7," he stated in a gravelly voice, meeting her eyes for the first time. "High xenotolerance, field sensitivity, and esper; reasonably intelligent for a Mu; work recommendations from ISA, EQU, and the *Mul Hunter* for services performed in transit."

Uneasy with the redness of his pupils and the yellowness that surrounded them, Kiondili, realizing that his statements required no answer, stayed silent.

"Recommended for posting as lab assistant, Federation

year 13114.'' He set the papers aside abruptly. ''Why did you not report here immediately on arrival? The trader ship docked over two hours ago.''

She stared at him. ''I waited for instructions,'' she said finally. ''There were none, so I stayed at the docks. Then an Einian told me to take a box of Johanson tubes to his lab in a hurry. I thought he was to be my adviser, so I did that, then I found out I was to come here.''

Dugan's yellow-red eyes gave the impression of a hunter who would be relentless even in tracking her through the free-boost chutes. ''I heard of your escapade in Chute Thirty-four,'' he said. ''As I am familiar with Argon's situation, and since you are new here, we will overlook the conflict this time, but it would be wise for you to remember that Corson is a Federation research outpost, not a supervising service.'' He paused and glanced at the paper on his desk. ''Since the recruiters gave you security clearance based on their evaluation, and because I have confidence in their judgment, you will not be deposted immediately but will only be on probation for your first quarter year light here.''

Kiondili stared at him. ''But I only did what the Einian told me to do.''

''The Einian is not your research posting, as you would have known had you come here for your assignment immediately upon docking. As is standard at other docks, you should have reported immediately upon arrival. You were a trader. You know the procedure.'' He dropped the flashpaper into the filing slot. ''After you turn in your profile cube to the psych—the xenopsychologist here—check in to your quarters, then report to Shyh Stilman's lab. His last assistant dispersed himself accidentally six cycles ago.''

Stilman—that was the name mentioned by the blue-skinned woman in the hall outside the Einian's lab. And Argon's tone had changed just after Stilman's name had been mentioned. Had she stepped into the middle of a problem between Argon and Stilman, providing Argon with a convenient weapon with which to score a point? Something like that would explain the director's comment about Argon. Then she snorted to herself. She had been at Corson less than three hours and was already guessing at the politics of the place.

She accepted the director's judgment silently. As she picked up her access and ID, she made her way out of the office, then to the corridor, where she dropped her profile cube off to the xenopsych as directed. She wanted a shower; there was plenty of time before she went in search of her lab assignment. She did not want to make as poor an impression on Stilman as she had on the outpost director.

By the time she found her quarters, she was ready for something of her own. But then she opened the door to her new room and saw the sterile area she was to live in. She stared at it blankly. It was nothing more than a junior berth on a trader: a bare, empty, six-walled cell. All that relieved the starkness of its walls was a small button-filled panel by the door. As it sensed her biofield, the control panel blinked briefly to tell her it could release the hidden furniture into the modular living configuration she desired. She ignored it, searching the walls for the patterns of the fold-out furniture. Ayara's eyes, even the shower was hidden in a slot in the wall! She stepped into the room slowly. At least at the institute she had had a room with a real chair and desk. And as a child on her parent's trade ship she had had quarters with colored walls. Here the walls were only gray, a light, uniform, uncompromising gray. She glanced at her travel pack, which contained her books and figurines and personal items. She wondered how they would fit into this sterile room. Finally, she ran her hands along the smooth surface. There was not one scratch or dent in the meta-plas walls to speak of the presence of another creature in any near or distant past.

She quit her quarters with a sense of relief. She hoped this Stilman to whom she was assigned was not as cold as everyone—and everything—else seemed to be. Corson was a long way from any reasonably habitable H'Mu planets. She could be stuck with Stilman for a long time.

The comlock to Stilman's lab released at her tap, but she

took only a few steps inside after the door shimmered open. In front of her, a man she assumed to be Stilman was standing in the middle of several piles of flashbooks, looking bewildered. There were tables around the edges of the lab, each piled with a combination of flashtexts, holotank controls, and hardware. Looking at the disarray, Kiondili stopped short. "Dr. Stilman?" she asked hesitantly. "I'm Kiondili Wae, your new lab assistant."

The human—he looked to be pure Terran stock—gave her a puzzled look. "Yes," he said slowly, pulling his thoughts back to the lab. "I needed one cycles ago. You can start over there." He pointed vaguely toward one corner of the room.

She hid an involuntary grin. At the very least, this man did not look cold. He wore green breeches like a Biluane would wear and a red-striped tunic that hung loosely from his lanky shoulders. A broad band of black, gold, and blue circled one wrist; his feet were bare, and his gray-white hair straggled to one side as if he constantly ran his fingers through it in one direction. His face was long, with a hawkish nose bent slightly to the right and quick, intense blue eyes that seemed to spear whatever they focused on.

"Shall I organize first?" she asked uncertainly.

"Yes. No," he corrected, locking his gaze on her at last. "I can't find one of my miniature beamers. It's a prototype. Find that first, then you can straighten up these files." He sighed. "I can't find anything since Perdue dispersed, and my notes are getting lost." He picked up a stack of flashbooks and thrust them at her. "These are full. You may as well store these before you get into the others."

Kiondili barely had time to nod before he turned abruptly and strode through the door to his office. She wondered for a moment if she should bring up the subject of her studies, the work expected of her, and her pay, but decided it could wait. Stilman did not seem the type to tolerate being interrupted when he was thinking, especially by a new lab assistant who did not know Corson protocol yet. So she sighed and sifted through the flashbooks instead.

Stilman strode back through the lab a few minutes later, disappearing through the shimmering door as it phased from solid to gas and back, and returning scant minutes later. She wondered if he expected her to find his beamer quickly. But as he did not address her again, she did her best to ignore the distraction of his continued popping in and out of the lab.

He had been gone for half an hour after one of his more abrupt exits, when Kiondili shivered suddenly. She frowned, shuddered again, and shook her head. But her skin crawled along her neck and then down her back as if sensing some unknown danger. She found herself backing hurriedly out from under the counter where she had been clearing out old flashbooks. Banging her head as she twisted around, she stifled an oath—and found herself staring into the hungry eyes of an alien predator.

The female who faced Kiondili had the aura of a hunter who had not eaten in a week. The eyes set in the spadelike face were mere slits of color. Laser-sharp teeth, slanted ears, retracted knuckle claws; the alien was an Ixia, Kiondili identified with a strangely exciting horror. She controlled her instinctive reaction with difficulty: The Ixia would sense her fear by smell alone. "May I help you?" she asked, carefully polite.

"Where is Stilman?" The Ixia's voice was luring, and Kiondili felt a hypnotic compulsion to lean closer.

Shaking herself, she dragged the words from her mouth. "He just stepped out. He should be back in a few minutes, if you want to wait." Was the predator as disturbed by the meeting as Kiondili was?

The alien met Kiondili's eyes with an agonized look and shuddered, her knuckle claws extending slightly. "Tell him to viscom me later. I'm Lan-Lu." She backed away, then turned and left the lab, the shimmer of the closing door outlining her muscles in a temporary shadow.

Kiondili stared after her. An Ixia—here. And one that worked with Stilman. How did he stand it? With an effort, she pushed her questions—and her discomfort—to the back of her mind.

It was just before third bell rang that Kiondili finally ran across the black box of the missing beamer. "Ha!" she cried in triumph, backing out from under a thick table. Having lost track of Stilman's comings and goings, she tapped the com for his office. When he did not answer, she went inside and set the beamer on his desk.

It was evening to her, so Kiondili went back to her cubicle and showered, then went in search of dinner. The cafeteria was crowded. With no one else to speak to and no desire to cross the room to sit with the few assistants she did recognize, Kiondili ate alone and listened to the conversations around her.

". . . hyperlight barrier ethics aren't as black and white as they want us to believe," said someone to her right.

"Yes," another voice answered. "But for us it's all a subjective question, anyway."

"It won't be for long. Coos made another breakthrough yesterday. It seems he finally figured out how to resolve sublight and imaginary mass for hyperlight transfer. Engineering already has the new design changes."

"That furball's going to rake in all the credit for the hyperlight drive by himself if we don't get moving . . ."

Other voices cut through the murmur at times, languages mixing where translators were reprogrammed to spit out their sounds more comfortably in one tongue rather than another. To one side a Moal was speaking, holding the entire table of H'Mu enthralled with its doubling tones. Kiondili wondered in brief amusement if any of them were listening to the Moal's words or if they just sat, mesmerized by its singing, as Kiondili would have had she been sitting closer to the creature. From the mix of aliens and H'Mu on the other side of the Hub, Kiondili picked up curiosity and flat indifference, calm meditation and intense paranoia, idle emotions and concentrated energies. There were even a few humans who projected E-blocks. Stilman, who entered with another researcher, projected nothing—just as a nonesper would—though he glanced in Kiondili's direction and waved briefly.

She wondered if the job offer to a researcher included a test for his E-rating, too. Did it bother Stilman to work among so many espers? She had sensed no envy in him, as she had with Argon. No fear, either. She half rose to join him, but he had already turned away. Uncertain, she sat back down, conspicuously alone, surrounded by crowded tables in the Hub.

She sat in the cafeteria long after she had finished eating. She was too keyed up to go back to an empty cubicle. She would just as soon stay here a little longer. If nothing else, she would get a good look at most of the people in her triad of the outpost.

To her left a large open space was laid out like a garden. That was where Stilman was sitting, still deep in conversation. The group was debating some point. One of the creatures at the flashtable motioned furiously with his arms and legs, and another was drawing just as excitedly on the table's large flashpad.

Overhead, the ceiling dimmed to show a projection of space, as if the outpost had a planetary day and night. It was not quite soothing. With the imaged stars as clear as if she were viewing them from a sky platform on Jovani, she kept waiting for the night scent of the planet to flare her nostrils, expecting the wind to pick up and the temperature to drop. Then she startled herself by laughing abruptly. She had been too long on-planet if she could not live without a planetary sky. Abruptly, swallowing the last of her drink, she dropped her glass in the dispenser chute and left.

The next day found her back in the lab, struggling with the mountains of flashbooks that filled the rooms. She had had her breakfast in the same isolation that she had eaten in the night before and did not feel like talking. Although a strange loneliness ate at her gut as if she had not had a meal in days, she was almost relieved to be in the calm atmosphere of the nearly empty lab.

When Stilman came in, she was staggering under a heavy pile of flashbooks and could only grunt a welcome that he did not bother to acknowledge. He walked thoughtfully through the room, his eyes on his feet in intense concentration.

Then the quiet shattered. "Wae!" the human's heavy voice roared from the office. "Wae, get in here!"

Kiondili froze, then dropped the flashbooks and leapt to the door. Had Stilman turned on the beamer with his hand in the field? Or had she erased some important calculations from a flashbook by mistake? She came to a breathless stop in front of his desk.

"What is it?" she asked, scanning the room with all her senses and finding no pain in the man and no danger that she could see.

"How did this get in here, Wae?" Stilman demanded, holding up the beamer. "It was on my desk when I came in."

"I put it there last night," she answered, bewildered. "I did not know if you would need it before I got in this morning."

"And how did you get in here to put it there?"

Kiondili stiffened. "The door was unlocked," she said in a low voice. "I touched nothing, just set it on your desk and left."

"Oh." Stilman seemed taken aback for a moment. "Well. Yes. I do need it this morning." He paused and shot her a clear, sharp look of piercing intensity. "What do you know about tachyon decomposition?"

Kiondili stared at him. Was he serious? First he almost accused her of being a thief—just as Argon had in the corridor—and then he asked how much she knew about mass behavior at faster-than-light speeds?

Stilman motioned impatiently.

"Just what I studied back on Jovani and what the hypnolibrary has in it," she said finally. "I have been taking in the latest hypnonet listings."

"Hmph." Stilman shot the next question like a firebolt. "So do you think the missing factor in the mass transference equation is in the energy conversion or in the acceleration of the mass?''

"Acceleration of the mass," she answered confidently.

"Why?" He was testing her. A flash of emotion told her he had been pleased at her answer.

"Because," she answered simply, "the energy conversion is a second-order equation. It's the acceleration of the drag field of the hyperlight matter that has yet to be compensated for."

"Your own thinking or someone else's?" he asked sharply.

She shrugged. "There aren't that many possibilities. I chose the one that seemed most reasonable to me."

"Hmm." Stilman turned one of the holotanks on and handed her a set of jacks. "Then how far could a standard Tore ship jump, given this set of equations and these trans-ference ratios?" He powered up a flashpad and scrawled a set of variables over the diagram that floated between them.

Kiondili studied the holo carefully. "The ship would boost to hyperlight," she said slowly, sighting her calculations into the tank with the floating ship. "But the mass loss in hyper-light space would be too great. The best they could hope for would be a jump of about thirty-one light-years." She frowned. "And the ship would recombine—" She nodded as if convincing herself. "—but there would not be enough energy to recombine completely. About half the ship would be lost at the lightspeed singularity."

Stilman studied her as carefully as she had studied the equations. "I understand you are esper. I'm not. But I can tell when you mean what you are saying. There are tricks you can play that would make it seem to me as if you told the truth, but I tell you now," he said, smiling, and she took no threat from his words, "I will throw you out if I find out that you used anything like that on me."

Kiondili started to reply, but Stilman forestalled her. "Do you know why we wanted you in particular?"

She shook her head. She had wondered about that herself. There were others more intelligent, others with higher esper, even others who had higher field sensitivity than she did. She was not so xenocompatible that aliens did not find her humanness disturbing and vice versa. The Ixia who had visited the lab the day before had reminded her of that.

He smiled briefly. "We need sensors to complete our experiments, as you'll find out if you stay here. But we've had a damned hard time finding sensors who are relatively xenocompatible and who have strong enough blocks to work closely with some of the others who are already here. This outpost is not like a Federation planet. As you know, onplanet, the species who are allowed to land are regulated carefully so that out-and-out conflicts don't occur. It's not that way here. This is a research outpost, one of the three administered by the H'Mu Guardians. And we accept anyone who can contribute to the work. The Federation requires us to wear our persona adapts, of course, and that lets incompatible life-forms know who is coming near them, but it still gets tricky. For instance, you met Lan-Lu? She's an Ixia. There aren't many H'Mu who can work with her. There are even fewer who can argue theory or application with her without triggering her dinner instincts. I have to work with her, so my assistant—that is, you—will also have to work with her and with others." He nodded at Kiondili. "You did well with Lan-Lu yesterday." She flushed slightly at the unexpected praise. "You also have an interest in physics. You're not outstanding in any of those areas"—he ignored her expression—"but most espers of your rank go into the reader trades. After all, you can make a fortune reading the history of an object or area. Half the Federation shields are readers, you know."

Kiondili quirked an eyebrow. Federation peace officers—readers? Shields were used for everything from armed confrontations to treaty negotiations. Each species had its own shields, unless it rented shields from the Federation. The shields who worked in H'Mu space were directed by the H'Mu Guardians—meaning that they were beyond the guild's long arm. She wondered why she had never considered becoming a shield. Then she flushed. The guild practically owned Jovani, the planet she had been on. They would not have encouraged her to find out about other options for work.

"Your combination of skills is one that isn't made up often enough," Stilman continued. "Still interested in the job?"

"Yes," she said, too quickly. Then she added, more easily, "Of course."

He nodded, then handed her a flashpad. "Put your ID on your contract and tubemail it to Central Control. I'll get a copy of it later."

She pretended to read it, but all she saw was the series of blanks that fell throughout the lines of tight print. It took only a second to put her ID on the largest blank. As soon as she had, the other spaces filled in automatically with her name, race rating, and ID number, and she stared at the filled-in blanks with satisfaction.

"Now," Stilman continued, "before I get engrossed in what I'm doing and forget my duties, I'll tell you what my responsibilities to you are."

Kiondili hurriedly collapsed the flashpad and stuffed it in her pocket. She would send it to Central Control immediately. Later, once it was filed, she would read the details herself.

"Corson is a fully accredited outpost," Stilman said, "so one of my responsibilities is to make sure you have adequate training in your field while you work for me. That field of study, of course, is your choice. Should you choose a field incompatible with mine, you will eventually be transferred to someone who would be better suited for your own studies.

"Room and board are included in the posting up to a limit of fifty credits a cycle, so if you want something more spacious than the standard cubicle, you'll have to pay for it. Something I advise you not to do, since every cubic meter costs a fortune out here."

Kiondili nodded, and he continued. "I understand you are already on probation, so your pay will only be half what it will be if I decide to keep you as my assistant: twenty-five credits a cycle for now, fifty later. If you brought any debts with you, you are responsible for them, not me. Got that?'' He looked down at his desk. ''I'm told you're quite talented with imaging and equations. Most of the theoretical work I do is based on the information stored in that stack of flash-books over there. I'll want you to be familiar with that material before you start on any real work. Oh, and Wae,'' he added, ''about the incident in the corridor: You'll find that there are some citizens here who provoke a response.'' He gave her a serious look. ''The most dangerous of them are not the Ixia or obvious predators.''

She met his eyes and nodded slowly.

''Now,'' he continued abruptly, handing her a note, ''take this message to Chute Eleven, outer triad; this to Chute Fifty-nine, central triad.'' He handed her a flashbook that registered full. He paused. ''And since no one knows who you are yet, give this—'' He set a small, dull-red box on top of the other things in her hands and pressed a black button set into its side. ''—to the assistant in the lab where you'll deliver the book. We call him Poole—no one knows what his real name is, but it's probably not pronounceable. He's the hairy one. His boss, who gets the flashbook, is a fairly normal Mu with red hair.''

Kiondili raised her eyebrow. What exactly did Stilman think made a normal Mu?

''Make sure you get the box there in exactly—'' He glanced at his chronometer. ''—Twenty-two point eight minutes.''

He grinned suddenly, and his face splintered from the severe look into that of a boyish human. ''The timing is important, Wae. Tell Poole—the assistant—it came in special cargo with your ship. Give him this message: Two raise twice, six over, point oh one eight, drive through and release.'' He gave her a sharp amused look. ''Stay calm, no matter what happens. It may not work, but I think I've finally hit on one he can't top.'' He dismissed her with a wave.

Kiondili juggled the objects in her hands and repeated the messages silently.

"Oh, and Wae," Stilman stopped her on her way out. "After you give the box to Poole, make sure you stand well back. And after whatever happens happens, give him this message for me: The minnow pulls back on the hook."

"You can't be serious," she protested. "He'll think I'm crazy."

"Poole will appreciate that it comes from me. Go on. Hurry. You've only got twenty-one point two minutes now, and you still have to go over that stack of flashbooks today when you get back."

She hesitated, then shrugged. Not wanting to be caught with the mysterious box in her hands when Stilman's clock ran out, she hurried. It was still early enough that few citizens were in the corridors, and she had no competition for the free-boost chutes. Apparently the outpost ran on individual, not standard, time.

As she dropped into the nearest chute opening, her hair floated out in the sudden absence of gravity, then she hit the acceleration pad and twisted into a dive.

Ayara's eyes, but she loved the boost chutes. Her field skills had increased so that now she could activate the boost pads before reaching them. That gave her a speed advantage that others could not duplicate and a sharpness to the cornering and braking that had won her the title of chute queen back at the institute. She hit the next redirection pad at an angle, branching off toward the outer triad just ahead of a pair of Mu who floated sedately into the intersection behind her. A double hit on the next two pads, then a right-angle bounce . . . She was in heaven, her hair streaming back and her shoulders taking up the shock of the next redirection. How fast could one go in the boost chutes?

Up ahead, she sensed several Mu shooting toward her, one after the other. They were preceded more closely by the flash of the biosensors, and Kiondili politely skimmed the yellow-toned side of the tube as they slammed around the corner pad and whipped past. She was almost sorry when she found her exit and had to leave the chutes to deliver

Stilman's note. Why Stilman did not just viscom the person to whom the note was to be given was beyond her. Humans, she snorted.

She trotted down the hall. There was plenty of time to make the second delivery and get the mysterious box to the alien called Poole. Perhaps she could get a tour of one of the other labs, find out about the other researchers' projects . . .

Activating the viscom at the lab, she hummed tunelessly, waiting for the woman inside to answer.

"Yes?" No image accompanied the voice—the woman who answered did not have the holo turned on.

"I have a note for Effi Ragan." She held it up; the light on the com indicated that the woman could see her even if Kiondili could not see into the lab.

The door shimmered abruptly, clearing to present an older woman—pure human again, Kiondili realized, just like Stilman. But the sharp mental probe that the woman sent stiffened Kiondili's own blocks, and the old woman's eyes narrowed as she recognized Kiondili's reaction. "Esper," she hissed.

A pure human with such strong esper? Kiondili shrugged mentally. Ever since the acceptance of esper as a marketable skill, more humans each generation were free to develop their senses rather than hide them. But Effi Ragan's probe had still been stronger than Kiondili had expected, though she had blocked it easily. She hesitated at the woman's hostile expression, then half held her hand out in esper greeting.

The white-haired woman ignored it.

Kiondili flushed. The envy behind Effi's rejection was palpable. Dropping her hand, she presented the note. "I'm Stilman's assistant. He sent this for you."

"I know who you work for," the woman said irritably. She saw Kiondili's eyes focus over her shoulder and immediately shifted to block the view into her lab. "You delivered your note," she said curtly. "You may leave."

Her cheeks darkening further, Kiondili turned away. The door was already shimmering shut.

The pounding of Kiondili's heated pulse filled her ears as she made her way mechanically back to the boost chutes. Fourth-class citizen. Mutant esper. Stronger sense than a human could have naturally, and strange-looking, besides. The human woman might as well have shouted it. Kiondili clenched the red box. It would have done no good to explain. The engineering that had created her mutancy had occurred centuries before, and Kiondili refused to apologize for what had been a talent from birth. For a pure human, Effi's esper sense was exceptional; for a H'Mu, it was strong enough to earn the H'Mu high-esper status, but it was still much less than Kiondili's talent. And though Kiondili could block her thought projections, she could not hide her E-rating from other high espers, no more than other high espers could hide their ratings from her. She wondered if pure humans should perhaps have been allowed a separate race rating instead of being included with their human-mutant variations as H'Mu. The jealousy in Effi's eyes . . . And what if Argon, her lab assistant, fed that envy with his own insecurity? The people Argon kept company with were nonesper themselves, or were half as strong as Effi. For Kiondili to become part of their group . . . She smoothed the fine, gray hair on the back of her neck with a tense fist. She could not help the challenge she represented. She had met those like Argon and Effi before, but it never got easier. Before her, the boost chute opened like a jaw, and she dropped abruptly in, hitting the first acceleration pad as hard as she could.

By the time she strode toward the lab where she was to deliver the flashpad and box, she had wiped the dark expression from her face and the resentment from her gray eyes. Effi Ragan was only one person. Argon, the H'Mu from her first day, was only one more. Stilman was fair, and so, too, was that female H'Mu with the blue skin. Kiondili would meet others.

She had six minutes to spare on Stilman's clock when she turned a corner and tripped headlong over a mass of fur. Falling into a diving roll, she managed to land on her feet without dropping the flashbook or disturbing the red box she was carrying so carefully. The alien Robul was not so lucky.

"You idiot!" The voice was a high chittering, uttered in a scream as the face shot out from one side of the furball. Legs and arms emerged from the alien's sides as the Robul tried to right himself. "What were you doing tearing through the halls like that? You could have bruised my retraction slots."

"Ayara's eyes, I—I'm sorry, citizen," she stammered. She tried to help him over onto what seemed to be his stomach. "Forgive me—I was in a hurry to a lab. I had no idea you would be in the middle of the hall."

"Where did you suppose I'd be when I was thinking? Somewhere convenient to your impatient Mu mind, I suppose." The chittering was fast, highly irritated.

"I'm sorry, citizen," she said quickly again. She had little more than five minutes before Stilman's mark. "But I am in a hurry. I have a time limit—"

"Time?" the chittering burst. Then the face retracted slightly, and the eyes focused on the object in her nervous hands. "That box looks like Stilman's work. Is it?"

"Yes, citizen. I am terribly sorry, but I've really got to go . . ." Less than five minutes now.

"To whom are you taking that?" he demanded, peering suddenly at the box.

"Chute Fifty-nine."

"To Battez?" he asked, the chittering sounding puzzled. "Or to Poole, that assistant of his?"

"The flashbook to the researcher, the box to the assistant," she said, edging away. Four and a half minutes.

"Instructions?" he barked at her.

"Two raise twice, six over, point oh one eight, drive through and release." She said it all in one breath. "Citizen, with all due apologies, I've got to go now . . ."

The chittering seemed to choke for a minute, and Kiondili was frightened that she had somehow hurt the alien with the tumble before she realized he was laughing. "Drive through and release.'' The Robul chuckled. ''Oh, Stilman's got him wickedly this time.''

''Citizen—''

''Let's go, Mu,'' the Robul chittered. ''It's primed, and you don't want to be holding it when it goes off.''

Kiondili glanced at her chronometer one more time and took off, surprised to find the alien loping gracefully and almost silently beside her on its spindly legs.

''You're Stilman's new assistant?''

''Kiondili Wae.''

''He did not tell you what you were doing, did he?''

She shook her head, then realized that the alien would probably not be able to tell if the motion was part of her gait or part of her conversation. ''No,'' she said. ''Just to give it with the message.''

The Robul dodged through an opening. ''Here, this is shorter. We'll go through my lab—saves about thirty seconds.''

''Citizen—'' she started.

''Coos, please,'' the Robul answered, skittering around a corner and emitting a high piercing noise. She almost dropped the box to cover her ears. ''Through here,'' he chittered. She dodged through the door that shimmered open at his whistle, catching the sharp tingle of the field as they passed through before it cleared completely.

She panted after him. The Robul was much faster on his four spindly legs than she was on her two. She caught only a glimpse of the lab as they dashed through, and then they were out into another corridor. One and a half minutes left.

Coos brought them up before a door and halted her with a gesture from his spidery arms. ''Be calm. Look natural— if a Mu can do that,'' he chittered. ''Otherwise, Poole will suspect.''

She controlled her breathing and put up her esper blocks tightly. Counting the seconds, she waited impatiently as the alien opened the door, then she followed him in.

The lab was painfully neat, opposite in appearance to Stilman's work area. At the counter to her left, examining a holo of equipment that was partially dismantled, was a red-haired Mu and a furry biped—a Dhirrnu. So that was what Stilman was up to. Dhirrnu were the practical jokers of the universe. This one must have pulled something on Stilman, and Stilman was getting him back. To have a Dhirrnu in an experimental lab—that took courage, she thought. And to make Kiondili part of a joke on one—that would put her in line for the alien's next retaliation. Stilman must have known the position he had just put her in. But the time on the box was running out, and she was curious.

"Excuse me, are you Poole?" she asked politely.

He looked her over, his yellow eyes sharp, and nodded.

"This came for you as special cargo with a trader ship that docked this morning." One minute to go. "With this message: Two raise twice, six over, point oh one eight, drive through and release." Fifty seconds.

The Dhirrnu took the box carefully, frowning. He gave Kiondili another glance, then shrugged and turned his attention to the object in his hands. "Two raise twice . . ." He tapped it twice and lifted it two measured distances into the air. "Six over . . ." He rotated it six times, end over end. Thirty seconds. "Point oh one eight—" He rotated it a precise arc before him. "Drive through," he repeated, pushing one finger into the black button on the side. "And release." He pulled his finger back and waited for the box to do something. Ten seconds. He frowned. Kiondili held her breath. Four seconds. The alien who had led her to the lab motioned casually to the other scientist and stepped away from the Dhirrnu. Poole opened his mouth.

And then there was a flash and a sound and a smell and a light. Kiondili stayed where she was, her eyes cringing and waiting for sight to return. The two scientists to her left were snickering—she could hear them over the startled sounds the Dhirrnu assistant was making. There seemed to be something wrong with the alien. His hair was growing. Not just his hair but his nails, his eyelashes—everything on the

Dhirrnu's outward body seemed to be lengthening. The body hair was already several finger lengths longer than it should have been, and now, sprouting from the newly luxurious growth of fur, were—Ayara's eyes, could it be believed?—plants. Flowers that intertwined with the assistant's fur till they made the whole length stand out on end, two hand spans from his normal hair length. His brows were hedges on his face. His lashes batted like unfamiliar wigs over his eyes.

Kiondili cleared her throat, her first instant of disbelief replaced by a bubbling laughter that threatened to choke her. "The minnow—" she said, trying to speak. Poole, who now looked like a walking meadow, stared at her, incredulous, as his hair stabilized two hand spans out from his body to support a still-growing mat of flowers that covered him completely. "The minnow," she tried again, "pulls back on the hook." Then she let loose and whooped so hard that she cried.

"Stilman!" the Dhirrnu roared, reaching for Kiondili. But he tripped on the flowers that stretched out from his feet and Kiondili took the opportunity to dash to the door.

She was a few steps away when she remembered the flashbook she was also supposed to deliver. Should she go back now? Why not? Another glimpse of that flowery assistant would keep her amused for days. She buzzed the lab door, and it opened to a vision she had trouble taking seriously.

"This is for Battez," she said quickly, shoving the flashbook at Poole and trying not to sneeze at his growth. "You look very nice, really," she added. "Is that what they call a spring coat?" The two scientists in the room howled, and Kiondili backed away quickly from the advancing Dhirrnu. She made her way back to Stilman's lab chuckling.

CHAPTER 4

Kiondili was still wiping the tears from her eyes when she got back to the lab and reported the success of the joke.

"Ha!" her new mentor said gleefully. "That will teach that hairy dog to leave my experiments alone." He paused and frowned suddenly. "Did it look like the growth was stabilizing when you left?"

"His hair length stopped at two hand spans, but the flowers were still growing when I ducked out."

"They should stop soon, although I have no idea how long the effects will last on a Dhirrnu." He saw the look on Kiondili's face and added, "I didn't have much chance to experiment. You do understand," he said suddenly, "that you are now a Dhirrnu target?"

"Dhirrnu retaliate only for the joke played on them. You played the joke. I just passed it on."

"Poole has a broad sense of humor, Wae, and you delivered the box for me. You will be next on his list until he thinks of a way to top my trick. Walk softly, Wae, and don't be too embarrassed by whatever happens. The Dhirrnu's jokes are pretty sophisticated now. After all—'' The older man grinned again. ''—this is Corson. He has genius to play with.''

Kiondili spent the rest of the day in the sanctuary of Stilman's labs, sorting, filing, and filling up flashbooks with compiled notes and old lecture material. As she went, she realized a grudging respect for the way Stilman kept notes. They were clear and organized, at least as far as the immediate discussion went. Sometimes there were leaps of thought from one book to the next, and with frustration, Kiondili found those holes filled in by other flashbooks. Organizing the notes was like taking three steps forward and two back.

As she worked, Kiondili began to realize how Stilman's work fit into the hyperlight drive project. His question to her about mass transference had not been inconsequential. Stilman was actually working on a beamer that would transfer the sublight mass into hyperlight mass. In fact, he was working on the main drive itself. That little beamer she had found for him on the first day was just one of a dozen miniaturized prototypes. She shook her head, reading another set of formulas and recognizing the sequence that computed the energy needed to send a ship to lightspeed and beyond.

She got her own half-empty flashbook, copying the formulas from Stilman's book into her own. She would go over this herself. To work on the beamer—this was the missing element of H'Mu space science. Her eyes grew dreamy. This might be the beamer that made it all possible—increased the energy of the ship to lightspeed, transferred it across the singularity at the light barrier, and then decomposed the ship into hyperlight particles. This might not just be another attempt at a hyperlight drive—this could be the drive that freed H'Mu from the onus of being a sublight race. Her hands clenching the flashbook, Kiondili's face took on a fierce look.

That evening, as she sat alone in the Hub cafeteria, she was not surprised to see Poole approach her table. She hid her smile. The trail of flowers he was shedding between the tables followed him like wilted grass cuttings.

"Kiondili Wae," the Dhirrnu acknowledged, seating himself opposite her.

"Citizen Poole," she replied, keeping a straight face with difficulty as a yellow flower slowly sprouted from his still-bushy eyebrow. Its petals waved at her with the movement of his head.

"Just Poole, please," he said.

"Then call me Kiondili."

Poole smoothed his fur wryly and grinned, his sharp teeth displayed in staggered rows. "It was clever of Stilman to use you. I did not know who you were or who you worked for. It will take me much *ti'kai* to get him back for this." He gestured at himself. "He is one up on me, and so you are, too. Welcome to the outpost, Kiondili Wae," he said expansively, getting to his feet. He swept a handful of flowers from his coat and bowed as he offered them. "May you live in luck." He handed her the flowers and left.

Kiondili gazed after him, amused, holding the tiny bouquet.

For a quarter cycle Kiondili had little conversation with anyone except Stilman. Poole's threat to retaliate did not materialize, and Kiondili was so busy that she did not speak to him or any of the other assistants. The flashpads and flashbooks she promised herself she would read piled up until she stored the information in her terminal. She would get to them eventually, she told herself. As for working with Stilman, the researcher was already bouncing ideas and theories off Kiondili as if she were a flashboard. Sometimes she pulled the answer to one of his questions from her own background. Other times the missing information was so obvious, projected from Stilman's subconscious, that she picked it up and slid it neatly into the conversation without interrupting Stilman's thread of speech.

At first he had seemed surprised when she supplied the factor or variable he could not remember. Then one day, when she murmured the missing constant from his side, he admitted, "It's very helpful but rather startling. Are you actually reading my mind?"

She laughed briefly and shook her head. "Of course not," she said, computing a new series of formulas for a modification to the beamer that they had just discussed. "But sometimes when you think, you concentrate so loud that I can't help hearing what you forget to say."

Stilman's laughter barked as shortly and intensely as his thoughts.

Other researchers came by, some waiting to talk with Stilman, some leaving messages, some just standing in the lab for minutes and then going away again without an explanation. The Robul, she recognized, and the predator she had met on her first day. She wondered about the predator. Lan-Lu held a fascination for her, and it was one she knew the Ixia was not blind to. With her blocks, Kiondili thought she should have been able to keep her feelings from the Ixia, even in an enclosed room. But Lan-Lu seemed to know every thought that struck her. It was not an esper sense—or at least esper as Kiondili knew it—that Lan-Lu used. Rather, it was a sixth sense of the hunter, something less tangible than an esper probe or block. Kiondili studied it, watched Lan-Lu, and pulled her emotions ever closer to herself as she sensed the Ixia's reactions. Though she did not want to leave Stilman, she knew that if she had to request a transfer to another scientist, she would choose Lan-Lu. It was not just her fascination: The Ixia was working on the sublight recombination phase of their FTL drive. If Kiondili could not work on the transmission beam itself, the sublight recombination would be her next choice.

Several times other assistants dropped things off or picked things up for Stilman. Of the three she had run into on her first day, she met on better terms with Tior—the H'Mu woman with blue skin and a thin set of water bags under her chin—and Jordan, the taller man whose triple-jointed limbs gave him a skeletonlike walk. Tior was from a dry planet. She said that when she was home and had drunk fully, the water bags hung down so far that they rested on her collarbone. Kiondili was not sure she believed Tior, but the other Mu's humor made her feel more welcome. Jordan made her feel welcome, too, though in a different way—he invited her to share a dreamer channel with him. Kiondili declined. It was not that she did not find the tall Mu interesting. It was that dreamer channels were only random guides. What she and Jordan shared in a dream could change her relationship with him into something awkward to work around, and she did not need more stress between her and the other assistants at Corson. Not with Argon around, anyway. Argon, the one who had picked the fight with her, came to the lab twice, but Kiondili did not speak to him. She would have to talk with him eventually. He worked with the same group Stilman did; in fact, he worked for Effi Ragan, the older human woman to whom Kiondili had delivered Stilman's note on her second day at the outpost.

By the end of her fourth week Kiondili was beginning to feel settled in. Her mornings were a routine of working for a few hours in the lab, making her way to the Hub for breakfast, then on to hypnotape reading, general applications—a class where they had to create problems as well as solve them—and back to the lab. In the afternoons she accompanied Stilman to the research discussions or worked with him on the hyperlight beamer. The afternoon sessions were draining, but it was that time she liked the best.

One day the afternoon session lasted a full three hours, and when Kiondili made her way back to her quarters, she was exhausted. Her brain felt as if it had been whipped up one side and beaten down on the other. Trying to keep up with the speed at which the scientists brought up, discussed, and discarded ideas could be blinding. Half the time Kiondili was not sure she understood why the idea was being tossed. Other times she was not sure she understood the entire direction of the conversation.

She sighed, coding her door to shimmer open, then scowling as she saw her room. She had forgotten to put away the retract furniture again, and her bed and dresser drawers were still out. And there was some sort of field transmission bleeding through the insulation again. She rubbed her forearms irritably where the hum of the field tickled her nerves. Tossing her flashbook at her chair, she turned to the control panel. But the sound of the flashbook hitting the floor stopped her, and she glanced over her shoulder. No, the book was on the chair. She must be hearing things. She played her fingers over the keypad—bed back in the wall, drawers down into the floor, and at last she could call out her reading couch. She reached for her flashbook as she sat down on the couch to relax. And landed on the floor instead.

Her rump hit with a dull thud as she fell through the holo of the couch. "Wha—" Her teeth clicked hard as she landed. She sat stock-still, staring at the perfectly formed hologram of the couch. "In all the realms of sixth-dimensional space, what is going on?" She passed her hand through the wall of the couch to make sure, and then a slow smile surfaced ruefully on her face. She groped through the shape of the other chair for her flashbook. This had to be Poole's work. She shook her head. "That hairy-toed Dhirrnu . . ." she muttered with a grin. She rubbed her buttocks. She had landed hard.

She could not see the hologenerators, but he would have masked them into the room with the furniture program. She grinned again. He was clever. The subfields were not distinct enough for her to sense their direction; he must have set up distorts to confuse her. She would have to search the entire room by touch before she could locate the boxes and disarm them. Very clever, she admitted again. "All right, Poole," she said to herself, "if it's *ti'kai* you're after here, two can play at this game."

Next day Kiondili showed up at the lab only to have Stilman tell her to cancel her morning's work and sit in on the rest of the meeting they had quit the previous day. She did not have a chance to tell him about Poole's trick, but she suspected that he would hear about it soon enough. She had found a viscom installed with one of the hologenerators. It was a sure thing that the other lab assistants had by now seen her fall through her furniture to discover Poole's joke.

Stilman motioned for her to hurry. "There will be some people you haven't yet met," he said over his shoulder, striding down the corridor. "Since we were able to make a decision about the test runs yesterday, we've finally gotten to the point where we can begin the real work." He stepped into the free-boost chute, hit the acceleration pad with a solid thud, and disappeared down the tube in a green-and-blue streak of tunic and breeches and bare feet. Diving after him, Kiondili caught up in a second, slowing to match his speed by triggering the local drag fields along the wall. She noticed that he had another pile of flashpads with his flashbook. They would not all be notes for the meeting. Some would no doubt be more deliveries for her. Why did he not use tubemail or the comlink for most of his messages? For his advanced work, she could understand—even tubemail could be tampered with. But personal delivery for everything?

In front of her, Stilman caught a redirection pad expertly on his shoulder and bounced into a branch tube, then stepped out of the grav-free chute without waiting for inertial compensation. His momentum caught up with him at the corridor opening, but he was already bracing back. He hardly even jerked. Kiondili, on his heels, had to admire his movements. It must have taken him years to acquire that grace. Most pure humans—and even some of the Mu types—had a hard time adjusting their equilibrium in and out of an abruptly grav-free environment. She would have asked him about it, but he was already greeting another researcher at the entrance to the conference room.

"Wae—" he motioned over. "This is Rae Arr. Rae's our field specialist."

The stubby woman scrutinized Kiondili carefully for a long moment, then smiled and held out her fingertips in esper greeting. Surprised at the courtesy, Kiondili reached out in response, not quite touching Rae's hand physically. Her esper impression of the short Mu woman suggested a bearing much taller than her actual body.

Stilman turned to introduce the other members of the small group. "You know Coos and Lan-Lu," he said, "and Effi." Kiondili smiled politely, but the other woman merely looked her up and down as if the Mu left a bad taste in her mouth. Flushing slightly, Kiondili sat down beside Stilman, avoiding Effi's eyes. Behind the human woman Argon dressed in his muted colors as usual, looked smug, and Kiondili swallowed her irritation behind her blocks. On the other side of the flashtable Effi brushed against Lan-Lu's shoulders, and Kiondili stiffened as the predator's wrist claws sprang out instantly. The sharpened scent of the hunter urge was unmistakable, and even Stilman glanced at the alien.

"Relax, Lan-Lu," he said shortly. "This is going to be a long meeting."

The predator let her breath out in a hiss, her slitted eyes glaring at Effi as she pulled her wrist claws back in. But Kiondili, feeling the heated urge of the alien's thoughts, noticed that the tips of Lan-Lu's claws continued to peek out of the predator's golden fur.

One more researcher arrived, and Stilman looked up. "Good, Waon is here. We can start. Kiondili," he said aside to her, "Waon is—"

"Waon is Waon."

Kiondili glanced up as the timbre of the newcomer's voice sent shivers down her spine, then looked again. Ruvian. Like the recruiter who had offered her this posting. The hair at the back of her neck prickled, and the short hairs on her arms stood out. At the same time her aura blocked instantly against an overpowering esper sense that was focused on her. Waon smiled—even his teeth looked as if they were field-generated projections, not solid mass, as did the dark opening of his mouth—and extended his fingertips. Mechanically Kiondili reached up and met them with her own, a full finger's length away. She sagged in relief when that focused energy was turned away as the Ruvian turned back to the table. Calling

Waon a strong esper was making fun of him, she thought unsteadily. She wished she knew more about the engineering of his mutation—the breeding must have taken hundreds of years. What did he eat? she wondered briefly, then flushed again as she realized her other, less discreet thought.

"Let's get on with this," Stilman said, tugging at his bright green tunic. "Clear the flashtable of all that gibberish, Coos. We're not discussing one of your dimensional gate calculations here."

Coos chittered, then stored his designs carefully before wiping the table. Setting it on automatic record, the alien retracted his legs as the others around the table settled.

Stilman tapped his flashwriter on the table for attention. "All right, our current problem is one of materials design. Some of our compounds are remaining too unstable at the singularity of the light barrier."

"We should reconsider using a new field," Rae Arr, the short esper, suggested. She coded her flashbook into the table and launched a diagram into the holotank. "A new field, generated in hyperlight space itself, could pull that mass through the singularity." She did not point at the design as she commented, but her mental projection was so strong that Kiondili saw exactly where Rae had focused. Kiondili wondered if Stilman could pick that up or if he had to guess.

Lan-Lu tapped her knuckle claws together, and Rae glanced at her. The Ixia ran her tongue over her sharp teeth. "We would still have to allow for another particle director," the predator said. "That would take care of the extra mass we would have to acquire to hold another field."

Waon stirred in his chair. "Cannot," he said flatly. He called up the engine design in another corner of the table and combined it with the existing ship design on the flashtable.

"Waon is right," Effi said, cutting Stilman off before he could respond to Lan-Lu's comment. Lan-Lu's knuckle claws gleamed before she pulled them back. Stilman looked at Effi irritably. Without showing her work to the others, the older woman erased the hastily scribbled computations she had drawn in her own flashpad and pointed to the previous projection on the table. "If we have to increase the slope of the energy gain, we can only do it here, at this point . . . ."

Kiondili listened carefully as Stilman directed the meeting. As fast as one person came up with a suggestion, someone else overrode it with argument. They picked holes in each other's theories and computations until each problem had been thrashed and cut down to components they could handle one at a time. Lan-Lu actually snapped at Effi, one hand full of bared claws and her pointed teeth gnashing. Then Stilman got so excited at one of Rae's comments that he lost his flashwriter in the air while waving his arms. The second time it happened, the writer got caught in Coos's body hair and had to be carefully disentangled by one of the assistants. Somewhere during the arguments Coos retracted his face and arms to think about something else.

"This won't be solved here today; that much is obvious," Stilman said finally. "Lan-Lu, pull in your claws," he ordered irritably. "And Coos, come out of your coat and listen. We've got a problem in pulling the ship's mass through the light barrier, and we've got a problem with the mass gain that follows once the ship passes into hyperspace. How much energy do we need to shed—how much actual mass must we lose to make a reasonable jump? And how much can we regain when we cross the barrier back into sublight spacetime? That is the problem now."

Rae frowned, and Coos chittered softly to himself.

"What about using a transitory field to support the ship?" Kiondili asked hesitantly. "See here—" She pointed at the design. "—you could hold the sublight matter in suspension while you cross the light barrier. It should take about a picosecond." She glanced down at her notes. "The energy gain would go to infinity right as the ship crosses the singularity. But the ship's mass would recompose again in hyperlight spacetime without having been completely disintegrated . . . ." Kiondili's voice trailed away.

Effi Ragan was staring. Behind the human woman, Argon's eyes were narrowed. Even Coos, his yellow eyes unblinking, regarded her curiously. What had she said? Was it so ridiculous a suggestion? Waon gazed at her thoughtfully, and Kiondili glanced around the room. She realized with a sinking feeling that during the entire meeting the other assistants had not said a word.

But Rae Arr was nodding her head, and Lan-Lu, her wrist claws preening her fur absently, was looking at Kiondili with new regard.

Stilman frowned. "Separate suspension?" he said slowly. "That close to light, the sublight structure's pretty useless, anyway. The computers could kick in on a preboost, start the transition, say, closer to this point—"

"That will scatter matter before the fields can control it," Effi snapped, still glaring at Kiondili.

"No." Lan-Lu reached across the table, one of her elbow claws dragging deliberately on the flashpad with a nerve-wrenching screech. Effi shuddered, and Kiondili felt more than saw Lan-Lu's sly expression. The predator crossed out one of Stilman's variables with her own flashwriter. "You are forgetting this term here." The images in the holotank shifted subtly.

Effi watched the computations warily. "If you do that," she said, pushing the white hair from her eyes, "you'll screw up the hyperlight decomposition just after you cross the barrier."

"Then start mass transference at this point," Stilman pointed out.

"That," Rae said, "will throw off the thruster support field."

"Look," Waon said shortly. He scrawled a few computations on the screen. "So, and so."

There was silence for a few minutes as the others studied his work. Coos chittered quietly to himself, and Stilman and Rae Arr murmured at the changes. Lan-Lu, her slitted eyes examining the design critically, finally nodded.

"Well . . ." Stilman said, "that looks like a go. Anyone

have any more objections? No? Then let's put that one down for now and go over it later. Nice idea, Wae.''

Kiondili flushed, ducking her head at the praise.

She was still feeling warm inside when they broke up for lunch two hours later.

"Wae," Stilman said, stopping her as she made her way toward the nearest boost chute. "What are you doing for lunch?"

She looked up, surprised.

"Join us," Lan-Lu hissed, gesturing for her to fall in with them.

Waon nodded at the younger Mu, his field-generated mass moving silently past, and Kiondili glanced at him uncertainly, her sensor skills almost overpowered by his nearness. She would need stronger blocks than she had now if she was to be around him much. Being with Waon was like standing within instead of outside an engine's field as she tuned it—each movement, each sound changed the field flux. Waon smiled as if understanding her thoughts, though she knew he had not read them—it would be the height of insult to do so—and Stilman motioned for her to catch up. She hesitated. He gestured again impatiently, and she made up her mind and trotted after the small group. Stilman motioned for her to fall in step with him. He was smug, she realized, and part of it was that he was pleased with her. Tior—the blue-skinned assistant she had run into on the first day—passed Kiondili and, blowing across her water bags to make them burble softly, smiled. Only Effi Ragan, who glowered behind Stilman, and Argon gave her pause.

CHAPTER 5

Tior poked her head into the lab a few days later. "Kiondili, did you hear the news?"

Kiondili, frowning at a holoprojection of the beamer she and Stilman had put together that morning, looked over her shoulder. "What news?"

Tior glanced at the holo with surprised respect, gurgling her water bags quietly as she took in Kiondili's work. "They're going to send the first Lightwing out one cycle—that's a month to you—from today."

Kiondili's interest sharpened, and she froze the holo, turning to face the other woman. "I thought launch was scheduled two full cycles from now."

"It was, but Lan-Lu just got the new field flux tested. They gave the go-ahead to schedule launch just a few hours ago." Tior blew across her water bags so that they vibrated noisily.

"You sound awfully pleased for just another probe launch."

Tior shook her head. "I get to send this one through."

Kiondili raised her eyebrows. "I thought the Lightwing launches were still restricted."

"Up until this morning, yes. But they're choosing up the launch teams now. And—my adviser just told me—I'm on the backup team."

Kiondili swallowed her sudden envy. "They've chosen the backup teams already?"

"Not all of them," Tior admitted. "Most of the slots won't be filled until the end of the week. Siln—the xenopsych—is still going over the recommendations."

Would Stilman recommend Kiondili for a launch team? Her sensor skills were high enough. But no, Effi would block any suggestion that Kiondili participate. She forced a smile. "Are you going to celebrate?"

"Tonight, at eighteen hundred. We're meeting at the Hub."

"Oh." Kiondili was put off further by the realization that if all the assistants were gathering, Argon, too, would be there.

"What's the worry?" The other Mu wagged her finger, and Kiondili half expected it to gurgle. "It's a party. No one is going to be nasty. Although you had better blast softly in Triad Eleven. Effi Ragan's out for your blood."

"What are you talking about?"

"I got it from one of the other assistants. Your theory— the one you spouted off about last quarter cycle—"

"I didn't spout off a theory. It was just a suggestion."

Tior shrugged. "Well, your . . . suggestion turned out to be right. Stilman had engineering make the modifications already. Argon, that snake-tongued warthog, was jealous enough to complain after yesterday's meeting. I didn't think anything about it at the time, but Effi Ragan was standing right beside him when he started shooting off his mouth. If he continued the way he was going, by now Effi probably believes that you are trying to discredit her boost-to-light design."

Kiondili stared. "You've got to be kidding."

Tior motioned at one of the screens in the room. It still displayed Stilman's recent work, and Kiondili's contribution was obvious in the detailed lines of beam transmission. "You're a strong esper, Kiwi. Effi is jealous. She doesn't want to believe that you could come up with a contribution to the project which she should have thought of first. And Argon was making sure she will blame you for her oversight."

Kiondili put her flashbook down slowly.

"You haven't actually worked with Argon yet, have you?" Tior commented. "He and Stilman don't get along."

"I noticed that," Kiondili said coldly, anger stiffening her voice.

Tior shrugged. "Argon was Stilman's assistant when he first got here. He made the mistake of using one of Stilman's computations to impress the outpost director. Next thing he knew, he was kicked out of Stilman's lab and barely got back on the project working for Effi. Stilman hasn't spoken to him since."

"So I have his position," Kiondili realized, "and his hostility is directed at me."

Tior nodded. "Effi and Stilman were in friendly competition for years. Since Argon went to work for Effi, things have changed. Argon has—" Tior hesitated and blew a soft bubble into one of her water bags. "—influenced her," she said finally.

"The competition isn't friendly anymore?"

"It's open war. Now Effi tries to get the upper hand on your boss, but Stilman is too savvy. His theories have been slower to come out, but they always work. Effi's theories fail about half the time when she jumps the blast before passing evaluation and test. Something I think Argon actually encourages her to do."

"To make her more frustrated?"

"Argon never dreamed he would have to work for Effi," Tior said dryly. "Sometimes I think he hates her more than he hates Stilman."

"And now that I'm here, he's using me to get at Stilman." Kiondili ground her teeth in frustration. "But I'm already on probation here. Discrediting my work won't hurt Stilman—it will just get me spaced off the outpost. And from what you said, Stilman would not take him back, anyway.''

''That is not why it would hurt Stilman.'' Tior watched Kiondili closely. ''Argon is claiming you misuse your esper.''

Kiondili stared. ''Then what he is really saying,'' she said slowly, ''is that I'm stealing Effi Ragan's work and passing it along to Stilman.''

''I believe his actual words were that you used her ideas as your own. You know, you gained a lot of credibility with the other researchers on that theory.''

''But—'' Kiondili was so angry, she almost sputtered. ''It's ridiculous to think that I would—that I could—''

''I know.'' Tior held up her hands. ''I read your E-status when I first met you. You couldn't read Effi unless she wanted you to or you forced her. Her natural blocks are at least as good as mine and probably better. After all, she's had to work with some of the predator species—like that Ixia, Lan-Lu—for more than eight years. If she could do that without becoming Lan-Lu's supper, how could she not keep you out?'' She stopped Kiondili's automatic protest. ''Try to see it from Effi's point of view. You come up with a theory that she probably could have thought up herself. Argon tells her that she did think it up and that you stole it. Effi's wide open. She's so worried that someone will get the credit for her research that she doesn't tell Argon or any of her other assistants half of what they need to know to help her. For Argon to tell her you picked her brains . . .'' Tior shrugged. ''Just thought you ought to know in advance, before you end up working with her on the probes. You and Effi are both strong espers. And incompatible espers make project meetings a nightmare, not to mention the mess you would make of a Blob launch together.''

''Blob?''

''When I first came here, we called the probes BLATs, for Boosted Light Acceleration Test. After we squashed a couple at the barrier, Stilman started calling them Blobs instead. It stuck, so blame your employer. Look, you know about Argon now, so you can watch your back. Let's drop this and go celebrate.''

Kiondili nodded, but the frown did not disappear from her face.

Tior triggered the door. ''Meet us at the Hub, Kiwi. You've got an hour to clean up. And get some of that steel out of your eyes,'' she ordered. ''This is supposed to be fun, not a fight.''

Kiondili looked after Tior without seeing her. Argon. It was not enough that she had few friends in this place. She had to make strong enemies, too. She tightened her jaw. She wondered if Stilman's previous assistant had dispersed himself accidentally, after all.

The next several days bore the mark of loneliness. Now that the schedule was beginning to quicken, she found herself working more closely with Stilman, eating at odd hours, and spending more time with his peers rather than her own. Coos, the hairy Robul, she liked. His chittering took some getting used to, but his sense of humor and sharp mind forced her to expand her own ideas and rethink her positions before she spoke. Rae Arr, the short, stocky esper, was quiet but steady. Rae was in charge of the recombination phase of the drive—the complement to Stilman's beamer—but her real love was theorizing about the hyperspace gates. The gates were the only recourse for those members of sublight species who could not afford the high cost of leasing an FTL ship. Too often, though, a being's perceptions were distorted by a gate. H'Mu were particularly susceptible. It was not always fatal—Effi Ragan had proved that when she had walked through such a gate to reach Corson—but as a trade route, the gates were useless to H'Mu. Too many who went in never came out. Rae thought that if she could just understand the time-space distortion inside such a gate, she could apply it to her research, combine Stilman's beamer with the concepts of the gates . . .

And then there was Lan-Lu. The predator always made Kiondili wary, but Kiondili had to admit that she liked the Ixia. Lan-Lu was objective, thorough, and sometimes cruelly honest. She attacked theories the way she would hunt her supper on her home planet. At the same time, she had a sensual streak that had startled Kiondili in those rare instances when Lan-Lu exchanged a greeting by touch.

There were others who ate with Stilman regularly, but the one who captured Kiondili's attention the most was Waon. Being near the Ruvian made her blocks tremble, and his biofields clashed with her senses, making her feel as if sandpaper grated over her skin. Sometimes she could almost feel a rhythm—like distant music—in his fields, as if he might change at any moment into something even more alien than he was already. He did not speak to her about it, but she set her persona adapt to damp all fluctuations when he was around. She did not want to inadvertently invade his privacy by reading his fields.

A few days later, as Kiondili was looking for a place to sit in the cafeteria, she was surprised to see Waon himself who, with one hand holding a thick, yellow, glowing drink, used his other to beckon absently to a seat at Stilman's table. Across from him, Stilman nodded a greeting without interrupting his conversation with Lan-Lu. Kiondili, stiffening her blocks against the presence of both Waon and Lan-Lu, listened with only half an ear to their ongoing argument. As usual, Stilman was trying to change Lan-Lu's mind about some issue that was, at the bottom level, instinctive to the Ixia. At least the silence directed at her by the researchers was comfortable, she told herself. She had waited an hour to eat because Argon was with the other assistants that day. Eating with Argon gave her indigestion.

"Wae?" Stilman asked again.

Kiondili started, realizing that Stilman had asked her a question. "I'm sorry."

"Didn't you have a berth on a trader at one time?" he repeated.

She did not change expression. "For fifteen years."

Lan-Lu glanced at her. "How much actual Contact did you have with other cultures?"

"I was a child. My parents were the ones to Contact and trade."

"But you were involved in Contact?" Stilman persisted.

Kiondili shook her head. "H'Mu like me can't get full guild trade ratings until we're fifteen. But I did navigate and pilot the ship and helped with repair because of my field sensitivity."

Stilman turned to the Ixia. "Wae is a perfect example of what I am talking about. Some Mu just are not as xenophobic as others. Wae was not exposed to Contact until she landed on Jovani. She just handles it better than others."

"She was born into a family of traders. She was raised with the knowledge that she would have Contact," Lan-Lu argued back. Her elbow claws poked out of her fur with her intensity. "And although she was not involved in Contact, she surely met and dealt with aliens. There is no surprise in her."

Kiondili frowned, but Stilman waved his hand. "Of course traders have some Contact, whether they negotiate or not, but Wae here had less actual Contact before going planetside than any other Mu I've known—didn't you, Wae?"

Kiondili nodded slowly. "I talked to many citizens on the holocom link, but they always spoke through translators and persona adapts. I only met a few face-to-face, and they were Mu, not aliens."

"Wae is a powerful esper," Lan-Lu returned disparagingly, her ears flattening. "Whether she had Contact within physical distance of another alien or not, the citizens' presence would have been in her mind."

"You're not esper, Lan-Lu," Stilman pointed out. "How do you know what Wae would have sensed?"

The Ixia hissed, her eyes going black and her knuckle claws flexing at Stilman's challenge. "I am not esper as you know it, Stilman. There are many senses other than those a human can experience."

Kiondili edged warily away from the predator's reach, but Stilman grinned and ran his fingers along his hawkish nose. "You're hunting, Lan-Lu," he teased. "Relax. I agree that xenophobia is as much a result of cultural training as physical reactions. But there are more species than H'Mu who are xenophobic, and tolerance can be learned."

"To what end?" Lan-Lu retorted. "Simply learning to cope with an alien does not change the inner feelings of a H'Mu. And for aliens who are esper, that is as much an insult as a claw in the nostril. Those H'Mu who are least honest in their emotions give the greatest insult with their esper probes and false projections. This outpost is an exception that cannot be repeated in your precious H'Mu colonies. Not, that is, without prejudice and bloodshed. And that is why there must be separate planets for H'Mu and those who are sensitive."

Stilman shook his head vigorously. "I could not disagree more. Yes, H'Mu are not honest in their emotions. But you are missing the point. What is the difference in a H'Mu keeping some feelings to himself and an alien offending a H'Mu by offering or identifying feelings that the H'Mu does not want to acknowledge? Both are boundaries of familiarity, and one is a breach of privacy."

The surge in Lan-Lu's emotions broke against Kiondili like waves, one of fear, the next of hunger. Did Lan-Lu worry about attacking a H'Mu here? It would not be because the H'Mu provoked the attack, she told herself. No one in their right mind would provoke an Ixia.

"An interesting thought," Waon remarked softly as he set his glowing drink aside and rose, "but narrow. The Ixia do not attack one who is not a victim. And H'Mu who are not honest with their feelings to others are hardly more honest with themselves." He paused, and his depthless eyes transfixed Kiondili's gaze. "Who is to say that a H'Mu does not want to become a victim? A hunter does not sense the why behind a victim's actions, only that the opportunity is there." He noted Kiondili's sidewise glance at Lan-Lu. "As for H'Mu, we are often afraid to think beyond our limitations, are we not? After all," he added gently, "it is so much easier to blame others for our lives."

Kiondili looked at him, startled. Then she stared, mesmerized by his depthless gaze. Her natural blocks dropped. She lost her train of thought. Her senses meshed with his fields instinctively, and suddenly she was sucked in. Hypnotized by the rush of sensation, her oversensitive mind automatically touched and cataloged the fields he generated, instinctively massaging those which seemed unstable and fighting away from others. Fields leapt; Waon's energy holes flared to brilliance; and she was cut off and thrown abruptly out.

Kiondili staggered mentally. Yet it had been barely a second, and her senses were still reeling. The Ruvian looked remote and closed off, and, frightened that his blocks hid anger, Kiondili felt a hot shame burn into her cheeks. How could she? she asked herself. To let herself be sucked in like that—would he ever forgive her crudity? She could still feel every nuance of his bizarre fields and knew he knew it. He had sensed her essence as well as she had his . . . The thoughts tumbled, disordering her composure more, but Waon was gone, disappearing through the cafeteria crowd as if to put as much distance between her offense and himself as possible.

Drained, she remained at the table after Stilman and the others had left. Those fields were so strong—had her psyche been affected? No, she decided finally. If Waon's fields had actually changed her, she would have noticed when she had cut in her own blocks. But she had *touched* him. He was not a Mu as she knew them. There was no substance to that body, no weight to his mass. He consumed food, liquid, as if he were as H'Mu as she. He spoke with true sound and projected his esper sense as others did. But he existed as—as some kind of vortex in which energy whirled and was created and killed almost at will.

"Ayara's eyes," she whispered finally, shuddering, "but he is alien."

CHAPTER 6

It was two days before Kiondili forgot the touch of Waon's mind, but the disturbing sensitivity to his moods did not disappear. In meetings, in the corridors, in the Hub—she could not help picking up on them. She was fascinated by the brief flash of insight she had had into the alien—the Mu, she corrected herself automatically when she read his fields in the Hub. Did his thoughts flow like hers? Was the pattern of his mass determined by his fields? Or did he determine his mass patterns himself? His bronzed skin and black eyes were striking and were not the result of body paint. Could he change color at will? With the strength of his fields, how did his will affect his surroundings? Did Waon consider her as far removed from his reality as he was from hers?

"It still bothers me," she complained to Tior. "I wonder about what he is. I even called up the library tapes to see what was written about the Ruvians, but they were engineered by a tangent group. The only information about them is so general that it seems insipid or so specific that I would need twenty years in biophysics to make sense of it." She motioned at her persona adapt. "I used to think this thing protected me from the aliens. Now I think it protects him from me. In the last week I upped my field damp twice just to sit in the same meetings as he did without upsetting his moods even more."

Tior belched unexpectedly, flushed, and tapped one of her water bags to let some air out. "I thought Waon didn't have moods."

Kiondili frowned. "I thought so, too, but he does. And they're like sitting in on someone else's nightmare."

"That will teach you to go around with your blocks half-down."

Kiondili flushed, her gray skin darkening. "Working around him is getting on my nerves. The worst part is, I know it's my fault, but I can't get near enough to him to apologize."

Tior shrugged. "You'll have another chance to say you're sorry at the control room. Waon is on the launch team, too. And we'd better get going. I don't want to be late for my own first launch."

In the control room Stilman latched on to Kiondili and put her to work setting up his instruments to monitor the launch. She glanced over her shoulder as Waon glided by. She almost wished she had found the time to talk to the xenopsych about the Ruvian. Waon had not spoken to her, and she could not avoid him; the disturbing sense of him made her shoulders itch.

She shook herself to clear her head of other thoughts. Perhaps Waon had not been as offended as she feared. Right now she did not want to worry about him, anyway. The unmanned Blob was sitting quietly on the dock, waiting for boost. And in the control room the human woman Effi Ragan was checking out her control panel. Kiondili watched intently. Effi would be monitoring and directing this probe through the sensor link. When the teams began using manned probes, the sensor link would no longer be used—and the

crew of the first manned Lightwing vessel would direct the
launch from the links inside the ship.

"T minus ten seconds and counting," the controller reported. Then, "We have blast. All systems go."

The Blob took off. Launching itself in a backblast of re-
burned, broken-down radiation, it disappeared; an image
appeared in the holo tanks of a skeletal ship with colored
lights for system checkpoints.

"Acceleration at point one lightspeed and climbing," Tior
reported.

"All systems go for blast."

"Acceleration curve constant. We have point three light."

"Switching in secondary boost. All systems still go."

"We have point five light. Acceleration climbing."

"What's the curve?" Coos chittered. "Readout is dimming."

"Boost is fluctuating," Tior cut in.

"Acceleration at point seven light," another controller
added. "We're losing acceleration."

"Backup boost is failing," the second one added. "Power
at fifty-two percent potential."

"Bring up the secondaries," Rae Arr ordered. "Come on,
Effi," she said in a low voice, "hold the boost."

Effi Ragan, white and straining under the headset, said
nothing.

"Easy. Take it easy," Stilman muttered as he set his measurements into the constantly changing screen before him.
But the needles dropped, and red lights flashed. Stilman
swore softly. The Blob was still accelerating, but not fast
enough to make it across the barrier.

"Holding at point seven three light."

"Direct more power into Drive Three!" Coos chittered
angrily.

"Shorting through the trace line. We can't hold the boost."

Lan-Lu ignored Coos, whose scrawny arms were waving
at one of the controllers. Her irritation was reserved for the
presence of so many Mus. She flexed her knuckle claws,

retracted them, then spiked them out again as she watched the controllers. What she could learn from an actual decomposition would help her finish the transference fields for getting the ship across hyperlight spacetime. But she needed the Blob to go hyperlight first. Her wrist claws tapped against one of the board panels, and she snapped them in abruptly.

Stilman groaned as he realized the ship was not going to make it. "Watch that overload—she's going to come down hot . . ."

"I can't hold it!" Effi gasped. The unmanned probe flashed into visible spectrum as it slowed.

Tior, tense as she frowned under her own headset, lost some water on the floor from one of her chin bags. "There's too much tope left in the tanks," she protested. "The tachyon compounds are unstable."

Lan-Lu hissed and said flatly, "Jettison the fuel."

"Acceleration dropping."

Rae shook her head, still staring at the readout of the ship's field flux. "We can't jettison the fuel. The controlling fields are unstable, and we've got a second oscillation on the beam. There's no clear path for the jettison to follow. It would disperse within the primary beam and break it, blowing the entire probe into base particles." She projected the flux readout onto one of the control room holotanks. "We've got to bring that probe back or boost her out of sublight. If we don't, we'll have a tachyon radiation patch in the system the size of a planet."

"Dropping to point seven one lightspeed," one of the controllers intoned.

"Damn it to a digger's hell," Stilman swore under his breath. "That's another half cycle of work wasted."

"Stress relief valves operating above redline. Overload imminent."

"Oscillation increasing in frequency—"

Effi wavered further. The Blob lost momentum. Stilman groaned as the fluctuating fields began to affect the ship's programming.

"Dropping to point seven light."

"It is lost." Waon's clipped speech was almost preempted by Effi's collapse. The two medics standing by took it as normal procedure, but Stilman swore again. The experiment was critical to his research. They had only so many Blobs, and wasting one of them hurt the whole program. Losing this one without attaining light would set them back a full cycle. And with the Federation breathing down their necks to produce results or give way to someone else's research program . . .

"Topes ready to jettison," Tior reported flatly.

"Dropping to point six nine lightspeed."

"Freeze the jettison," someone snapped. "One of the drive programs just dumped. We've got no control over the release valves."

"Warning across the drive chambers."

"Holding. Holding."

"I can't keep power in the primaries—I'm losing beam control."

"Get that drive back up," Lan-Lu hissed. But the tenuous contact between Effi Ragan and the Blob had been broken abruptly when the old woman had collapsed.

"Dropping to point six six light."

"Hold the drive as long as possible," Rae instructed. "We've got to figure out that fluctuation."

"Rebooting now," the controller repeated.

"Topes unstable into redline."

"Damn those drives," Stilman muttered.

"Dropping to point six four light."

"Reboot completed. Drive active."

"Flux still unstable," another controller reported, watching the field graphs dip farther as Rae Arr took over another console.

"We're losing it."

"Tachyon isotope leak across the primaries."

Rae flashed up the images of the topes in a second holotank. Their instability was obvious. In the third holotank the projected breakup turned the unmanned Blob into a bomb. "Block those topes," she snapped. "Short across the secondaries and fix that leak."

Without thinking, Kiondili, her hand gripping the control panel of Effi's now-vacant chair, reached out along the beams undirected by the unused headset. She jammed her own jacks onto her temples, unseeing. Focusing, she steadied the flux that threatened the speeding unmanned ship with destruction. The boost stopped slowing. As she guided the beams, Kiondili felt the interference lessen. There was a break, then the ship's programming snapped back online. The code whipped in, draining the topes from the tanks that were bulging like a bomb about to explode, sucking the energy from the atoms and boosting the ship faster and faster through space. Speed, she told herself. Light . . .

"Hold that jettison!" Stilman shouted over the controllers. "We've got acceleration!"

Rae glanced at the first holotank. "Acceleration in the main drives!" she snapped at the controllers.

"Stop the jettison!" Stilman yelled again. "We're on boost again!"

"Acceleration?" "What's happening in the secondaries?" "Who's on the Blob?"

Kiondili ignored the voices beating at her as she concentrated on the tiny unmanned ship. *Light*, she thought.

"We're go for boost." "We're on the boost!" Voices clashed as all the controllers tried to get their messages across the sudden din. "Power in Drive Three. Power in Drive Four," one of the controllers cut in excitedly. "Power in secondaries. Power in Drive Five."

"Who's on the Blob?"

"We've got a green light across the beamer chambers."

"Watch that flux . . ." Rae glared at her screens.

"Flux nearing normal."

"Who's on the Blob?"

"Acceleration in all drives," the controller reported.

"We've got point seven light."

"We're on boost. Mass is increasing at normal slope. Repeat, we're go for boost."

"Shielding weakening over the secondaries . . ." The warning cut through the crowd.

"We've got a heat leak in number twelve."

"Hold the boost, Wae." Waon's voice cut across the noise like a knife. "Control the secondaries."

There was no time to register surprise. "Strengthen that shielding," Rae snapped at one of the men at the console. "Steady, Wae. Hold that boost."

"Holding," one of the controllers murmured. "Holding."

"Give it some power . . . right . . . *now*," Lan-Lu muttered from somewhere beside her.

Kiondili *pushed*.

"Spectrum shift at the mark."

"We've got point eight light."

"Holding."

"Steady that flux," Stilman muttered.

Kiondili *reached*.

"Boost it, Wae," Waon muttered. *"Boost . . ."*

She felt his strength added to hers in an indefinable way.

"We have point nine light."

"Bring it up. Bring it up." Stilman's fingers were flying as he set the Blob's measurements into the program before him.

"Going to point nine-seven light."

"Keep it constant," Waon muttered.

"Mass transference is a go."

"Start the breakdown," Rae ordered, her eyes never leaving the charts. The holotank blurred; the Blob darted through space in a rainbow as light lengthened to its tachyon sensors.

"Programming kicking in. Breakdown starts at mark."

"We have point nine-eight light . . ."

Kiondili *pushed*.

"Mark. Breakdown begun."

There was an audible gasp as the Blob's recordings pushed

needles into the breakdown phase. Closer, closer to light. Kiondili seemed to touch the Blob as its matter began to separate and decompose into pure energy.

"Decomposition kicking in. Matter transfer going on *now*. We have point nine-nine lightspeed. We have lightspeed at the mark . . ."

Kiondili *reached*—

"Mark."

—and disintegrated . . .

The Blob disappeared in a backflash of energy. Kiondili followed the beam's burst into hyperlight space. Her mind fragmented, and she sagged, exhausted. The control room was in an uproar. Stilman and Rae ignored the commotion, frantically scribbling notes into flashbooks as they checked and rechecked the screens. But the other Mu danced around the consoles as the controllers sought vainly to report the track of the first successful Blob run.

"Status, transference."

Tior's fingers flew across the control panel. "Transference at ninety-two percent efficiency."

"Status, field disturbance."

"Negative."

"Status, transmission and decomposition."

"Transmission at ninety-five percent efficiency. Decomposition at sixty-seven percent efficiency."

"Record that decomposition. It's foul. Tracking?"

"Negative," the other controller reported. "Hypercom reports the Blob dispersed immediately in hyperlight space-time. The Blob was destroyed. There was no debris, just a wash of tachyon particles that is gone now."

"Secondary burnout?"

"Negative."

"Backlash?"

"Negative. Particle reactions well within limits."

There was a reverent silence for a moment.

Rae looked around. "We did it," she said in a stunned voice. "We made the first real step to light."

"We made light!"

Everyone looked stunned for another moment. Then Stilman grabbed his flashbook and Kiondili at the same time, hugging her as if he wanted to crack her ribs. One of the assistants pounded another on his shoulders in excitement, and Waon flexed his personal fields with his emotions. Persona adapts whirred into the redline as they tried to accommodate the fluctuations he sent their way.

All except Effi. The old woman sat, hunched and somehow much older, ignoring the festivities of their first successful hyperlight decomposition. *It was supposed to be my success, my moment,* she shot bitterly at Kiondili. *Now, when I was so close, to have it taken away by a self-centered, arrogant, trade-spawned Mu . . .*

The hatred in the thought shocked every sensitive in the room, bringing a second, jagged silence. Effi, already mortified by her weakness, blanked her thoughts instantly and slunk out.

"Effi . . ." Kiondili reached out.

"Back off, Wae," Rae said quietly, stepping between the two. "She's better off taking time to think."

Kiondili almost flared, but a look from Waon quelled her response and left her feeling somehow cheap. She could not take heart in the celebration that followed. Even Stilman, excited about the first actual use of his beamer, could not clear her depression or shake her conviction of doing the old woman an injustice.

CHAPTER 7

Two days later Kiondili stared intently at the lab's main holotank, where the spacedock for the outpost was duplicated in tiny scale. From the varied shapes of the ships to the tiny movements of the ships' crews, the holotank gave her a complete view of the dock. She tapped the temple jacks of her headset, frowning as she zoomed the holotank view around the dock area.

Tior, standing beside her, gurgled absently into her water bags. "You can't get beam access to a dock without going through Central Control, Kiwi. They don't let anyone beam transmissions into Control without clearance. And they are going to ask why you need the access. What is it you are trying to do?"

Kiondili studied the docks, ignoring her question. Instead, she flashed in on two tarnished silver ships whose irregular sides appeared to be warped and buckled. "What about going through a low-level cargo access?"

"Won't work. All access for transitory beams—even

cargo—is scheduled through Control. This has nothing to do with your lab work, does it?''

Kiondili tightened the focus of the holotank without answering.

"Those are Dhirrnu twister ships."

"I know."

"This wouldn't have anything to do with Poole, would it?" Tior guessed.

Kiondili bit her lip. If she was going to get dock access, she would have to tell Tior at some point, and it looked as if that point was now.

"If it's *ti'kai* you want," Tior said, "why the dock access? Poole doesn't work on the docks."

Narrowing the holotank view farther, until only the base of one of the twister ships floated in the tank, Kiondili froze the image and looked over her shoulder. "I checked the records. All Dhirrnu on the outpost meet at the docks when a Dhirrnu ship comes in. Just because Poole was assigned to a research team doesn't mean he will miss meeting a ship at the port. Poole has met every ship but one since he's been here."

"Since when do you know so much about Dhirrnu?"

Kiondili said wryly, "Since Stilman made me a target for Poole's *ti'kai*. Besides, I was curious. They already have an FTL drive. Why send Poole and the other two Dhirrnu to this outpost? It turns out," she said, rotating her view of the dock, "that they assign a Dhirrnu to every research project they can. Even if it looks like it would duplicate their own technology, they want to make sure they don't miss anything. In their own way, they are collectors of knowledge."

"I would say that they are more often collectors of practical jokes."

Kiondili shifted the images in her holotank. She wanted to filter out some of the transmissions her program kept simulating from the active beams at the dock. "Just think," she said as she worked, "they understand all three methods of faster-than-light travel. Ayara's eyes, but I don't understand why they don't sell their drive knowledge to anyone—what could it hurt to sell a few tidbits of knowledge to a species that already has FTL and just wants to upgrade its ships?'' She vented her frustration on her holotank as she killed first one excess beam, then another.

Tior frowned. "If that is true, Kiondili, why hasn't anyone kidnapped Poole—or any other Dhirrnu—and used drugs or esper to take the FTL knowledge from the Dhirrnu mind? After all, they have racial memories—if the knowledge is known by one Dhirrnu, it is known by all its descendants.''

Kiondili shook her head. "Only one family line among the Dhirrnu has complete knowledge of FTL beyond the rudiments. And nobody would need to talk to any other Dhirrnu to get the rudiments of FTL—you can get that information from a low-access library, even if you don't have citizen status. But the drive secrets—those are known only by that one family line, and the Dhirrnu in that line never stir from their home planet. They assign the younger ones from other family lines—like Poole—to work on Federation projects like the Lightwing. So here is Poole, working with us—and Ayara knows he's practically indispensable—and at the same time, passing information about our progress to the other Dhirrnu.''

Tior scowled. "If all this is true, I don't see why Poole or any other Dhirrnu is allowed to work on the Lightwing project at all. We ought to tell the Dhirrnu that if H'Mu can't have any of their information about other drives, they can't have any information about ours.''

Kiondili gave a short burst of laughter. "It's part of the Federation contract that he is here. I found a reference in the Dhirrnu files. The Dhirrnu get to place at least one of their own at every trade outpost to which they have access. It makes sense, Tior. If you want to trade with the Dhirrnu, better to communicate it through one of their own than through what to them would be a supply request from an alien.''

"Poole isn't Supply.''

"No, but there is a Dhirrnu down in Supply. It's not Poole's fault that he doesn't know anything about FTL that would help us. So why not use what he does know? It isn't going to hurt H'Mu that the Dhirrnu know what we're doing. As long as he helps us make lightspeed, I don't care how much information he passes along."

Tior raised her eyebrow, one of her water bags tightening across her chin.

Kiondili, intent on her holotank, was not watching. "He already met the two ships that unloaded yesterday, but another ship is due in three days. Here—" She pointed. "—and over here. This is where I want to set up a combination of holograms and local field stimuli. But I need access to run the beam transmissions through."

Tior frowned. "Beam access to the Dhirrnu portions of the docks is usually restricted—the Dhirrnu take advantage of everything they can get their fuzzy hands on. Control always shuts off the systems they don't need."

"For all that I'm glad Poole is on our team, it must be hell trying to trade with a Dhirrnu."

"It isn't too bad. They have decent business practices, compared to some species. They just play so many tricks with deliveries that they rarely deliver more than half of what's ordered." Tior motioned at the Dhirrnu vessels in the holotank. "They have the fastest ships in the Federation. Sometimes you don't have a choice."

"We might have a choice once we get the Lightwing through the barrier." Kiondili glanced at Tior slyly. "If you get access for me, I'll let you watch the fun."

The other Mu blew water bubbles out to her lips and sucked them back in. "Give me a day to see about the access," she said finally. "I'll let you know what I can do."

"Thanks." Kiondili turned back to the holotank.

Tior turned to go but paused at the door and looked back. "Kiwi, don't blame yourself for Effi."

Kiondili flushed slowly, her gray skin darkening with the pink flush that fled across her cheeks.

"Effi knew she might not be able to handle the strain, but she would not let anyone take her place as sensor. She wanted to do it all." Tior paused. "What was important was that we made it past the light barrier—not who pushed the Blob."

Kiondili nodded slowly, but as the door shimmered solid behind Tior, she sat lost in thought for several minutes. Finally she rose, turned off the holotank, and left the lab, dropping into the nearest boost-chute opening. She was hungry, but it was to Chute 11, not the Hub, that she directed her momentum. She would see the old woman now.

However, it was not Effi who met her at the lab door but Argon. The assistant gave her a long look of disdain, and Kiondili stifled the slow burn of anger that swept through her.

"If you have a message for Effi from Stilman," he stated rudely, "I'll take it to her." Disdainfully, he brushed imaginary dust from his dull-colored tunic.

"I'm here to see Effi myself," she returned steadily.

"Why? You aren't happy enough that you kicked Effi out of her own experiment? You're here to gloat, as well?"

She stared at him, damping her feelings automatically as he tried to read her face. "I stepped in after she stepped out, yes," she said. "But no, I'm not here to gloat. I'm here to apologize if what I did hurt her."

"Effi doesn't need any more of your meddling," he drawled slowly.

"Argon, what is it with you?" she snapped finally. "Are you just prejudiced against Mu that don't look like you, or is this all because I have your old job and you want it back?"

He merely raised one eyebrow and mocked her with another look.

She stifled her own projections, furious that she had given in to his prodding while he had kept his motivations hidden. Taking a step forward, she said flatly, "I'd like to see Effi now."

"You could have apologized to her yesterday at the shake-down meeting." He glanced over his shoulder and raised his voice subtly. "I think you just want into this lab."

She bit back her rejoinder. "I came to apologize to Effi in private," she said stiffly. "If she's not here, just say so."

"She's not here, but," he said, smiling unpleasantly, "I'll tell her you dropped by."

Kiondili turned abruptly and retraced her steps to the free-boost chute. She no longer felt hungry.

She did not try to see Effi again. At the end of the week, when the rest of the launch team assignments were posted, she avoided the listings as she had avoided Effi. Her name would not be on any of the launch teams: Effi would certainly block anyone who tried to add Kiondili's ID.

She worked through that afternoon in a foul mood. She ignored even her hunger until her stomach began to growl incessantly, and finally, swearing under her breath, she threw her flashwriter in a corner of the table and got up. She was in no better mood as she entered the Hub.

Jordan, the tall Mu, waved from her right. "Put your drive on low, Kiondili, and dive on in!"

She waved listlessly to him and turned away but then changed her mind and crossed the crowded room instead. The lilting voice of a Moal cowering as it moved out of her path caused her to pause for a moment, but even the beauty of its greeting was lost on her mood. As she reached the table with the other assistants, Tior shifted to give her a seat across from Poole.

"Did you hear the news?" Tior asked quickly. "They think they know why the Blob dispersed as soon as it hit lightspeed. So we're dropping the Blobs and going to manned ships—the Lightwings. And the launch team lists are already out."

The Dhirrnu stroked his thick fur and watched her punch her dinner out on the dispenser. "Did you see the lists, Kiondili Wae? You are on Team C as backup."

She waved him off. "Great joke, Poole. That's about as lame a trick as any you've tried to pull."

But the Dhirrnu grinned, his teeth displayed in sharp, even

rows like a shark. "It is no joke. You are on the backup team."

She stared at them. "Stilman put in a recommendation for me?"

There was silence for a moment, and then one of the others answered. "No. The posting came from Rae Arr, Lan-Lu, and Waon."

Jordan unfolded one of his long legs and stuck it out to the side of his chair. Even after punching in his adjustment code for the Soft, he never seemed to get comfortable. "You should have seen the look on Effi's face when Lan-Lu put up your ID," he said slyly at Kiondili's look of wonderment. "She was about to throw a fit, and then Waon punched in his recommendation. There was not much she could do about it then."

Tior agreed. "The Ruvian is the top sensor at the outpost. With his approval, no one else could object."

"Except Stilman." Poole stroked the fur on his arms and gave Kiondili a long look. "I think it's the only time Stilman and Effi Ragan argued on the same side of any question."

Kiondili, not yet believing that she was really on one of the launch teams, protested, "Why did Stilman object?"

"Stilman argued against it because he's lost the last two assistants through dispersal." Tior pressed her fingers into one of her water bags and swallowed the fluid that ran into her mouth. "He's not too excited about your posting. Ayara's eyes, Kiwi, he doesn't want to lose a third assistant the same way."

Jordan grinned. "If he does, we'll just give him Argon back." He glanced at Kiondili sideways. "Someday," he said under his breath, "you'll have to tell me what Ayara's eyes are, Kiondili. Everyone has picked up that oath from you, and no one has any idea what they're swearing to when they say it."

She raised her eyebrows and whispered back, "They're the two main stars that outline the trade routes on the Rim. You can't miss them if you're there."

"Me? Out on the Rim? Not likely. Though I'd rather be

there than here if I thought I'd have to be the one to tell Stilman, even in a joke, that Argon was coming back to him.''

Tior made a face at them. "Stop whispering, you two. Shyh Stilman would rather disperse Argon himself than hire him back.'' She caught a speculative look on Poole's face and said sharply, "Don't go getting any ideas, Poole. There are too many cross-threads between Argon and Kiwi. You do something to Argon, and Kiondili could lose her job.''

The Dhirrnu wrinkled his nose, snorting softly as the fur bunched up at his nostrils. But he raised his glass and said, "To the backup team. May they launch in luck.''

Kiondili grinned and raised her glass with the others. Team C—that meant there really was a chance at a launch herself . . . "Who else is on the team?'' she asked.

"Me as controller.'' Tior pointed at herself. "Of course, you knew that a while ago. And then you as sensor, and Xia, the one in Rae Arr's lab, as pilot, and . . . Argon.''

Kiondili choked. "What?''

Tior caught her expression and shrugged. "He's your systems link.''

"I see.'' That meant Kiondili would have to work through him as much as with him. Xia, the fourth person on the team, she did not know well, but the woman seemed efficient.

"Don't worry,'' Jordan added. "After seeing what you did on the probe launch this week—well, I'm sure you've got enough power to boost Argon hyperlight himself if he doesn't watch his mouth.''

Poole chuckled, his yellow eyes gleaming, and Kiondili wondered what he was thinking, until someone passed her another drink and someone else toasted the backup teams. Team C—the words echoed in her head. Backup for launch. That meant she would be in the ship itself, should backup be called. She clenched her hands around her glass, accidentally flexing the fields of Tior's and another Mu's persona adapts. But she did not care. Backup for a Lightwing . . .

The next morning Kiondili was sorry she had gone to bed

at all. Her head felt as if it were swollen out a hand span from where it should have been, and her stomach felt as if it had been turned inside out and smeared around in her belly. She triggered the automed without wincing too much at the noise of the click and managed to wait the scant seconds impatiently for its dispenser to pop out the prescribed hang-over pill, which was duly tallied for the medic to note. Sometimes she wished the H'Mu Guardians had not prohibited the brewers from making drinks that gave no hangovers. They had locked those synthetics out of the dispensers, too. She could understand their reasons, but still . . . Luckily she did not have to think too hard that day, just transcribe and finish the rest of Stilman's equations from the Blob run a few days before. She groaned, waiting for the pill to take effect. It was going to be a long day.

Stilman did not show up in the lab till late afternoon. When he finally did appear, he did not even greet Kiondili but stomped his way through the now neatly stacked flashbooks and flung himself in front of his computer, muttering something about Thygerson functions. Fingers flying, he cursed under his breath, designed a four-deck equation, wiped it out, smoldered to himself, wrote another equation, flashed his screen blank, snarled half-loudly, and finally hit the kill button.

"Damn it, Wae." He turned angrily in his seat. "Why by all the frigged hairs of a foltor's nose did you pull that stunt in front of everybody?"

"What stunt?" she asked innocently.

"You know exactly what I mean. Three days ago at the launch—boosting that Blob where everyone could see it."

She refrained from pointing out the fact that since all in-struments had been on the probe, and the probe had been on a prescribed course, she could not have boosted it where no one would see it. "I thought it was critical to your re-search," she said quietly.

"Yes, well . . ." Stilman ran one of his hands through his white hair, then tugged irritably at his red-and-chartreuse tunic. "It was. But that does not excuse you or answer my question." He tugged angrily at a loose thread on his violently orange trousers.

"Look, Dr. Stilman, what's the problem? You needed those measurements to set up the mass ratios for your beamer—"

"That's exactly what the problem is," the researcher said, pouncing angrily. Gesturing jerkily, he leapt up and began to pace the room. "Waon was impressed. Rae was overjoyed. DeNusien was awed. Even Lan-Lu had nothing to say. And I—" He jabbed a finger at his chest. "I, Shyh Stilman—your counselor, *if* you haven't forgotten—and your adviser, your teacher, *and* your boss—am beset by these aliens with their bizarre hairdos, stink-rot breath, and field-generated fangs while they tell me they want you for hyperlight backup."

Kiondili grinned. "Isn't it great?"

He sputtered. "I said you'd never consider it. They said you already had. I said you'd turn it down. They said don't be a fool, you'd blast at the chance. I said you had more brains than to commit suicide. They said that's exactly why they want you. Damn it, but Perdue dispersed only eight cycles ago, and I've tried out four assistants since then. You're the only one who works, and you're the only one who actually helps me with my research. The Federation is breathing down my neck for results, the outpost director is dogging me right and left, Effi Ragan is claiming first test run, and now you're going to go off and play suicide scout at the light barrier. No, it isn't wonderful or great or *tejonki* or whatever word you know-it-all institute punks are using these days. I find it highly inconvenient, frigged-back frustrating, and inconceivably wasteful."

"Is that all?" Kiondili asked calmly.

"No. There's one more thing." He stomped to the door. "Congratulations." The door shimmered shut abruptly—Kiondili wondered briefly how an automatic door could reflect such emotional feelings—and Stilman stalked off down the hall.

The next day, as she was coming back from the gym, Tior caught her in the corridor.

"Kiwi, it's in," the blue-skinned Mu said in a low voice. "A day early, but it's in the docks right now."

Kiondili glanced around quickly. "The Dhirrnu ship?"

"Uh huh. It's a twister model, and it will be ready to unload in an hour. Poole should be down there already."

Kiondili nodded. The twisters were the spacetime converters the Dhirrnu used. Able to go through a warp to jump light-years at a time, the twisters were the fastest ships in the Federation. Any normal ship would buckle under the strain, but the twisters had a suspended frame that twisted, passed through itself during warp, and snapped back. And Dhirrnu, with their oddly modular cell structure, could do the same. There was no mutation of H'Mu yet that could survive a ride on a twister. She had asked Waon about it once—she thought if anyone could do it, a Ruvian, with his field-manipulation skills, ought to be able to—but Waon had given her a strange look and said that Ruvians, being partially field-generated, would be absorbed into the twister fields like so much extra energy. It might be interesting, he said, to know the sensation, but it would certainly be death. She wondered what the Dhirrnu felt when they went through the jump . . .

"I got the access codes this morning," Tior interrupted her thoughts. "Do you want to try now or wait?"

"Now," Kiondili said firmly. "The program has been burning up memory in one of my flashbooks for days."

Tior gave her a curious look. "What exactly are you going to do?"

"I'm going to drop a shoe on their loading ramp," she teased. "They have an extended sense of humor. At least half of them will laugh." She grinned slyly at the look on the other woman's face. "I'll tell you when we're back in the lab. I don't want anyone to overhear."

An hour later Tior and Kiondili were scowling in front of Stilman's terminal.

"This is going to take a while." Tior fidgeted, her fingers drumming absently on the temple taps of her headset. "I don't want to leave traces . . ."

"It might be better if you did," Kiondili said slowly. "I want them to know who did this, or Poole won't know who earned his *ti'kai*."

"We can try it," Tior said slowly. "I just hope no one is on this access already. Here, I can sensitize a general dock area, but I won't be able to program anything else. It should be enough. There, I think I'm in—oops—" She belched, losing water. "Blaster burns. They might have traced it."

"Someone on?"

"Not only on but using that line, too."

"Better wait a few seconds, see if they put a trace on."

Tior stared at the screen intently for a moment. "This could lose me a cycle of pay, Kiwi."

"It'll be worth it to see the look on Poole's face."

Tior sighed. "I don't suppose I have anything to spend my credits on, anyway." She burped again. "I'll consider it a donation to the cause."

"What did Poole ever do to you?"

Tior flushed. "My first real presentation to the board, he gassed the podium so that every time I breathed in, I got some helium. I thought it was the translator at first because every time I opened my mouth to speak, I sounded like a Freafish out of water. It took me a few minutes to figure it out. I was so nervous about speaking that I just kept trying till the board lost it. They ended up canceling the meeting. Poole got enough *ti'kai* on that one to last half a year."

Kiondili pointed at the screen. "There's been no trace so far on that line you tried earlier. It must be safe to try again."

"Not on that line, but maybe if I—"

"If you try that again, I'm going to let Lan-Lu have your ears for dinner," Rae snapped over their shoulders. The two Mu whirled.

Rae gave them a sharp look as she stalked over to them and read the codes on the console. "Exactly what are you doing with the dock access, Tior?" she demanded coldly. "It's a serious offense to break through the control net, and you, Tior, of all people, should know that. Do you want your control privileges cut off for a year? Do you know what that would mean to my project?"

Tior opened her mouth to protest, but Kiondili cut in first. "It's my fault, Rae."

The esper ran her eyes over the younger Mu. "So. You're taking advantage of the launch stunt already? I thought better of you, Wae. What do you think would happen to Stilman's work if Control traced your line to this lab?"

"It's not what you think, Rae."

"Then what is it?"

Kiondili fidgeted. "We're not trying to get full access, Rae. We just want a few minutes on the docks. It's for a joke."

The researcher looked her up and down coldly. Then a corner of her mouth began to twitch. "I should have known," she said sourly. "For two days you've been projecting a smugness that's been irritating the hell out of me. I suppose this has to do with Poole."

"Why is it that everyone thinks jokes only have to do with Poole?" Kiondili complained.

"Because he's generally the cause or effect of them." Rae looked at the other assistant. "Your link wasn't clean, Tior. You had better brush up on the system for the next few days."

Tior, knowing that Rae's suggestion meant that her after-class time would be spent studying beam links, made a face.

"And next time," the researcher continued, "check the status of the lines before trying to read them."

Tior looked at her feet, one of the tiny water bags under her chin sloshing quietly with her embarrassment.

"And as for you . . . ." The researcher turned to Kiondili, glanced at the codes again, then leaned between the two assistants and tapped a sequence of keys sharply. She strode toward the door. "We launch again in two days," she said sharply. "Stay out of trouble."

Tior and Kiondili stared at each other for a long moment after Rae had left. "Ayara's eyes," Tior breathed. "At least it wasn't Lan-Lu who caught us."

"Or Waon." Kiondili slumped. "Hells. How are we going to get access now? I just spent two days rigging this up, and now I'm going to have to throw it all out and start over."

Tior sighed and glanced at the screen, then sat suddenly straight. "It's not a complete waste, Kiwi." Her fingers flying, she traced a new map of access lines. "Look at this!"

Kiondili stared at the flashscreen. "But those are the access codes."

"Rae must have coded them in for us through her own link."

Kiondili grinned slowly. "I wonder what Poole did to her."

"Let's not ask. Let's just grab this access and go." Tior paused. "What do you want to do with this field?"

"Set it to be sensitized to Poole's footpads."

"Current?"

"Sensory stimulation to alpha point oh six two. That's as close as I can get to the setting of his biofield. Now set the sensitivity low—I only want to tickle his feet when he sets them down on the deck, not jolt the humor out of him. No, don't kick it on yet. Set this program to execute," she added, handing Tior a flashpad with another access code.

Tior entered it dutifully and set it to run, asking, "What is it?"

Kiondili grinned again. "It takes a holo of each person who walked by Poole, squashes the holo, and puts the image of the squashed alien on the bottom or side of every object Poole drops."

Tior chuckled, then laughed out loud. "You owe me for this, Kiwi."

"Your pleasure is on my credit chit," Kiondili returned magnanimously.

Tior grinned slyly. "I haven't had Sowfi cake in over a year."

Kiondili wrinkled her nose, but eight and a half credits for one piece of cake was going to be more than worthwhile if she pulled this off. "It's your tonight. If," she added, "this works."

"It will work. Watch. All I have to do is erase my path—"

"No," Kiondili interrupted. "Freeze that path."

"But the Dhirrnu on the ship will know in minutes who's doing this."

"That's the point." Kiondili triggered the holotank beside them to track the unloading, then tagged Poole's shape with color so that he was unmistakable. "If Poole has *ti'kai* on that many people at this outpost, I want to make sure he knows who got him here."

Tior shook her head. "When the shipmaster finds out who's behind this—"

"He's a Dhirrnu, too."

Tior stared at her a moment. "You really are crazy, Kiwi. What if the entire ship declares *ti'kai* on you for this?"

"It will be worth it," Kiondili reassured her friend. "Look, Poole's starting to react. And there's a H'Mu going by."

At first the Dhirrnu on the screen shuffled his feet, then he stamped them as he balanced his load of crates with the cargo beams. Finally he jerked the beam, and one of the crates tilted, dropping to the dock with a dull thud that was duplicated in the holotank in perfect, tiny scale. Tior held her breath. Kiondili stared in anticipation. Still fidgeting, Poole lifted the crate again, then froze. On the side of the crate where it had first landed was the squashed shape of a human-mu. Kiondili could almost see the shock on Poole's face. Another Dhirrnu stopped what he was doing and stared at Poole, who still stood, stamping his feet as the fields Kiondili had set tickled his senses. A second crate crashed down as he lost more of the cargo beam. This time the shape of the second Dhirrnu was on the bottom. Poole stared. He stopped twice, then almost jumped as he got a jolt on his feet, and as the rest of the crates tumbled, they, too, picked up squashed aliens. There was a Trident, another H'Mu, a Greggor, and a Robul. Kiondili had to look quickly to figure out where that one had come from, but then she caught sight of Coos disappearing into a nearby free-boost chute. Poole, dancing as his feet were tickle-scratched, began wheezing.

"He just got the joke." Tior pointed. "That's the way he laughs."

The Dhirrnu beside Poole began wheezing and coughing with him, and Kiondili motioned for Tior to cut the field before Poole started dancing on the dock. Gasping and bending over back and forth, the Dhirrnu did not seem to notice at first that the sensations had stopped.

"You're a dream, Tior," Kiondili said fervently. "You did that to point nine efficiency."

Tior grinned smugly. "I always have point nine efficiency. That's why I'm in Control." She got to her feet. "I expect my Sowfi cake after theory class tonight, Kiwi. Don't be late. I'll be starved."

Kiondili, still watching Poole and the other Dhirrnu, said with a shake of her head, "If I had simply hung a shirt on Poole's chair, he probably would have laughed as hard."

"Yes, but this took work. He'll appreciate that." Tior glanced at the screen. "I asked Rae about their humor once. She said they are born with racial memories. Every child has an adult mind, but it takes decades to teach them to use it. In the meantime they confuse all the signals and call it funny. They grow up, but there's still so much information in their heads that they never quite lose the humor."

"Maybe he didn't lose his humor, but he sure lost *ti'kai* on this one. Though I'm sure he'll make up for it with his next trick."

Tior grinned slyly. "And I'll have a ringside seat for that, believe me."

CHAPTER 8

It took concentration for Kiondili to get back to work. That image of Poole . . . She found herself grinning at odd moments. That and the fact that she really was on the backup team. The words kept echoing on the tip of her tongue: backup for launch. A Lightwing launch of her own.

She did not notice what the hypnotape lesson was for the day. She went through her theory class without paying attention. Finally it was time, and she met the other assistants for the first gathering of the launch teams. Effi Ragan was there, too, ignoring Kiondili as usual, but Kiondili did not care. Eagerly, she filed in with the others. There were a few moments of noise, smell, and prickling senses. It always took a few seconds for a persona adjust to reset its fields and projections when aliens and H'Mu mixed randomly. As she waited, Kiondili took the chance to use her own persona adjust to set up a dispersal field around her Soft. She did not want her excitement to project strongly. That, and she was definitely not in the mood to be distracted by the two Greggors behind her. Greggors were lazy about keeping their subsonics to themselves. With her persona adjust working overtime to keep her personal space clear in this crowd of sensors and espers, it would have a hard time filtering out the Greggors' irritating and unpredictable sonics. Although, if the esper fields got too strong, the sensors would trigger a weak esper net—just enough of an overall damp on the room to calm everyone down and keep all those probes and projections soft.

"Attention," a huge Mu boomed from the front. "I am Funda, in engineering. The analysis of the last Blob launch has been completed. We are most confident." He noted the smiles. "Rae. Stilman, Effi. Waon—the entire team has agreed that it is time to cancel the rest of the Blobs. We will be going directly to the prototype ships—the Lightwings—one half cycle from today."

There was a sigh that drifted through the complete range of sonics. This was the news everyone had been waiting for.

"Prime One—or Team A; Prime Two—team B; and backup teams have been scheduled. Drills begin tomorrow at first quarter. Yes?"

"Have the Federation observers been notified yet?" an alien who sat to Kiondili's right chittered. "My research—the grants are running out."

"Yes," another alien chimed in from across the room. "And I've got to be able to order more equipment for my next experiment. These plans are well and good, but where are the credits coming from if the Federation revokes my grant anyway?"

"Where is Dugan?" another demanded, searching the crowd for the outpost director. "Have you set up the launch schedule yet?"

"And what about the new proposals?"

The Corson director stood up. He turned his yellow-orange eyes on those who had asked the last questions, then swept the quieting room with his baleful gaze. "The Federation is *always* kept up-to-date on our progress." He paused. "Or lack of it. Financial questions can be addressed later, in regular staff meetings.'' He paused again, letting that sink in as some members shifted restlessly. ''This meeting,'' he continued, ''will be restricted to a discussion of how the Lightwing will operate under a combined drive. Funda? If you will continue, please.''

The massive Mu nodded, then continued as if he had not been sidetracked by the questions. ''The first three Lightwings, as you know, have brought us through the prototype phase of this project. We have studied and refined the engines, drives, shields, and structures based on information from the Blobs. *Lightwing IV* is ready for its crew . . .''

After the meeting Kiondili barely had time to change jumpers before Stilman called and complained that her work on his equations was not done. As she hurried out, she made a face, then grinned. At least, with her sensor status, she had one of the highest access codes for the free-boost chutes. She could be at the lab in two minutes if she pushed the boost-chute fields just a bit. She dove into a chute, hit a redirection pad hard, and accelerated quickly.

Flipping through another opening, she twisted around an Umbor clinging upside down to the shaft while it searched its back pouches. Her diving roll took up most of the shock of slowing down, and the stiffening redirection pad took the rest. Good thing she had a sense of timing. Some people triggered the inertial field too late and continued to bounce or jerked with an almost audible slam out of the grav-free tubes while the redirection pads rebooted.

Smoothing her hair, she made her way to the lab. She wished she was already working in the simulator. Launch . . . She could see herself in the sensor's chair, pushing the ship on, reaching light. The only darkness in her daydream was Argon, and she could not quite calm the sense that it would be Argon around whom her problems would center.

CHAPTER 9

"A little more power," Rae Arr was saying to Kiondili. "There, you've got it now. No, don't go beyond that level. The way you handle the sensor lens, it isn't even half-maxed-out, but we're working as a team. Stay with the others."

Kiondili relaxed her pressure on some of the delicately focused beams. "Steady?" she managed to say.

Tior, staring at the holotank, replied. "Steady. All systems on green. We're approaching light."

Rae glanced at her, then brought her attention back to the other woman. "Watch your course, Xia. You're veering toward that gravitational well."

"Corrected," the woman returned. "On course."

Rae touched a button under her hand to throw another problem at the assistants, and a light flashed on Argon's ship screen.

"Stress overload in Drive Chamber Six," he announced. His fingers flicked with blinding speed through the console functions. At the same time, he sent his mental images and commands through the temple jacks into the system. The

113

holotank configuration shifted, and he said with a trace of smugness, "Rerouted through Chamber Eight with his dull, brown-and-black jumper, he faded almost completely into his console."

Rae looked up, her eyes flashing. "Dammit, Argon, you never listen. That's the third time you've had this problem, and each time you jury-rig a fix that creates a dozen more blips. Last time it was a diversion that almost dumped the main drive. The time before that you started breakdown two-tenths of a second early and practically tore Kiondili away from the sensors while the ship's mass shifted out of phase. And this time you need Chamber Eight free for the second-stage decomposition or you're going to lose the probe completely."

"The odds are ninety-three percent for my decision," he said stubbornly.

"What about the other seven percent?" she asked, touching the button again. Another light flashed. "Stay on the boost, Wae," she reminded sharply as Kiondili was distracted by their argument.

"Fracture in Chamber Eight," Argon said tightly, reading the new images. His frustration at Rae's action forced him to think faster, more clearly. "Stress at one point three oh. Beams beginning to fall apart. I'll have to bridge—"

"If you bridge, you'll bring the brunt of the primary stress down on Six again," Tior protested.

"I've got to do something," he snarled.

"Mass disintegrating fast," Xia snapped. "Velocity holding at point nine eight lightspeed."

"Try looping the fields," Kiondili said in a strained voice.

She hoped the emotional shield was strong enough to get her through this lab session. The other launch teams had had problems with it that morning, and Effi had been pulling her hair out by the end of the session. With Xia as competitive as Argon was antagonistic, Kiondili was going to be in for a rough ride on this team. It had not escaped either Kiondili or Rae Arr that Argon worked more against than with Kiondili. At one point, Rae had shrugged and said that Kiondili would learn a great deal by working with Argon. Kiondili thought it was a waste of her energy. She worked just as hard to maintain her blocks around the man as she did to control the ship's sensors. Even with the field amplifier and the sensor lens, her focus faded as soon as Argon started sniping at someone. She was beginning to see Rae's point, however: the struggle to maintain her blocks while she focused through the lens had already upped her biofield power by half a level.

"Xia," Rae directed absently, "watch that gravity well again. You're skewing."

"We're on course," Xia repeated tersely as she shifted again. "It's pulling too hard. I have to keep correcting."

"That is the point of the exercises," Rae said dryly, "to learn how to correct automatically."

Having watched the other teams go into the sessions first, Kiondili had an idea of what to expect, but even so, the hours were draining. By the time the fourth quarter was over, she was ready for a mental massage. She sighed, swung her stiffened legs to the floor, and staggered. Thankfully, no one offered to help as she picked herself up and steadied herself against the nearest console. No one in the room was shielded enough—they would shock her in this state of heightened sensitivity. Or she would disrupt their persona adapts. She straightened wearily.

Tior's own irritation was as palpable as scorched oatmeal. "Dicti's dowers, but I'm glad that's over," she muttered, setting the last of her notes in the flashbook.

"At least you don't have to feel everything Argon and Xia send while you're working," Kiondili returned sourly.

"I may not be top esper," Tior retorted, "but even I can get half of that through my blocks. If they weren't so expensive, I'd build a persona damp into my adapt and program it to filter out the both of them."

Kiondili glanced back at Xia and Argon. They were still bickering, and everyone else was giving them a wide berth. Tior, glaring at the two, suggested to Kiondili that they have a drink in the Hub before taking off. But after sitting through two sessions of observation, one of lecture, and one as a sensor herself, Kiondili was ready to call it quits. She had never worked her field skills so hard for so long before. Rubbing her temples where the headset pressed against her skin and her aching pulse threatened to break through, Kiondili made her way almost blindly to her quarters. She should have taken the esper training at the institute while she had had the chance, she admitted silently, groping for the automed's discharge and rubbing the sticky paste over her temples. Leaning back gingerly on her bunk, she admitted that her blocks could use some work. If she had not refused the training back at the institute, she would be in a much better position to take this level of punishment now. Ayara's eyes, but her *brain* felt sore.

The Soft beckoned to her as she opened her eyes again, but she resisted the temptation to sit. She wanted to go over the launch sequence in her mind before she forgot Rae's comments. Right now a hundred threads of sensitivity still seemed to be stretched between her and the stimulation probe, and Rae's voice echoed in her head. She closed her eyes. She had done the overall field manipulation well, but she had to admit that she had not controlled the inner stresses of the mass at all, especially when the ship had started collapsing in hyperlight spacetime. Had the simulated lens been real, it would have fractured. Rae had not said anything to her, but Kiondili was sure that she would hear about it from Stilman or Lan-Lu or Waon. Waon's field computations were exact, and his silent disapproval was worse than a year of complaints from any other H'Mu. And Stilman, that infuriating human, was constantly critiquing her performance second by second, as if she were a flux chart he could control by pushing the right buttons harder. On top of that, Lan-Lu kept demanding perfect control of the mass decomposition. But no matter how Kiondili tried, she could not seem to control two decomposing beams at once. The beams frayed; they fractured; they crossed in the lens. And she knew it was her fault. Her control was not strong enough.

She sighed, picking up one of her figurines—an ironwood

dolphin—and turning it over in her hands. The smoothness of the wood was soothing to her fingers, and she rubbed its coolness against her temples. It did no good to talk to Effi about Kiondili's problems with the beams. Effi spent enough time with the two prime teams to show them how to match their sensor nuances to every aspect of the lens, the amplifier, and the Lightwing itself. But then she ignored Kiondili's own efforts to copy their exercises, even though Kiondili got farther with her lack of focus than the other sensors did with their perfectly guided touch.

Well, why should Effi spend time with Kiondili? She pressed the dolphin against her forehead as if it would refute her thoughts. Kiondili was on backup, not a prime team. Effi's priorities were Prime Team A, then Prime Team B, and if there was time, then backup. That there was little time was not in dispute. But was there really no time at all for backup?

In spite of the old woman, Kiondili had to admire Effi's drive. The human woman had actually come from Earth through a hypergate eighty years ago light, one of the few H'Mu to make it through such a gate. Effi's personal account of the trip was in the hypnolibrary and on the dreamer channels—a nightmare entry. She had been restricted to sublight travel ever since; she would never go FTL again. To work her entire life on a hyperlight drive she could never use . . . never to see Earth again . . . never to return home . . .

A ghost spoke in Kiondili's mind. If not for her professor and those two recruiters, she would not have gone FTL again, either. Not unless she caved in and rejoined the Trade Guild. Her bitterness surged, and she savored the emotion briefly before shoving it abruptly down with the rest of her memories.

Four long, drawn-out, dragged-on days later Kiondili had to admit that she was too tired even to dream about breaking the light barrier. Working on a backup team had sounded like the perfect opportunity to learn what she wanted to know, but she had not realized how little sleep she would get. Eight hours in Stilman's lab, then four hours watching Teams A and B work on the simulator, then another four hours trying to imitate the other teams' work with the rest of the backup team.

"It's driving me into a black hole," Tior confessed. "I feel beat. Like I was flattened with a Gol whipper's tail."

"That would be interesting," Argon said snidely. "If a Gol whipper hit you with its tail, it would push your water bags out on the other side. You would look as if you had body warts."

"You're one to talk, Argon," she flared back. "If a Gol whipper ever caught hold of you, it'd asphyxiate itself popping your gas follicles."

"Keep it to yourself, bubble brain," he snorted. "With all that water you carry around, I'm always amazed that you don't drown yourself when you try to insult someone."

Kiondili did not wait to hear Tior's retaliatory snipe but escaped instead to the sanctuary of one of the upper-level float rooms. In an hour she would have to go back and report to Stilman, and a scant hour after that she would be back in the lab with Tior and Argon. She closed her eyes. The low-grav suspension of the float room was heavenly after the last session with Argon and the rest of the backup team. Like Tior, Kiondili felt physically bruised. Hitting acceleration badly in a simulator felt the same as hitting acceleration badly in a ship, and Kiondili was still learning the controls. And Argon, jury-rigging every solution for the textbook problems, was not helping. Each solution he found created a new set of problems, and the result was that they usually blew up going through the light barrier singularity. With Xia hissing and snarling indiscriminately at every good or bad turn and Tior so upset over her own mistakes that she was losing water right and left, Kiondili was not sure how she would make it through the next quarter cycle.

Even the other researchers seemed to be on edge. Rae snapped at Kiondili four times the next day, and Lan-Lu prowled the lab as if hunting. Only Argon seemed immune to the strain. Twice he had even come to Stilman's lab, nosing around the stacks of flashbooks until Kiondili had asked what he wanted. His manner irritated her, and the looks he gave her made her wary, but she could not put her finger on a reason why. It was as if he were waiting for her to misstep, to give him an opening. And the sensation persisted, even into the meetings she attended with Stilman. She would find herself sitting silently among the researchers, offering no input until afterward, when she and Stilman were back in their lab.

"Dammit, Wae, why didn't you say that during the meeting?" Stilman demanded after a particularly difficult discussion. "If you had spoken out then, we would not have gone through that entire hour of argument."

Kiondili looked down. "I didn't want to cause problems."

"It's a problem when you have a suggestion and don't say anything. That discrepancy in timing wasted half the meeting."

Kiondili said nothing. What could she say? That she could sense Effi waiting for her to open her mouth? It was like a trap that she could see and her friends were pushing her into, while Argon waited on the other side of the trap to keep her from getting out again. He was not even trying to be polite anymore. She had even more proof of that when, on her way back to the lab, he passed her in the free-boost chutes and unexpectedly shoved her out of a jumpline. Her flashbooks went flying, chute to chute, and she slammed into a redirection pad without warning.

"Maghoul maggots in his ear," she muttered, clinging to an emergency wall guard after hitting with bruising force. Tior, who was free-boosting behind her, gave her a sympathetic look but said nothing, just triggered the Objects-Free button on the nearest panel. The flashbooks were sucked to the wall and held in place till Kiondili could pick them up. She could not get them all—she and Tior were in a hurry to work cycle, as usual—but chute cleaners would return the books to her at the end of the day.

She was surprised when, barely two hours later, Argon

came to Team B's practice session and pulled Effi out of class. They conferred in the observation closet. There Effi grew more upset, until she stormed back in, followed quickly by her assistant.

"You Mu-spawned worm!" Effi snarled at Kiondili when she burst through the door, barely waiting for it to clear. "You thief! Stealing my research and feeding it to that shyster Stilman!" She launched her hate like a blow, and Kiondili, shocked, barely jerked her blocks up in time. Even so, she reeled under the force of Effi's emotion. "I'll teach you to rip me off!" Two needles seemed to pierce Kiondili's brain like a pithing, and she stiffened her blocks desperately. Only in the back of her mind did she realize that half a cycle earlier that blow would have stunned her and possibly damaged her permanently.

Lan-Lu's hunter voice lashed out like a tangible whip. Kiondili had never been so glad to hear that ghastly sound as when it struck Effi and paralyzed her into silence and immobility. And then one of the other researchers jumped between them with a growl, grabbing Kiondili by her arm and holding her up. Argon was touching Effi now, seeming to calm the woman, but even through her haze Kiondili could feel him subtly egging Effi's emotional tension on by encouraging her outburst. Effi tried to launch another blast, but not before Rae punched the E-button and threw an esper net on the room. Kiondili dimly realized she should protest. The triggering of an E-net was always registered by the outpost director. He would be on his way even now, and she was still on probation. Dugan would space her without a suit before thinking twice when he found her in the middle of this mess.

Trembling, Kiondili sank down. Her blocks shuddered under the strain of fighting the E-damp. Effi was sobbing, unable to focus more mental shafts in the mind-crushing weight that had settled over them all. In the moments of stark confusion that followed, Kiondili picked up many more thoughts than she had ever wanted to. Lan-Lu was hungry, and both

Effi and Kiondili would be easy prey right now. Rae was running through the outpost laws for thievery. The flood of energy to Kiondili's blocks was being sucked away by the net. And then slowly, ever so slowly, the net dissipated.

"You," Rae ordered one of her assistants, "keep Effi quiet. You—" She pointed at another one. "—see if Kiondili is in shock. Argon," she snapped, "get away from Effi. You've already done more than enough to precipitate this."

And then the outpost director, Dugan, flashed through the door and seemed to impale Kiondili with his glance. He *knew*—the accusation of thievery—she could read it in his eyes. Would she even get a trial before she was judged?

"Tior," Dugan said flatly, taking the room in at a glance, "this will require a Testing. Get Waon."

At Dugan's words, Tior looked frightened. Water soaked her chin as she turned and ran to the viscom, and Kiondili's nerve slipped. This was happening too fast. Then she froze. Waon? The Ruvian was the strongest esper at the outpost. And Dugan had said a Test, not a trial. Gods, but a Test was not a light challenge! And for Waon to be judge . . . She had done nothing! "Dugan," she croaked.

Dugan ignored her. "What is the charge, Effi?"

"Esper theft of—" Argon started in.

"Effi," Dugan cut across Argon's voice mentally and psychically. "What is the charge?"

"Theft." The old woman pointed viciously at Kiondili. "Esper theft of my research. She's been reading my mind—she stole it all—all of it—"

"The proof," Dugan cut in coldly. His orange-red eyes seemed to smolder but there was no real emotion there.

"The flashbook—here—this one." Effi thrust it at Dugan. "Is this yours, Wae?"

Kiondili stared at it. She could not deny it. The flashbook was one of the ones she had lost that morning in the free-boost chute when Argon had slammed into her. She nodded mutely.

Dugan glanced at her. "What code, Wae?"

Kiondili frowned, then winced as the muscles seemed to pull at her brain itself. "No code, sir. They're just notes from the lab."

Dugan flipped on the flashbook and scrolled through the pages. "I find nothing amiss in these notes," he said flatly.

"That's because they are *my* notes," Effi spit venomously. She tore free of Argon and flung aside flashbooks of her own till she found the one she wanted. "See this—"

Dugan took the proffered book and flicked it on. "Code?"

Effi, with a long glance to either side, carefully punched in a sequence of color and light too fast for anyone to follow. Then Dugan examined the book.

"I find these identical." He met Kiondili's eyes squarely. "What is your explanation, Wae?"

Kiondili almost gaped at him. "But that can't be! Those are *my* notes, the experiments we ran fourth quarter—my notes from the lab—"

Dugan cut her off. "What level are you, Wae?"

"E-7," she stammered, her eyes going automatically to the shimmering door through which Waon was gliding.

Dugan set both flashbooks down. "Then I hope you are innocent."

Kiondili sickened. Her hand held out in a half appeal, she tried to reach Dugan—anyone in the room—but they all had closed their minds. Even Lan-Lu, her predator instincts raised as she sensed Kiondili's terror, was closed, fighting her own battle not to attack while Kiondili pleaded for Dugan's mercy.

For Dugan meant for her to be Truth Tested. For a nonesper, it was an invasion of the mind, a sickening touch that crawled through one's thoughts, reaching even one's deepest self. A surface probe revealed only that an esper had guilt, not what the guilt was from, and all H'Mu had some guilt in them—for a fight with a sibling, a debt not repaid before a friend died, an insult never retracted. The Truth Test tore that guilt out and exposed it as irrelevant. For a nonesper the probe was unpleasant—it left one feeling unclean—but for an esper such a probe could kill. Espers could not be read honestly until their blocks were down—they were just as good at projecting emotions and images as nonespers were at lying—so the Federation used judges to break down the blocks. Some Federation species could open up to a judge's probe; others could not. H'Mu were among those who could not, even if they wanted to. And not only could H'Mu espers not help blocking those probes, whether they were innocent or guilty, but their blocks strengthened the deeper a judge reached. The more sensitive the esper or the stronger the blocks, the harder the Test. And when the blocks were destroyed, the esper could be destroyed with them.

Kiondili shivered, the chill that crept into her back crawling down her spine to her thighs. She was innocent, she told herself. Waon would try to protect her mind from the probe as soon as he knew that. But there was no expression on his face as he looked at her. His eyes were only dark spots of energy in which she could drown. *No!* she cried out mentally. She had done nothing. Waon would not let her die in the Test . . .

But—the realization would not go away—if Waon even suspected she was guilty, then Kiondili Wae would not only go insane, she would probably die. Waon was rated E-10. He would smash through her blocks as if they were soft like clay, not solid like stone. And she would die only after every dark thought, each nightmare emotion, every guilt in her life had ripped through her person and blasted her mind, her psyche, and her soul.

Waon nodded at Dugan that he was ready. "Test for theft," Dugan ordered the Ruvian.

No! Wait! Her voice made no sound. She was frozen.

He reached out. She whimpered. At the first touch, her bruised blocks stiffened. The gentle probe became a lance, piercing her mental shield and blasting through her mind. She screamed. *I've done nothing*, she shrieked. *I'm innocent!*

She blocked Waon once, twice, three times, only to find the white-hot shaft of his thought stabbing again and again, around, under, through each wall she slammed up. His unemotional attack was even worse than a normal H'Mu's—it had no feeling for her at all. It examined, discarded her innermost thoughts, picked at her embarrassments, tore out her insecurities and threw them back at her in nightmare shapes and touches. She pleaded, she begged him to stop. Terrified, frantic, she attacked back. He absorbed the shaft, launching back a blast that shattered her mental shield like a stone through glass. Then he broke into her mind like a corer. He used an ax to smash her thoughts; he burned her dreams in a stench of sulfur; he tore her private self apart under a spiked foot that ground back and forth over her soul like a heel over the broken glass of her mental shield. She writhed on the cold meta-plas floor of the lab while her mind was dissected as the Ruvian probed and burned back her blocks with infinite patience. The time she lied about the credit chit on Dith; the fire she set in the hold when she was careless with the cargo beam; the tuva gem she lost and never told her mother about . . . He beat her down further, searching, seeking a thread that would tie her to the flashbook Effi had held out. The time she broke into an alien's house to hide from the three who had chased her from the job pool; the time she cheated on a lab experiment by manipulating fields . . . His lance became sharper, probing more deeply. The time she fought with Argon because she did not report to the director right away . . . The probe steadied. Her mind lay open in shock, cowering. The time she stepped into Effi Ragan's place on the probe launch . . . Waon paused. Terror-stuck, helpless, Kiondili watched as the Ruvian stopped, his lance of power a talon that would taste each guilt. He spitted a thought, a memory, a feeling, and then, with an infinite wrench, tore the truth from her mind.

CHAPTER 10

There was a dark energy in the beams that Kiondili guided. It was a resentment she wore like a robe, so that even her silver-gray skin looked tarnished. Like pools of ashes, her eyes took in nothing but the screens before her, and the burning in her head was a heat that clawed and tore at the few thoughts she could stand.

Yes, she had survived the Test. She could say that now. Her esper was not burned out of her—she had not gone E-blind, though she thought that Effi would not have been sorry if that had happened, too. Her blocks? They were coming back. Slowly, painfully, she rebuilt them out of the esper ashes Waon had left in her brain. She could not even face him now without a rage burning in her gut. And there was still Argon. Effi would not have to pay for what she had done to Kiondili—Argon's false evidence had seemed to justify her accusation. But Argon—a superficial fine, some loss of trade access . . . Their work was important; their team could not be broken up at this stage. It was for the good of the outpost, Dugan, the director, had said. Kiondili snarled at him in her mind. Blast, probe—she jammed her power through the lens. The prelens amplifier, overwhelmed, shut itself down. Kiondili did not notice. Blast like a neutron wave through Argon's face—

". . . mass transference in one minute, ten seconds." Tior's voice went unheard by Kiondili.

"Tracking stations online," Xia, the other Mu on the team, reported. "Ready for transmission . . ."

Kiondili pulled her lips back and gnashed her teeth. Against the pull of her temple jacks, the fields of the simulated Lightwing jerked and snapped like a chained dog. Rae glanced warily at the stress curves in her holotank. If Kiondili went much farther, Rae would have to start cutting in an E-damp just to protect the weaker espers. But Kiondili did not let the beams fracture out. Reaching for the fields, she flexed them hard, forcing them to speed the ship toward the blast point. Her brain burned. She wanted to ram the blast up Effi's nose. The beams separated. The sensors pulled. The simulated Lightwing hesitated, and she jammed more power into the phasing. Blast, damn it—

Rae's voice was like cold water in the background. "Bring it back in line, Xia. You're losing mass too fast. You're throwing off the acceleration curve. Tior, control those secondaries."

"Acceleration still increasing at a factor of four."

"All systems at ninety-eight percent efficiency."

And Kiondili pushed her fury farther into the Lightwing. Blast, she raged. Blast to burn her memories into Effi's brain. Effi Ragan. The name was a curse. That woman ignored Kiondili's work with the backup team, praising Teams A and B instead. She scheduled work sessions so that the backup team members had to stay up later and get up earlier to do the same work as the other teams. Effi's work was important, the researcher said, more so than an extra hour of free time they would only waste. As for Kiondili, Effi had nothing to say. No apology for what she had put Kiondili through with the Testing. No asking how Kiondili was.

And how was she? Kiondili raged. First there had been a mindless pain for four days, days that Kiondili did not want to think of. Then there had been the wakening, with the blinding voice of Siln, the xenopsychologist. No sight, no images, just a voice piercing through that animal darkness, a voice that forced a sanity back upon her. And when sight finally returned, there was only the rawness of her memory to hold her rage: a burning paste that scorched and cracked her brain waves like mud searing in the desert. Something had changed for her. Her edges were sharp. Her blocks were tempered. And there was a strength and focus to her core that had not been there before. But she *burned*.

Tior glanced at her flashscreen. "Phase one breakdown complete. Phase two starting at mark."

"Perfect decomposition," Rae breathed. She cataloged the numbers with flying fingers, her temple jacks almost sparking with the speed of her imaging, as her eyes jumped from the holotank to the flashscreen and back. Even Teams A and B had not been able to get that far. And for once Argon was almost silent, his systems uncritical and stable.

"System efficiency ninety-seven percent," Tior reported.

Argon directed the next sequence, muttering, "Ready for transmission."

"Breakdown at the mark. Starting countdown."

Kiondili glared at the screens and deliberately tore open a mental scar, thrusting her wrath at the ship's fields.

". . . Seven . . . Six . . . Five . . ."

Blast like a laser cutting across Argon's spine—Kiondili snarled.

". . . Three . . . Two . . ."

Light, damn it! *Blast!*

"We have breakdown." Tior could not keep the excitement out of her voice. "We have blast—we have light!"

"Transmission is on the beam," Xia reported. "No, we're losing it. The beam is fouling."

Beside her, Argon swore silently as his own systems began to blink into red. Lan-Lu moved to his holotank, flexing her knuckle claws irritably as she registered his antagonism with her slitted eyes narrowed. "What's the percentage?" she snapped.

"Beam dispersing at twelve percent per second," he returned shortly. "Thirty-one percent per second . . ."

Stilman, who had been silent so far, watched the breakup with a frown. "The field factors are all wrong. Lan-Lu, pass me those decomposition stats. Rae, when did we make light?"

The short esper registered the last figures. "We hit light-speed immediately at breakdown. Not bad," she said approvingly to the backup team. "With these readings Lan-Lu should be able to compute the next launch twice as accurately."

Lan-Lu nodded at Rae's words, her sharp teeth gleaming in a smile until she stiffened. Rae, following her hungry gaze, looked at Kiondili. The younger Mu was disentangling herself from the sensors, and the violence that colored her thoughts flooded the room.

As her claws sprang out, Lan-Lu snapped the filters on her persona adapt to full strength. Kiondili, switching the console off, noted with dim surprise that the prelens amp was burned out. She must have focused her sensor's skills too sharply. She took a step, staggered, then pulled herself up and stalked to the door, brushing insolently by the predator.

"Careful, Mu," the alien warned with taut control.

Kiondili turned slowly. The tension in the room was palpable. "Sorry."

Stilman frowned after his assistant, and Coos, moving off with the other researchers, retracted his arms and chittered quietly.

"Give her a few days, Coos," Rae Arr said. "She is doing well, considering."

The other assistants gathered their notes and made their way from the control room. Coos, watching them go, blinked his yellow eyes thoughtfully. "I'm not esper," he said in a soft chitter, "but even I could see what her Mu eyes were hiding."

Stilman gathered his flashbooks. "Hate, anger, and pain, Coos. That is what you see and what I have to work with."

Rae gave him an odd look. "It is exactly that, Stilman, the hurt, which is driving Kiondili Wae and forcing her to focus her power. A focus you have been using as much as any of us."

Stilman looked skeptical.

Rae nodded at the holotank and called up a series of graphs. "I have been plotting each team's efficiency against the individual improvements in each of these areas. Note that each time Wae is in simulation, the use of the sensor lens increases by a factor of more than two. The rest of the team, after a slight delay, is forced to keep up. It is your assistant, Stilman, not me, who is driving the backup team so hard."

Coos chittered, swinging his head from Stilman to Rae. "She's right, Stilman. Right now, backup is leading the project, not Teams A and B."

Lan-Lu's wrist and elbow claws snaked out of her arms as her eyes shuttered. "And Kiondili Wae is leading the backup team."

Stilman examined the graphs with interest. "Hmm. Based on our output for the last two days, if she continues to push the backup team to improve at the same rate as they have been—"

"Stilman," Coos complained with a burst of chittering, "stop talking like a flashtext. We're talking about a person, not a meson particle—and not a meal, Lan-Lu," he added at the Ixia's still-extended claws.

Tior, escaping from the control room, let her breath out in relief as the voices of the researchers were cut off behind the door. Poole, who had been watching the team, was waiting for her at the free-boost chute. "Ayara's eyes," she said as she caught up with him. "The atmosphere in there was rough enough to rock a Tore ship."

"I'll put a rock in your water bags if you don't stop burping like a Biluane," Poole returned.

"It's not my fault," Tior complained. "I lose water any time Lan-Lu gets her ire up. And with Argon and Kiwi in the same room, there's no way to avoid it." As they reached the meeting room, Tior filed in behind Poole, who paused. She followed his gaze to the left. Effi Ragan was just sitting down, and Tior belched again in disgust. "Hot scientists get all the breaks," she muttered to Poole. "If I'd been in Dugan's spot, I'd have sentenced Effi to personality erase and given Argon a memory wipe. But," she mimicked, "their work is too valuable to the project right now." She slipped into a chair and nodded toward Kiondili, who was sitting next to Stilman's empty seat. Stilman and the other researchers would be following soon, and she glanced over her shoulder to see if they were at the hall yet. "Even I have trouble speaking to Argon now, and how Kiwi works with him is beyond me. Dugan must have laid down the law for her to leave him untouched." She frowned. "I wish we could do something for Kiwi. She looks terrible."

Poole brushed his arm fur down. "Enough has been done to her. We should leave her alone."

"You're hardly one to talk, Poole," Tior retorted angrily. "Your jokes haven't helped a bit. Setting her Soft so far down that it practically melted into a puddle at the last meeting? And digitizing that rainbow to appear over her head every time she spoke? In your own way," she snapped, "you are just as insensitive as Argon."

Poole stopped short so that Tior paused and looked back. His fur rippled strangely. "I am not now," he said quietly, intensely, "never have been, and never will be like Argon. As a student here, I may be conceited; as Poole, I may be smug; and as a Dhirrnu, I may have a sense of humor that is not always appreciated, but I have *never* abused anyone the way Argon did Kiondili Wae."

Tior was startled. Poole being serious? She recovered her

composure with little grace, adding petulantly, "Waon was not easy on her, either."

Poole looked at her, his yellow eyes gleaming. "How could he have been easier on her than he was? Perhaps you should use some of your brains for something other than blowing bubbles, Tior." His lips quirked at her expression. "If it had not been for the Ruvian, Kiwi would have been spaced without a suit more quickly than Dugan could have called for the chute guards. And don't think Stilman could have helped to keep her on. Dugan knows that Stilman worked without an assistant for months. He would just tell him to do so again. Use your head, Tior. Effi made an accusation that could not be proved except by Test. And Waon is the only esper strong enough to test an E-7. Each line in that flashbook pointed to Kiondili having entered the material, even to the way she color codes her notes. Argon got her pegged, and then Effi pushed the button. And it would have worked, too, if it had not been for Waon. If Argon had been esper himself, he would have understood what it meant to have a high-level esper like Waon do the testing. As it was, Argon had no concept that an esper test by someone of Waon's level could destroy Kiwi's mind—or her own esper. Had he known, I am sure he would simply have figured out some other way to help her crucify herself."

Tior opened her mouth to retort, but the meeting was called to order, and she had to subside.

"Attention," the Corson director said from the front. He expanded the holotank above them, and the room quieted as sound and sight depressors were turned on. "It's no secret that the Federation is pressing us for results," he said without preamble. "What we are considering today is an advancement of the Lightwing schedule to try to meet those deadlines. So far, there seem to be no overwhelming obstacles to pulling the timetable in a cycle. Training on the simulators is progressing faster than expected." He nodded at Rae. "The preliminary ship design is almost completed. Before we discuss this, however, several of us will present views on the progress of individual and team projects. Dr. Stilman?''

Stilman, who had sat down only a minute before, got up, his chair's fields collapsing behind him as he made his way forward. He always preferred to stand when he talked. He hated having his image projected while he sat in his Soft.

He cleared his throat. ''As you know,'' he began, ''the Lightwings appeared to lose energy when they reached hyperlight spacetime.'' Touching his temple jacks absently, he sent a string of images into the holotank. ''I stress the word *appeared*. If energy is being lost, we cannot find out where it is happening. You can see the path of the ship here. Even our tracking stations tell us that the ship does not lose energy during transmission. This means that the beam exists—the ship is being transferred to hyperlight spacetime. So it must be corrupted—not,'' he added strongly, ''dispersed.'' There was a murmur, and Stilman nodded. ''Once the beam is corrupted, the ship can recover only part of its mass. Without the right mass gain, the energy held back to slow the ship will be too great. That energy would be released at a single point at sublight speeds.'' The room seemed to rustle at his words. He nodded. ''Yes, an explosion with the force of a small nova would go off right under the nose of the Lightwing.''

He switched off the holotank. ''Now, if Coos will show us the new ship design for the Lightwing, I will be able to show more clearly how I think we can focus and control the boost to hyperlight.'' He strode back to his seat.

Behind Kiondili, the Greggors' subsonics surged carelessly while the next speaker took over, and she lost track of the discussion. Why in all the digger's hells on the Rim did the Greggors always have to sit next to her? They knew their alien sonics irritated H'Mu, and right now Kiondili was not just irritated but annoyed enough to wrench the controls on her persona adapt so that the field filters were on maximum. And still, the hair on the back of her neck stood up while the subsonics that shot through her filters sent fingers walking up and down her spine. She struggled to hold her temper. If the meeting had not been so important, she would have walked out.

By the time the talk was over and she could escape the range of the Greggors' fields, Kiondili was mentally inflamed. Her strengthening blocks kept much of her emotions from leaking out, but her frustration and festering fury were obvious. She had to be careful, she told herself. There were others as sensitive as she. Were she to lose control, the other sensitives would be disturbed. And Dugan, the outpost director, had made it clear what he expected from her. It was an esper's responsibility to control herself.

Esper responsibility, she spit in her mind, dropping into a boost chute. What responsibility had anyone shown when she had been Tested? Had anyone requested that Effi be Tested for the truth behind her accusation? Kiondili slammed through the free-boost chute and almost shot out at the opening near her room, stalking down the hall and shouldering her way through the still-shimmering door, gloating in the sparks that leapt from her arms in the still-tingling field as the door tried to go from its evaporated state to its solid form and encountered her body still within it. Dropping across her bunk, she stared at the random holomural on the wall. It swept from planet to planet until it showed a blue depth that only Terran seas could contain. Kiondili reached out mentally and flexed the mural's fields, holding the graph to Earth scenes. She stared at it. Then she exploded in rage, grabbing her dolphin figurine and slamming it across the room.

"Damn you!" she screamed. Her voice choked, and she pounded on her bunk. She could not escape her thoughts. Truth—yes, she could see the truth of herself now. More clearly than a H'Mu should ever see. With Waon's Test, she saw the shell of herself without value, without strength, without a core. There was only emptiness there. And she hated that emptiness—that weakness—even more than she hated Argon and Effi. Was she bitter? Was she dark? Before her, the holomural shifted as a school of fish dove deeply, dragging the images into a blue-green depth. Where the carved dolphin lay against the mural, the colors shifted into shadow to merge with the rich brown of the statue. Dark—yes, like a shadow across her mind. And driven? Even more so. Driven by anger and hate for the traders who had killed her parents. Driven by the fear that she would one day realize that without her anger, she was even more alone than when she had had her rage to sustain her. Kiondili stared at the dolphin. It lay silent and unmoving, but its lines were clean, smooth, gleaming in the light. Kiondili, seeing its grace, made a low, guttural animal sound before burying her head in her arms.

Team A was scheduled for the first manned launch ten days later. Kiondili, finding out, could not even congratulate her counterpart on the team. In a foul mood, she took to the free-boost chutes. It was off-shift, so the tubes were nearly empty, and Kiondili slammed into the redirection pads carelessly, manipulating the boost fields to augment her speed. She worked her way around the entire outpost before slowing and making her way to the upper triads. One of the float libraries was empty. Kiondili set the door to occupied as she entered, then set the spheroid grav control to encompass the whole room. With the gravity at zero, she drifted, exhausted physically, drained mentally. For the first time in days she felt tired and empty of hate.

She barely saw the stars that floated around her head as she bumped into the window. Insulated as the glass was, a frigid draft still swept away from the pane. Above her, the galaxy's rim was only a radiant swirl made up of pricks of light. Close by, the tiny shapes of solar surfers and space walkers darted among those steady stars.

"Mu." The soft voice slid into her consciousness.

Kiondili stiffened. It was Lan-Lu's voice. She twisted her body around slowly and warily to face the Ixia. She said nothing, but the return of her resentment at the intrusion was hard to miss, and Lan-Lu did not mistake it for a welcome.

The Ixia forced her elbow claws in until only their tips

peeked out from her fur. "We have to speak, Mu," Lan-Lu stated.

"I don't see that there is anything to say that has not been said in simulation."

"I did not come to harass you."

"Really? Then why follow me to a float library in the middle of night cycle?"

Lan-Lu tensed while her wrist claws flexed involuntarily in and out of their sheaths. "Because we must speak, Mu."

Clearly the Ixia would not leave until she had said what she had come to say. Kiondili ground her teeth and motioned abruptly for Lan-Lu to begin.

The predator's teeth gleamed, and her tongue flicked their tips as if testing for blood. "I have been working with all three launch teams, Mu." She gestured at Kiondili with one of her fingers, the knuckle claw jabbing out, as well. "Backup has been more noticeable than the others for the last two quarter cycles."

Kiondili's eyes were hooded. "It's nothing I've been doing."

Lan-Lu's slitted yellow eyes regarded Kiondili until she shivered; then the predator said, "You are pulling your team together better than the other sensors who are leading the prime teams."

Kiondili stared at her, suddenly furious. What right did Lan-Lu have to search her out here? What right did she have to tell Kiondili that, once again, she was being noticed? Was she going to tell Kiondili to back off now, make the prime teams look good? Whose setup was Kiondili walking into now—Effi's? Or Argon's? Or that of someone new? Ayara's eyes, but she just did not give a flash anymore. The next Mu that tried to force a Test on her would be cinders as soon as she could focus her fields. Subconsciously, Kiondili reached out across the fields and flexed the float library's sensors. She glared at the Ixia.

The alien's neck ridges became taut, but her voice was calm. "Your strengths as a sensor on the team have not subsided, Kiondili Wae,'' she observed. ''They have grown since the Test.''

''Make your point, Lan-Lu.''

Lan-Lu said softly, ''Your hostility arouses me, Mu.''

Kiondili's eyes narrowed. She pulled on the fields generated by the float library so that they pulsed, then condensed, stronger now and easily within reach of her sensor skills—like a weapon.

The Ixia struggled to keep her elbow claws from flexing as she sensed the Mu's challenge. Her yellow, slitted eyes locked on Kiondili's own gray glare. She breathed sharply, forcing her wrist claws to retract as her elbow claws had. ''You are dangerous to me, Mu.''

Kiondili fought to stifle her hostility. She shot a mental probe at the alien. ''This is a threat?'' she demanded coldly.

The Ixia clenched her fists until the skin whitened and the tips of her wrist claws slid out of their sheaths. ''This is a warning, Mu.''

Kiondili snorted.

''This is not comfortable for either of us, Kiondili Wae. There are many species I must hold myself back from hunting. And lately you have made me aware of them all.''

Kiondili opened her mouth, then closed it slowly. Warily, she withdrew her deliberately careless probes behind her blocks.

The Ixia shuddered in relief. ''Your strength is growing, Mu, and your anger helps you focus on the project better than the others at this time.''

Kiondili stared at her, repressing her instinctive retort. ''Then why does Effi discard my work as meaningless?'' she demanded finally. ''I passed her flash-damned Test, and the backup team does better on the launch than the other teams put together—the teams Effi herself trained. But she won't even acknowledge that half the progress we've made so far is due to my team's effort.''

''She is H'Mu. Your success only gives her greater reason

to hate you. Envy is a powerful motivator, Wae, and Effi is not jealous but frightened.''

''Of me?''

''Of her age.''

Kiondili tightened her jaw.

''She cannot force the other teams to make the progress your team has made. She does not have the strength to work as the sensor for one of the prime teams. She sees that you have everything she does not. So she pushes the prime teams to catch up, to reach beyond you, to beat you—as if this were a game or race. And so you and your backup team go to Rae, Coos, even Waon and me for your training.''

''And you came here to complain,'' Kiondili scoffed.

''From experience and from Effi's training, the other teams have more knowledge of the physics, of the drive theory, of ship control. That experience, applied, is what I need to complete my own research.'' Lan-Lu adjusted her persona adapt to turn her personal grav sphere off. As the zero-grav field in the float library picked her up, she floated toward the nearly invisible pane that held back the stars. ''It wastes my time to duplicate Effi's work with the prime teams.''

''Then why don't you go back to working with the other teams to finish your research?''

Lan-Lu looked at her. ''I am a hunter, Mu. And the espers on the other teams have less effective blocks than you. My research is crippled by their crudely blatant emotions, and my instincts disturb my thoughts.''

Kiondili said nothing. Lan-Lu mistook her silence for a lack of comprehension.

''The urge to hunt is heightened when the prey projects certain emotions,'' the Ixia explained tightly. ''Frustration, which makes them careless; anger or hostility, which challenges; and helplessness, which makes them such easy prey that my claws come out each time Effi spurs them to feel they have lost control or failed. The tension on the prime teams is eating at their nerves. And so it eats at mine.''

''And I'm not stressed when I'm around Argon?''

"Your hostility behind blocks is less . . . provocative," Lan-Lu said, "than the other espers' tension leaked through their blocks. Ce'eldi, the sensor on Team A, makes my teeth want to sharpen. And Arond, on Team B, sweats so that I desire nothing more than to chew his spindly arms off and gnaw on his bones. Also," she added as an afterthought, "neither has the potential that you do."

Then why was Kiondili on backup and not prime?

Lan-Lu answered as if Kiondili's thought had been spoken out loud. "Because you lack the emotional maturity to be prime."

Kiondili stared. Emotional maturity? Since when did that matter? Sal, who was as emotionally unstable as they came, was on Team B as controller. Kiondili was at least as emotionally mature as he.

"Are you sure?"

Kiondili opened her mouth to retort, stopping only when a movement by the predator reminded her of what the alien could do. She set her jaw. If Lan-Lu wanted to play rough, fine. Kiondili had not honed her sensor skills for nothing. She could manipulate the fields in this float library without half thinking, tighten the grav sphere around herself and leave the rest of the room in no-grav. She would drop to the floor while Lan-Lu sprawled in the air. And Kiondili could manipulate those fields all day. Then see what Lan-Lu thought of her lack of experience in field control.

Lan-Lu did not need to be esper to read Kiondili's intention. "I am not here to fight, Mu. I am here to offer a compromise. It will help my research and ensure the success of the program. And," she added, "gain you greater prestige at this outpost."

Kiondili had to laugh. "Prestige? All I want is to get out from under Dugan's eyes and out of range of Argon and Effi. As for the success of the flights, as Effi said, the prime teams are supposed to do that, anyway."

"Backup is the only team to reach recombination phase," Lan-Lu spit. "Your fields hold together tighter; your blocks stabilize the tension on your team. And I must be able to train at least one team to go through recombination properly. Effi will not agree to put you on Prime A or B, and I cannot work with the espers on the other teams amplifying each person's stress.'' The Ixia's muscles rippled tautly under her golden skin as she shoved off from the window toward the door.

''I will think on it,'' Kiondili said finally.

Kiondili was startled at the expression on the Ixia's face. When Lan-Lu next spoke, the softness of her voice betrayed her intensity. ''My people need this drive, Mu.'' Her slitted lips were tight. ''We Ixia would never have stooped to working with H'Mu—or any other species of prey—had it not been for our need for the Lightwing drive. We have little left to trade with the Federation for the lease of their ships. Without more development, without the ability to explore what we have already discovered, we will be condemned to sublight status.'' She touched her chest. ''H'Mu, Ixia, Robul— we will all share the Lightwing drive if it succeeds. My work must not be wasted. Nor your talent.'' She regarded Kiondili with a challenging look in her eyes. ''We will work in my lab. Surrounded by food and comfort, I will be less likely to snap at you.''

Kiondili stared after the alien. She had not suspected the Ixia of offering to help—or of having a sense of humor.

She told herself as she went to sleep that night that she did not need prestige. That she did not care what Effi or the other researchers thought of her. Stilman had never complained about her work; in fact, he had praised it. She had passed their Test. She had taken the backup team farther than Effi could take the others. She did not need Lan-Lu's help to prove herself.

But the thought of the Ixia's offer nagged. As she turned on the narrow bunk, twisted back, and readjusted the Soft controls for the third time, she admitted that with Lan-Lu's training, she would be able to take the backup team to launch status even before the prime teams made that goal. She might not get to take a Lightwing out, but her team would be ready.

She lay for a moment in the dark, then startled herself by laughing bitterly. Kiondili would take the backup team beyond the level the others had reached, yes. And then Effi would use Kiondili's effort for Teams A and B—in effect, steal it—just as the old woman had accused Kiondili of stealing Effi's research. Except that in this case Kiondili would give Effi the work freely. The irony of it choked her. She tightened her grip on herself rigidly, but her thoughts wound around each other like snakes. Effi and Argon. Argon and Waon. Argon—she told herself she could deal with the fury he raised—she could block her emotions and work with that worm. She had no choice in that; Dugan would have spaced her had she refused. And Effi she could tolerate. It was not the old woman's fault she was so unbalanced; the others who had walked through that hypergate fifty years earlier had suffered similar problems. Yes, she could still work with Effi.

And that left Waon. Kiondili stared at the depthless blue of the holomural on her wall and shivered. The cold crept into her skin and turned its silver-gray warmth to ice. Waon. The Ruvian had ripped her blocks down as if they were nothing. He had torn such truth from her that she could barely tolerate her reflection in a mirror. It was no longer herself she saw there; the face that stared back at her was not her own. The gray eyes in the glass were only a thin shell. A shell that hid the terror that others could now walk in and demand what Waon had wrested from her mind. Each guilt and fear and insecurity beat at her consciousness. She could not hide them anymore. There was no longer a depth in her mind that she could not see: Waon's touch had reached her core, and she saw—could not help but see—the ugliness of her person in every insult breathed and every thought suppressed. And if she looked too closely, the insecurities that coated each guilt ruptured and burst up into her mind like geysers, blinding her with their rush.

Yes, there was fear behind her blocks now. A fear that

Waon could step in again and tear her apart. She would not be able to stop him. One word, she knew, and he could force her to look at herself again. Hide, she could not. Her own mind was her enemy. Her dreams relived each truth he had pried away. And now she knew and saw herself and hated herself for what she had hidden throughout her life.

She sat up suddenly, her back to the wall of her bunk and her fists clenched against her temples. The harshness of her breath clung to her memories. She did not sleep again that night.

CHAPTER 11

"Pass me those last figures again, Wae," Stilman said as he adjusted a critical field point in the lab.

She adjusted her temple jacks and murmured the string of numbers as directed. Beside her, the image in the holotank fleshed itself out, and Stilman nodded with satisfaction.

He picked up his own headset. "All right, give me the next set."

She listed the next string and then hesitated, Lan-Lu's offer on her mind. "How much do you need me in the lab in the next cycle?"

"Give me the horizontals next. Why do you ask?" he returned absently.

"Lan-Lu thinks I need more help on field control in simulation."

Stilman looked up. "We're on a tight schedule, Wae. I need you here in the lab, not off in some Ixia's lab. Next set," he prompted.

She bit back her retort and repeated the numbers. She paused. "The launch is important, too," she said, adding bitterly, "Effi doesn't show me anything. If Lan-Lu is offering to give me the training I'm not getting elsewhere, I want to take her up on it."

Stilman stopped fiddling with the beamer and stood up. "Wae, look around you. Right here you are working on one of the most important components of the entire Lightwing project. You are learning at a phenomenal rate, must faster in fact than I expected for your native intelligence level. I realize that being on backup is exciting to you, but Prime A and B have a much greater chance of succeeding than you seem to be giving them. And as your adviser, I have to tell you that I think you'll get more out of staying with your scheduled studies than going off on a tangent with Lan-Lu."

"Prime A and B haven't even reached recombination yet," she said in a low voice. "I have. My team has. If we don't continue collecting information like we have been, what kind of chance does that give the primes in real space?"

"Simulation isn't everything, Wae."

"But it's all we have to judge by," she retorted. "Lan-Lu can't work with the other teams as well because their blocks leak more than mine. She's offering the help. She just wants to make sure the Lightwings work."

He raised his eyebrows.

Kiondili met his gaze stubbornly.

He bent back over the beamer. "I believe your confidence is misplaced, Wae. If we get this prototype to transfer mass consistently, *Lightwing IV* will be on the beam and hyperlight before your backup team gets a chance to think of stepping out in one of those little tin cans."

Kiondili controlled the burst of emotion that swept through her until she felt calm enough to speak. "Do you have any objection to my working with Lan-Lu after lab hours?"

Stilman looked up again. "I need you here full-time, Wae. And as we come down to the deadline, you're going to find yourself living in the lab. There will be hardly time for you to eat and sleep, let alone work extra hours with Lan-Lu."

Kiondili stood her ground. "The design computations

could be set up as easily by another assistant as by me. I want the beamer to work as much as you do, Dr. Stilman. All I'm asking is that you schedule the lab hours so that I can have some time for my own studies. After all,'' she said sarcastically, "that's part of your responsibility, too.'' As soon as the words were out, she regretted them.

"Are you telling me how to do my job?'' the scientist asked coldly.

She licked her lips. "I'm telling you that I want to take the opportunity Lan-Lu is offering me.''

He glared at her. "Perhaps you want to be her assistant, not mine.''

Kiondili forced herself to laugh, but it came out a short, sharp sound. "We both know that I would rather be dispersed by you than be an assistant to an alien who would rather have me for supper than teach me.''

Stilman jerked his hand through his hair angrily. "And I'm not teaching your impatient Mu mind enough.''

Kiondili pulled her blocks tight. "I have learned more from you than I ever thought possible,'' she said at last. "I— I just want . . .''

"You want the glory that goes with the launch,'' he finished for her.

"What if Lan-Lu loans you the Lemer she works with so that I spend time with her? It could set up the design calculations easily while I get in a few hours in her lab. The computer could run them until I got back from Lan-Lu's. Then I could test the results with the new prototype.''

He snorted. "Lan-Lu never gives up her Lemer. It took her two decades to get one on order and another decade for it to get here. She doesn't let it go, and she doesn't loan it out. She doesn't even let it leave the lab.''

"Well, what if she did?'' Kiondili persisted. "You would have the designs that much faster, and I would have time to work on my sensor skills, as well.''

"Lemers can't image into a holotank,'' Stilman said flatly, but Kiondili could tell he was intrigued. A Lemer would guarantee that Stilman's designs would be done on schedule; Lemers had an incredible capacity for multitasking. They had little ability for physical tasks, though. The aliens weighed tons. They could not move quickly, and they had no adaptable limbs. But they could think better than most species in the galaxy—and they got along well with the Ixia, to whom eating a Lemer would be like biting into a hunk of rock.

"It doesn't need a holotank. It can use the flashscreens to set up the base designs for me to build the beamer," Kiondili said persuasively. "Then I could work on the designs in the holotanks to put each version of the prototype together."

"Hmmph," Stilman snorted.

But he had not actually said no. Kiondili nodded, satisfied that he would think about it, and read off the next set of measurements as if the matter were settled.

The next night cycle found Kiondili and Stilman in Lan-Lu's lab, the white-haired scientist standing with his arms crossed and the Ixia pacing irritably before a bank of computer terminals.

"The Lemer is not part of the deal, Stilman," Lan-Lu snapped. "I need it for my work. You do not."

"You want Wae to take extra training, and I need her in the lab. If she cannot find someone to do her work while she is wasting time with you, the deal is off and she stays with me."

"No," the alien said sharply, flexing her wrist claws so that they dug into the soft plastic of the lab table. "She must learn the recombination phase. She is the only one who is ready for it, and the launch depends on it."

"Well, I depend on her," the human retorted. "She's the only one who fully understands my designs now. I have four more prototypes to complete, and without them there won't be a beamer to drive the next launch hyperlight. Of course—" Stilman paused. "—the Lemer could set up the basic designs in a fifth the time it takes Wae to do them . . ."

Lan-Lu glared at him. "The Lemer is needed here."

"Ah, well. I tried." Stilman gestured abruptly for Kiondili to follow him out. "I'll need the breakdown of the mass transference ratios by tomorrow—"

"Just a minute, H'Mu," the Ixia hissed. She was angry, and the claws on her toes dug into the floor as she rocked from one foot to the other. "You can use the Lemer for one hour each day cycle," she said finally.

Stilman shook his head. "Wae is spending three hours each night cycle with you. The Lemer will spend exactly the same time on my prototypes."

"The Lemer can finish the design sets in half that time. One and a half hours. Including transport time."

"Two hours. Excluding transport time."

Lan-Lu hissed. "One and a half hours," she spit, "excluding transport time, to be done on a cumulative basis every three days."

"Agreed. I'll expect the first work to be done two day cycles from today." Stilman winked at Kiondili as he left. "Get to work, Wae."

As Stilman left, Lan-Lu muttered something unintelligible. Kiondili, left by the holotank, pulled her temple jacks out of her jumper pocket and held them awkwardly, waiting for Lan-Lu to tell her what to do. The Ixia looked at her through slitted eyes, then turned abruptly and switched the lab's local E-damp on high. The resulting depression of the atmosphere felt to Kiondili as if she were seeing and hearing the alien through a wall of cotton.

"Sit," the Ixia ordered as she motioned for Kiondili to put her temple jacks away. She handed the Mu a larger pair instead. "Put these on and tune them to your comfort."

Kiondili nodded and adjusted the jacks, but the background fog remained. She frowned. "My jacks would cut through this."

"That isn't static," the Ixia said coldly. "I adjusted those for the purpose of training sensors. Most sensors are esper, and H'Mu can hide too well behind their E-ratings. The

E-damp will let me see how well you understand how to apply the principles of recombination. Once I am sure that you are not working on instinct, we will gradually shut off the E-damp and allow you to work unhindered under a pre-lens amplifier.''

''I don't need an amplifier. I haven't used one for a quarter cycle.''

''I am aware of that. But that is why we will do it this way. You are pushing your biofields too hard. You burned out the prelens amp in simulation, but that amp is weaker than the one on a real Lightwing. I want you to know what a properly set amplifier can do for you. Later, you can choose to have one implanted in your brain to give you greater control over the Lightwing fields.''

''Implantation was not part of the team option package,'' Kiondili said warily. To have something as powerful as an amplifier available to her all the time . . . She was not sure she could be trusted with such power: There was still Argon.

Lan-Lu understood. ''That is why it would be tuned only to the lens built into the ship's engines.'' The Ixia adjusted the settings in the simulator. ''This first problem will be trivial so you can get used to being E-blind. You will be in a full damp in a minute.''

Kiondili's blocks tightened. Esper-blind? As the damp increased, she felt suddenly lost, her blocks vague and only semisolid. Then she saw the look on Lan-Lu's face. She closed her mind to her fear. Lan-Lu could smell fear, she reminded herself harshly. She flicked the switch on the temple jacks. A silence invaded her mind. Motion seemed to disappear. Sound? No, the world was mute. She opened her mouth to cry out, but the movement itself was shortened and dulled by the absence of esper depth. She took a breath and could no longer taste the other creatures that had breathed that air in before.

''Lan-Lu?'' she asked with a shake in her voice. It was curiously dull and flat.

''You have never been in a hundred percent damp before,

have you, Mu?'' Lan-Lu smiled, her eyeteeth gleaming, and Kiondili had a sudden realization that with her esper cut off, she would not be able to sense when the Ixia was hungry. Was this how Stilman lived? How Argon and Coos sensed their worlds? Ayara's eyes, but this—this was—

"Get used to it," the alien said maliciously. "We have only a half cycle left to work before your backup team will be called to launch."

At the end of two hours Lan-Lu was pacing the lab. "No, no—you cannot focus the beam after it comes out of the prelens amp," she repeated for the third time. "You just have to do it again when the lens kicks on."

"I *know* that," Kiondili said tersely.

"Then concentrate," the Ixia snapped back.

But drenched in sweat, the Mu was so tired that she could no longer keep from tightening her muscles each time she reached out through the simulator to the beam. With the E-damp still clogging her senses, she tried again to grasp the unfocused beam, failed, and dispersed the beam before it reached the lens.

Lan-Lu's elbow claws snapped out against the cabinet. "It is enough," she said abruptly. She shivered as wisps of the scent of Kiondili's sweet perspiration flowed into her nostrils. "Tomorrow," the alien managed. "Same time."

Kiondili, staring miserably at the efficiency graphs, did not trust herself to speak. She shut the simulator down, took Lan-Lu's temple jacks off in relief, and gasped as the E-damp dissipated and her esper sense flooded back in. The Ixia still stood where she was, trembling, her wrist and finger claws extending and retracting uncontrollably. Kiondili dropped the temple jacks in the Soft and fled the lab.

Outside, she sagged against the wall of the hallway. Wiping the moisture off the side of her face, she stared at her shaking hand. When she reached her quarters, it was on weak legs, her blocks tight around her blank thoughts. She did not look at her messages, only curled up on the bunk, twitched twice, and fell asleep.

It was dark when she woke. Around her, the room was silent except for her breathing and the familiar subtle hum of the outpost fields. It felt so right to sense the fields again . . . The thought of the E-damp quickened her breath, and she turned the lights on abruptly. She had used, had been in, partial damps, but this had been her first experience with a full damp. Never had she felt so suffocated, so dulled. And not since Waon's probe had she felt so alone with herself. Those two hours with the Ixia— She had sensed nothing of Lan-Lu or of anyone else at the outpost. The emotional blanket of hundreds of minds that had always been with her had disappeared with the damp. All she had felt was herself— her own rage and hate, her own desire to hurt Effi and Argon as they had hurt and humiliated her. Kiondili dragged herself up and stared into the mirror across the room, her silver-gray face a caricature in three dimensions. Even her expression was hard, like revenge cast in steel. Her straight, black hair made the tightness of her mouth seem more drawn, and her cheeks were only harsh shadows that showed the tension of her pain. Her eyes—only her eyes were alive in that gray, shadowed face.

A mask. That was what she saw when she looked in the mirror. There was no dimension to the surface of that face. Was this what she had become? A shell of revenge? Had Waon wrenched every other emotion from her mind, stripped her memories of even the good things in her life? She reached her fingers toward the mirror, stopping halfway as they began to shake.

This launch—what was it worth? Could she face herself again in Lan-Lu's E-damp? And what would she gain if she did? A chance to go light? Not unless both Team A and Team B failed. And she would not, could not wish that on them. So why was this training so important to her? Was it because of the Truth Testing, the probes that had reached beyond her blocks so easily? Was it that memory which drove her now? She stared at her eyes, searching for a sign that it was more than that, that it was hope for a dream, not fear of the past that had pulled her to the predator's lab. She found no answer in the taut expression on her silver-gray skin. But she knew that the answer did not matter: She would go back to Lan-Lu, anyway.

The next nine days were a blur—classes and lab work and sessions with Lan-Lu. Kiondili spoke to almost no one. Only Tior met her for meals. Tior, as controller of the backup team, had been working as late in the simulator lab as Kiondili had with Lan-Lu. They went together to watch the first launch of a manned Lightwing.

As she sat in the observation lounge, Kiondili's stomach twisted up as she watched Team A's main controller down in the launch room. The central holotank was replaying the images of the team's shuttle as it sped out to the Lightwing. As the three-man team transferred to the ship, Kiondili gritted her teeth. This was the goal that had sustained her throughout the institute and its threat of the job pool; this was the goal that had given her back her sanity after Waon's test. This—the first manned Lightwing—was her dream. The holotank switched over to real time. The Lightwing was go for launch. "Thirty seconds," she whispered to herself.

Tior's attention was riveted to the holotank, but hearing Kiondili's voice, she stirred. Unwilling to miss her counterpart's actions, she did not look up as she asked, "This is the first launch that uses your new beamer?"

"We put in the new oscillation damps just last night."

Tior nodded absently. "Fifteen seconds."

In the holotank a tiny white-blue flame signaled the launch, and a blue-purple flare marked the first-stage boost. Below the two H'Mu the control room was orderly, the holotanks merging and splitting as one tracking station and then another picked up the ship. Status reports bounced from flashscreen to flashscreen and fleshed out the holotank images as they watched.

"Yellow light across Field Four at the sensor lens," one of the controllers said, breaking into the steady stream of reports.

"They are not ready for this," Coos chittered suddenly.

Rae barely glanced at him. "The decision was made, Coos. The launch is a go." She turned to the controller and motioned at him to split his holotank. As he did so, the stats began to flow into the tank, creating a brilliant display of lines and curves. "Acceleration constant," he reported. "We have point five light."

But next to him, the main controller's voice cut suddenly and sharply across the noise. "Energy flux is shifting out of phase." He glanced at his flashscreen and merged his holotank with that of the controller next to him. The curves blurred. As the phase shift grew, each line split into two, one marking the original path and one marking the error.

"Red light on the flux," he warned. "Red light."

"Flux out of control on primaries."

"Tell the pilot to cut the secondaries back in," Rae ordered. Behind her, Lan-Lu paced first one side of the lab, then the other.

Coos squatted in the middle of the room, limbs and face withdrawn into his body so that his head jacks seemed to sprout from featureless fur. Only his muttering was audible. "If the fourth flux is controlled by— ow!" the Robul chittered frantically, surging up from the floor as Lan-Lu trod on him. "My leg slots. It isn't enough to have to watch this farce of a launch with a team that is only half-trained—"

The Ixia whirled, but Stilman was already there, easing the predator away from the scuttling furball. "Back off, Lan-Lu," he snapped. "Supervise the secondaries."

Lan-Lu snarled at him, one of her elbow claws raking across his arm and snagging his tunic.

Stilman ignored it. "The secondaries, Lan-Lu."

The main controller ignored them both. "Primaries under stress . . ."

The Ixia stalked over to one of the other controllers' seats and stared with narrowed eyes at the man's flash-screen.

"Secondaries starting backup procedures now," the H'Mu reported nervously.

"Get that predator something to drink," Coos ordered one of the standby assistants testily. "She's enough to disrupt the launch by herself."

"Zingar's balls!" Stilman snapped, "Will you watch the launch and leave Lan-Lu alone!"

"Secondaries taking up stress." The controller cut across their voices again. "Repeat, secondaries taking up stress. The beamer is starting the transfer of the blast beam to the lens."

Rae tapped her fingers irritably on her headset, listening to the rush of numbers and watching the holotanks at the same time.

"Hold that transfer. We've got a red light on the secondaries now," one of the other controllers cut back in remorselessly. "We're losing the secondaries."

"*Red* light?" Effi snapped. "Check the mass transference system for a leak."

"It's not transference. Look at the decomposition beamer."

"Secondaries beginning to fracture the blast beam . . ."

"The lens is not activated. Repeat, the sensor lens does not sense enough power to activate."

"Control, this is the Lightwing. What the hell is going on?"

"Control to Lightwing. Drives are fracturing. Repeat, the primary and secondary fields are falling apart."

"Secondary stress at ten to the fourth," a controller repeated.

"Primary drives holding at redline," a second assistant added.

"Control, this is Lightwing. Do we have a go or not?"

"We have a go," Effi snarled into the com. "Boost it out."

"Secondary stress at ten to the twelfth. Primaries' efficiency dropping below eighty percent."

"Control, we're losing mass as we gain it. Repeat, mass transference fields are going down. My sensor lens isn't drawing enough power to pull a shuttle through, let alone this ship. We *can't* boost—"

The controller's voice cut over the com. "We've lost the secondaries. Secondaries going down."

"Control, this is Lightwing. We have no drive fields. Repeat—no hyperlight drives."

"Flux shifting. Stabilizers off center," the controller announced.

"Control, requesting permission to abort."

"This is Control," Effi snarled. "Dammit, focus that beam, Ce'eldi." The woman stabbed her wrinkled fingers at the holotank. "What's blast status?"

"Blast on yellow alert. Loss of control imminent."

"Requesting permission to abort," the Lightwing captain repeated. "Acknowledge, Control."

"Acceleration jumping. Loss of control eighty percent."

"Course veering . . ."

"Control, acknowledge," came the disembodied voice from the Lightwing.

"Hold a moment—" Effi started to say.

"Control," the disembodied voice came urgently over the com. "We've got less than two minutes to abort safely. Stop hanging on, Effi; we're talking lives here. There are other Lightwings."

"Main blasters going to red light," the controller said.

"Acceleration system on red alert. Loss of control ninety-two percent."

"Control, acknowledge abort status. Acknowledge abort—"

"Navigation systems core-dumped."

"Oh, damn it all to hell," Effi snarled. "Abort the launch." She sank down trembling against the console. "So close . . ." she whispered, staring at the screen. Three small blips burst away from the Lightwing twelve seconds later, a puff of burning matter marked the end of *Lightwing IV*, and the control room was silent. Only the continually reported status of the fleeing crew was visible on the screen as the controllers murmured their numbers and tallied their stats.

CHAPTER 12

"So, what went wrong?" Dugan demanded flatly, surveying the assembled group before him. "Rescan shows that the problem was not crew fault." His orange-yellow eyes looked angry, but Kiondili knew there was no emotion there. Dugan's eyes tracked motion, not color or changes in light, so there was no reason for her to feel so uncomfortable when his empty gaze slid over her and went on. "Let's have individual status first."

Dugan listened impassively through the long list of researchers until one of the ship designers, the Moal, spoke.

"Elim Qu-Ibis sings status
  Status design preliminary.
             Preliminary design incomplete.
                incomplete gives birth
                    birthing weakness.
                    birthing weakness.
                    loss of mass complete."

The Moal subsided almost before she finished, cowering back into her seat. Her discomfort at speaking in front of so many people added an almost discordant tone to the doubling and tripling tones. Kiondili, entranced by the effect, realized suddenly that the Moal's tension was a reflection of its mood, not of its message. She shook herself to make sense of the song's array before she lost the gist of those notes. But Dugan motioned for the alien to continue. "Explain further, Elim," he ordered.

"Elim Qu-Ibis sings weakness
              weakness tears fields
                        fields flux handless
                                  handless gives birth
      Beamer pulls on fields   birth weakness
              fields yield to yearning space
Elim Qu-Ibis sings   yearning space
      weakness
Elim Qu-Ibis sings   mass fields lost in place
      corruption
Elim Qu-Ibis sings   energy dispersed
      yearning space
                        mass lost to yearning space."

The medley of tones reverberated. Kiondili tried to make sense of it, but she had already lost the thread of tone. "Did you catch what she said?" she muttered to Coos.

The Robul chittered irritably. "Of course. She is much easier to understand than you. Qu-Ibis said that when building the preliminary design, time constraints did not allow them to fully develop the stress connectors for the primary fields. When the acceleration reached a certain stage, the mass-to-energy conversion was uncontrolled. This caused a fluctuation that tore the primary transmission fields apart. When the beamer kicked in too early, mass was volatilized before being focused through the sensor lens. With the resulting energy dispersed in space, the crew was forced to abort before the fuel topes exploded."

Kiondili stared. ''I didn't catch even a quarter of that.''

Coos snaked his head out and glanced at her. ''Listen to the fourth and fifth harmonies and ignore the double stops under the message. Elim Qu-Ibis always gets verbose when she's asked to speak.''

Kiondili raised her eyebrows.

''So what is the problem, design or miscalculation?'' Dugan was asking.

''If the beamer had not kicked in too early, we could have saved the Lightwing,'' Effi sniped with a sideways look toward Kiondili.

''If the beamer had not kicked in at all, we would have lost the crew,'' one of the other ship designers cut in. His voice was as flat as the Moal's was musical but carried just as well. ''Besides, the beamer was recalibrated just last night.''

''Yes,'' Effi agreed, pointing viciously at Kiondili, ''by her.''

Kiondili opened her mouth but shut it without speaking.

Stilman stood abruptly, silencing the crowd with a sharp tapping on his flashbook. ''Kiondili reset the beamer last night as I directed,'' he said testily, straightening his violently colored tunic. ''Yes, we put in the new damps, and I supervised the testing myself. I also certified the beamer one hundred percent. Unless you have some doubts as to my competence, too, Effi, we can continue without the harassment.''

''Effi will keep her mouth shut unless it spews forth something constructive,'' Dugan cut in equally coldly. ''If the beamer is not the problem, that leaves the fields and the design itself. Rae, I would like you to work with the design team on this. Elim, Kiet,'' he said, nodding to the two designers, ''how soon can you modify the three Lightwings we have left to work around the variance for now?''

''Elim Qu-Ibis sings stress
         stress to strength
                  strength for handless flux

> Elim Qu-Ibis sings space   flux a cycle
> Elim Qu-Ibis sings light   flux a cycle.''

The other designer nodded ponderously. "I guess that is about right. Half a cycle, give or take a few days. We will have to cannibalize *Lightwing VII* to refit *V* and *VI*—we only have a few flux adapters in stock. Also, I'll want to run a few tests. I caught some other readings that may have predicted more trouble if we had gone farther to light."

Dugan tapped his fingers on the console, and a modified schedule appeared on the room screen. "Then this is the current schedule we will work within. Design by Cycle 15.2; next launch scheduled for Cycle 15.4 after test. Any questions? Yes?"

A four-legged alien chittered to his mate, then addressed the room through his translator. "If this launch is also unsuccessful, which according to my calculations is a seventy-six percent probability, what is the date by which we must achieve FTL to keep our funding?"

Dugan tapped his fingers irritably on the podium. "Racing light is a sure way to make mistakes."

"But also a way to keep our goal in sight," Coos murmured, projecting his face halfway toward the front of the room as Dugan hesitated.

Dugan let his eyes meet those of each life-form in the room. "The drop-dead date," he said deliberately, "is the first day of Cycle 16.1."

"But," Tior protested audibly, "that's only three days after our next shot at light."

Dugan swung his glance toward the Mu. "That is correct. We have a total of twenty-seven days to make light." He paused. "And if we do not reach our goal, the outpost will be returned to the Federation and assigned for other research."

Twenty-seven days, Kiondili thought as she threaded her way out of the meeting room. Twenty-seven days was barely time to redesign the Lightwings, let alone leave leeway for a second or third launch if Team B's launch failed. And if the third Lightwing was torn apart to make the other ships work, there would be only two chances to reach light. Two chances that the backup team would not be part of if Team A recovered in time to launch again.

And Kiondili had not missed the fact that the designers had glossed over some of their answers. The compute power alone that was required for such a redesign would cripple half the computers in the outpost. All other research would be brought to its knees while the Lightwings were revamped. Brooding, she made her way to the Hub, then changed her mind at the door and went instead to Lan-Lu's lab. She entered hesitantly when the access lock opened.

The Ixia, having just returned to her lab, looked over her shoulder from the flashscreen she had turned on, her knuckle claws half-extended. "What is it, Mu?"

Kiondili hesitated. "I just wanted to talk, Lan-Lu."

The predator turned back to her flashscreens. "We can talk during our work session."

Kiondili steeled herself. "I saw the boost go down. I'm sorry."

Lan-Lu swung around slowly. "Why? Failure is not a unique experience. This emotion you call apology seems to have no other function than that of sharing blame. If you must feel blame, keep it to yourself."

"Ayara's eyes, Lan-Lu," Kiondili burst out, "don't you care about it at all?"

The Ixia let her slitted yellow eyes bore into Kiondili's. "I have no feeling for H'Mu on board the Lightwing except that of hunger. I have no feeling for *Lightwing IV* because the launch was premature." Lan-Lu took a step toward Kiondili, who took an involuntary step back. "*My* work is on schedule in spite of these ridiculously hurried launches." The Ixia let her wrist claws flex. "I am not in the mood for talking, Mu."

Kiondili cleared her throat. "I saw the trouble the other field sensor had holding on to the ship. I know the beamer came on early, but her control slipped long before the beamer kicked in.''

"So, you have eyes and know how to use them. Why did you not bring that up at the meeting?"

"Ce'eldi deserves no blame. She was not up to the boost, and neither was the Lightwing. Besides, we found out enough about the design to know we have to redo part of it, anyway."

Lan-Lu merely looked at her, and she shivered.

"I saw enough to know that—" Kiondili steeled herself to continue under Lan-Lu's bored gaze. The Ixia was not making this easy on her.

"Why should I make it easy for you?" The alien had picked up her thought easily. "I called up your records. You turned down the training that was offered to you freely at the academy. You could have had more training than most sensors ever dream of, but you preferred to wallow in sentimental pity. You have wasted my time by forcing me to teach you elementary skills that any true sensor would have had by the time they were sixteen years old. The only advantage to your ignorance is that it allows me to mold your skills to the application in front of us."

"I need more help than that, Lan-Lu," Kiondili said in a low voice. "Ce'eldi had the sensor training I did not take, and she still could not control the fields when it came to the stresses of boost."

"So you see your inadequacies. What do you expect me to do about them?"

Kiondili took a step forward but stopped as the Ixia's elbow claws began to unsheathe. "I need more training than this. I need you to teach me more so that I can handle the stresses."

"You are a H'Mu and esper enough to provoke me without thinking. If I taught you what you ask, I would kill you."

"But Lan-Lu, you know the techniques."

"I am hungry, Mu," the Ixia said in that soft, subtle voice. "The techniques you speak of must be taught through a merging. If an Ixia merged with a H'Mu . . ." The words trailed off, but Kiondili's imagination filled in the picture. To merge with Lan-Lu . . . The instinctive half of the Ixia would not know that Kiondili was not prey; the other half would not care. In the midst of the merging, Lan-Lu would kill Kiondili and feed on her body.

"Then who can I learn from?" she demanded.

"Waon. The Ruvian is the only esper strong enough who also knows field manipulation beyond your level."

A tremor ran through Kiondili's frame. "No," she said flatly. "No, I won't do it with him."

"That is your choice. The work period is scheduled for tomorrow, Mu. I have much to do before then."

Kiondili clenched her fists, then spun on her heel and left, not bothering to hide her anger at Lan-Lu's suggestion. Waon—how could the Ixia even say such a thing? The Ruvian had Tested her, ripped out the cells of her mind and burned away every defense she had. He had forced her to look at herself, to hate herself. Lan-Lu could not expect her to go crawling to that Ruvian and beg him to merge with her to teach her. Kiondili spit at the walls and threw herself into the free-boost chute with a vengeance. To work with Waon now . . . No. She still had some pride left. She would rather spend a week learning on her own than ask for an hour of his time.

In the next few days the schedule tightened around the researchers like a noose. Kiondili, after snarling at Rae one day, requisitioned supply for a personal E-damp. She could no longer stand the dullness that accompanied the other, and if she could get one tuned to her own persona adjust, it would be less obtrusive. As if any E-damp could go unnoticed, she thought resentfully. But she was not the only one irritated. One of the Greggors' subsonics provoked another alien so much that the alien tore a flashtable apart. Not even the astrogators—both of a race that thought it distasteful to show emotions outside family ties—were immune. Dugan, pulled aside by Siln, the xenopsychologist, had to agree that the tension was beginning to affect everyone's work.

"Yes," he repeated at the next meeting, "all schedules will be slipped out one day cycle. Anyone who wants to solar surf can sign up through Central Control. They will arrange for shuttles to take you out to the surf arena." He smiled humorlessly. "We need a break before Siln has us all in for therapy."

Kiondili ignored the excited murmur. She had too much to do to go surfing. But as she left the meeting, she changed her mind and took a boost chute down to supply instead. It had been a full year since she had put on a pair of solar wings. Now that her biofields were stronger, she would have to have her solar suit refitted.

"Aren't you ready yet?" she viscommed Tior irritably when she returned with her new gear. "The flux will drop if you don't hurry, and I want to feel it in my hair while it's still strong."

Tior belched, remembering that to Kiondili's ultrasensitive structure, a solar wind would stimulate the Mu's follicles everywhere, just as a real planetary wind would ruffle a normal citizen's hair. "I'm getting there," she returned. "I've got to get this sensitizer adjusted before I go. I think a Greggor used it last."

"Greggors are the last to use everything," Kiondili retorted nastily.

"Stilman going?"

"Says he's too old." Kiondili ticked off the various excuses from FTL team members on her fingers. "Jordan says his arthritis gets worse if he surfs; Waon is too close to some sort of Change to get into a strong field without special shielding. Ruvians go through a metamorphosis every couple decades—it's violent," she added as she saw Tior's consternation. "I looked up a record of it in the library. Changes their entire field structure. They have to hide out in a completely shielded area to go through it without warping into something unpredictable. Anyway,'' she concluded impatiently, ''Waon isn't going, and neither is Rae, although Rae never cared about surfing, anyway. Lan-Lu is too unstable with all of us fleeting to and fro to be out unguarded among us. If you're going to take all day cycle, I'll meet you in the pod or else I'll see you after. I want to get going now, while the flux is up.''

''I'm going to be at least another half hour.''

But Kiondili had already cut out. She made it to the first pod before it filled up and squeezed in beside the shapeless blob of Coos's suit. Ignoring his chittering, she sat back and waited for the pod to launch, bracing herself for the inevitable corkscrewing motion so typical of the smaller ships going out of the crowded Corson docks.

The holotank in the front of the pod showed the current map of the solar wind, and Kiondili studied it carefully. ''Looks good across the sixty-fourth quadrant,'' she murmured to Coos.

Coos chittered a protest. ''That's where the most powerful surging is going on.'' He clacked his teeth together. ''I'll probably take the forty-first quadrant myself.''

''The forty-first looks smooth,'' she agreed, ''but I like it as strong as it gets.''

''If I had your control, I'd feel the same way,'' Coos retorted. ''Just remember—it's an eighty-credit fine if you can't make it back to a pickup point on your own.''

But Kiondili's seat had already dropped into its ejection well. The locks clicked shut, air was sucked back into the pod, and the temporary blast stasis held her safely through the few seconds of crushing boost that thrust her out into the glorious wind.

She let the ejection path take her out to where the solar wind's flux was strongest, and her scalp was tingling so much that she felt like laughing with the sheer joy of it. She stretched out her arms, letting her surf wings expand and energize with the particles spewed off by the sun. It took only a moment to adjust the wings to nearly maximum power.

Then she tucked and twisted until she was riding headfirst into the stream.

Darting and swooping, the silver flashes of surfers dodged in and out of the meteoric debris that cluttered space. Kiondili felt the particle wind die back—the tingling of the nape of her neck decreased—and adjusted the gravity attraction field to high. The trick was to balance the gravity wells of the individual asteroids while getting the most out of the wind. Picking up speed, she shot between a slower surfer and two tumbling asteroids, defying them to close with her.

Her entire body was a sensor, and she reveled in the feel of the wind. She sank into the pleasure of raw solar power, surging with it, then cutting away from the stream as another solar flare died back. She laughed. She danced. She screamed her latent fury to the stars as the fields surged around her. She hung on the critical edge of a gravity well where her surf wings strained against the pull and the power gauge clung stubbornly to redline until she arched away.

Finally she slowed. Gently at first, then more quickly, she dropped her speed and came to rest on an asteroid. Her wings collapsed automatically, and, shaking from exhaustion, she folded them back into her suit seams before tuning to the pod's pickup frequency. It was with surprise that she read the detect. The pod was on the other side of the solar system collecting the last surfers from the beginners' runs. She had been out almost six hours.

She leaned back on the rock. She could feel its sharp edges grit against her suit and could almost sense the frigid cold of space through its solidity. Beyond the asteroids, the flares of ships going in and out of the outpost caught her eye, and she idly watched them as she waited for the pod. It would take at least twenty minutes to reach her. The solar wind still tempted her, but she was too tired to give in and go out again. She felt good, she acknowledged. Probably for the first time since the Test.

She stared out across space at the too-bright image of the sun. Lan-Lu was right. Here, away from the outpost, away from Effi and the pressure of the launch teams, she could admit that the Ixia had seen through her as clearly as Waon had with his Test. If Kiondili wanted to know how to beat Effi at the human's own game, she needed more training. Training she had turned down at the academy because it would have been bought with her parents' blood, bought with the debt settlement of the Trade Guild. Training that Lan-Lu could not give her because the Ixia was a hunter. Training that only Waon, who had ripped her mind apart on Argon's say-so, could provide. She ground her teeth. She could not help it. By the time the pod picked her up, the tension had already crept back into her shoulders.

By the next morning the stats for each team were posted, and Kiondili saw that the teams were on schedule. But Kiondili, even after a day of solar surfing, found herself curiously depressed. Between Stilman's work, the backup training, and Lan-Lu's lectures, she was exhausted. She dragged herself to her quarters each evening. She dragged herself back to the labs every morning.

"Ayara's eyes," Tior exclaimed one day. "I'm going to need a cycle off just to sleep after this."

Kiondili rubbed her neck with one hand. "I wish we had more shielding to work behind. These fields are driving me up the wall."

Tior nodded. "My persona adapt has been picking up static all day. If this keeps up, I'm going down to storage and have them swap out my damp for a stronger one."

"I never thought I'd say this, especially now that I hate them after working with Lan-Lu," Kiondili muttered, "but I'm inclined to agree with you. I'm so sensitive to fields now that even the one I'm wearing is hardly strong enough anymore."

"A damp would be nice," Tior said, "but a Division beer would be heaven. My treat at the Hub?"

Kiondili hesitated, then nodded and threw her flashbooks down the nearest mailtube. "I'll race you."

Tior laughed. "You've got to be kidding. Challenge the Jovani institute's chute race champion?"

Kiondili did not bother to answer, but she howled when Tior passed her in the boost tubes. The other Mu had emptied her water bags and used her persona adjust to flex the chute fields, just as Kiondili did instinctively. Tior beat Kiwi to the Hub with seconds to spare. Kiondili did not mind; Tior paid for her win by buying the brew.

The next day Kiondili awoke feeling irritable. She snapped at Stilman, then at Tior on the viscom. By the end of the day she had gotten nothing done, and there were only two weeks left before the next launch. On top of that, she was due in Lan-Lu's lab in another hour. Glowering, she made her way to the Hub cafeteria. With the field fluctuations in the outpost systems prodding and teasing her temper, the continuous subliminal harassment made her snap at everyone. She joined Poole and the other assistants at a table, but she had to bite back a snarl as the Dhirrnu bumped against her and subtly adjusted her persona adapt so that the voices she heard were in nothing but low frequencies. Just wait, she thought at him, turning the frequency adjustment back up. He had yet to regain full *ti'kai* on her for the stunt at the docks. And she had more in mind for him yet.

"So it was decided, Jordan?" Argon asked, ignoring Kiondili as she sat beside Poole. "Team B takes the next launch?"

"Looks that way." Jordan nodded. "Team A won't recover for some time. Ce'eldi's confidence is shot, and the psych hasn't got her out of her depression yet."

Tior glanced at him. "That means, if this launch is successful, we might get to be the first passengers on a hyperlight ship of our own making."

Jordan nodded. "What do you think your chances are of being in on the Lightwings, Kiwi?"

The field in their dispenser surged as it generated Argon's drink, which was as drably colored as his clothes, and Kiondili bit back another snarl. "About nil," she said shortly. "Do you really think Dugan's going to allow a bunch of half-educated assistants to play with an experimental ship like that, especially when he's got Effi's prime teams on ready status?''

"With or without *your* half-educated self, we've got as much chance as anyone,'' Argon retorted.

"In your dreams,'' Kiondili turned away and punched the dispenser for another drink.

"Well, don't bother waking up from your dream,'' Tior said sharply. "You'd probably kill yourself with the shock of realizing there's a real world out here.''

Jordan agreed, nodding at Kiondili's look. "If you put as much effort into the Lightwing as you do into being permanently ticked off, we'd have made light already.''

But Kiondili did not respond. She sat almost frozen, alternately stiffening and shivering.

"Stop fidgeting and flexing those fields,'' Argon snapped. "Jordan is only telling you the truth. If Poole had pointed it out, we might have at least had a laugh at your expense, as well, but it's still true.''

But Kiondili's jaw was tight, and her hands clenched. "It's not about the truth,'' she returned through clenched teeth. "If they'd control these friggin' field surges . . .''

Poole rippled his fur down to his belly. "I wouldn't—'' He broke off and stared toward a table behind Kiondili.

But Kiondili was no longer paying attention. A surge in the free-boost fields below the Hub had just hit her.

"Trouble,'' Jordan said urgently, even as Kiondili felt a more powerful surge.

Poole caught the paralyzed look on her face and half rose, his fur rippling across his chest. "What is wrong?''

"Never mind Kiwi,'' Argon snapped. "Check out Waon.''

Tior twisted, her eyes widening at the Ruvian's shimmering form. Her chin bags tightened, and she lost water, but she ignored the fluids that dripped down her neck. "Get the medic in here fast,'' she said.

Poole wrinkled his lips back from his teeth. "Hit the E-damp!''

Argon hit the emergency damp with his fist, and others who recognized the trouble did the same at their tables. "Get under the local shield while you've got a chance. Let the chute guards take care of Waon—if they can."

"But look at him." Jordan half rose, and Argon grabbed his arm and pulled him down, closer to the center of the E-damp's field.

"He's melting," Tior whispered.

Kiondili was released from her thrall as the second surge lessened and the local damp at the table cut in. She started to turn but was interrupted by a high-pitched frequency that pierced her temples from under the sonar depressor. Clutching her ears, she writhed with the sudden surge of power. It was Waon, she realized suddenly, recognizing the power of that scream with an intensity that startled her. So close to his Change, he had been pushed too far by the increased field fluctuations.

There was not enough shielding in the Hub to keep the fluctuations from tearing at the Ruvian's body mass; the surging of the fields must have set him off. Had they not warned him? The Ruvian *was* melting. His field-generated mass was oozing and pulsing as he tried to re-form into—something. But there was no shielding to protect him from the outpost systems, no buffer to keep his shape separate from the fields snapping and shifting in the Hub. In the agony of the Change, he lashed out, blasting apart everything he touched. E-damps, persona adapts—everything fried in the power surge. Even under the depressors, Kiondili could sense thousands of inaudible screams. Aliens and H'Mu collapsed right and left. Those still standing were already in shock. The tiny E-damp in each citizen's persona adapt was useless in the strength of Waon's blast. Not even the table damps were strong enough to stand, and two of them went down, leaving the people huddled under them to faint or retreat into a coma. Kiondili punched frantically at the medcom button; she could almost see lances of power stab the people around him. Why had the esper net not kicked on? In the blast of Waon's Change, the net should have automatically killed all esper transmissions in the entire area.

Across the room, the Ruvian writhed. His fields projected through the floor to the free-boost chutes below. Then they flexed above him to disrupt the lighting and circuitry in the Hub. Behind her, a shock and a burst of blankness cut through her mind, and Kiondili knew suddenly that a Mu had just died. As the horror hit her, another burst of blankness snapped across her, and her fury surged. Did Waon not feel what he was doing to these people? Or did he just not care? Her rage exploded, and Waon's fields encompassed her, pulling on her nerves, and she realized with a shock that the esper net was not on because Waon's own out-of-sync fields had jammed it.

"Waon!" she screamed. *"Stop it!"*

She leapt in slow motion, buffeted by the fields he had generated. Cells along her skin and then deep into her body ruptured where the Ruvian's fields pulled her apart. Had she been wearing her temple jacks, they would have melted onto her head. No, she would have to use her sensor skills in a more physical way. She would have to generate her own paths, her own lens for the focus of the fields.

She forced her way forward, beating her own space into his field. There was no light in this flux. There was no sound except for a roaring that was not in her ears but her mind. And then a rage surged into her own and fed her, and she dimly recognized Argon behind her, his presence joining hers and their conflict strengthening her focus. She forced herself forward another meter, her feet slipping on a body she could not see. "Waon, control yourself—"

The Mu writhed, oozing up against a table and shattering it with his touch. "Ahh . . ." She did not hear her own gasp as the shards of plastics flew like shrapnel, cutting her unprotected face. "Waon, damn you, control your fields!"

His darkness ate her. She drank in her own hate to advance, the emotions bolstering her momentum. She screamed as he slid along the floor, burning out the circuitry in the

Hub and shocking her field-sensitive nerves as he went. Under him, through the door, she could sense the free-boost chute out of control, hurling bodies through like comets. His face turned to her. It was only a maw—

She retched, fighting forward another foot. An acrid smell cut through the din and cleared her head for an instant. "Control the fields," she heard herself say. Was it her? Or another voice—that of Tior, who stepped in behind Argon and steadied them both. And then Poole's strange mixture of thoughts and memories meshed with Tior's and seemed to cement them all together. Behind them, using them as anchors, she built that corner of safety like a silent wedge. But in front of her Waon lifted up like a snake, boneless and wispy in the core of his fields. He reached for her team . . .

"Damn you . . ." Reaching, cursing, sobbing, she grabbed at one of the wild fluctuations and soothed it. She grabbed another field and pulled it in close, forcing the Ruvian to relinquish control. Behind her—

Behind her a sudden hunger fed strength to the four, and Kiondili surged forward. Lan-Lu . . . Her wrath rose again, stronger and brighter than the flames that licked at the Hub. "I'll beat you, you tath-eating alien!" Kiondili screamed silently. "I'll jam you back into yourself so tight, you won't get out for a century light . . ."

She warped her control to darken the wedge of blankness that grew behind her like a support as well as a drain. Lan-Lu was like a cat, slinking through Waon's fields to get ever closer, guiding Tior, Argon, and Poole. And in front of that hunt Kiondili built a wall of her own through which Waon could not strike. A distort—she forced the thought out. Protect . . . She did not look—she could not—but in that wedge she had formed, some of the creatures were stirring: Jordan and a dozen other H'Mu . . . One of the aliens was dragging some of the bodies away. But before her . . .

She cried out as Waon's wild energy sucked at her like quicksand. It was all she could do to strike out at him, throwing herself at his fields till his surge fell back and then back again. "You life leech," she snarled. She caught his outbreak sharply and turned him back into himself, pounding at the flux and forcing him to retract his fields as his energy gates closed. Her hate was still too new. He solidified for an instant but burst out into a metamorphic mass again until she squashed his power, dimly sensing that the E-damps had come on in the far corners of the Hub. Lightning crackled around her in a continuously lessening sphere as she cursed and shrieked in her own insanity. A lust for the hunt fed her, led her on. Lan-Lu . . . She was almost within the Ruvian's fields. His field extended—

She screamed. Within her anger was still a fear, and this close to Waon it crippled her suddenly. Lan-Lu was flung away; Argon and Tior cut off abruptly. Poole's presence disappeared. Kiondili screamed again. But it was too late for her and for Waon. Their fields merged, the younger esper fighting for control, and the two raging minds struck with a clash of energy that tore at them both. Waon shrieked in pleasure. He—it—reached for her. She slapped him down with a bolt that should have killed, but their energies coalesced into a ball of force that fused each cell, each thought. Change . . . She was blinded. She split out from him, hurling another blast. She wanted to hurt him, to destroy him as he had tortured her. She flexed his fields, smashing him back, cutting him off from the boost chutes below, from the circuitry above. There was death behind her, and Waon was the cause. He struggled against her, but she could crush him now.

There was a maniacal strength behind her blows. She battered him, beat him back until they were almost touching. Then she was on her knees, staring blindly at the pulsing darkness that was Waon. Hurt him— The thought was behind her. It was in agony that Waon now cringed and flexed. But the merging was on her. From behind, the aggression that was Argon and the steadiness of Tior flowed back into her. And in the midst of her strength she suddenly saw the truth that Waon had forced her to see before. Through his eyes, she remembered. He surged, and she forced him down. But the visions of herself remained. Hurt him? Hit him back? What she was in his eyes was only what she saw in her own. Herself. Her truth. Her heart. She hesitated, and Waon broke away, but she slammed him back, and then, with Argon's anger fueling her to revenge, she turned away and then simply held him.

CHAPTER 13

Kiondili was on her knees, blood trickling from her face, her joints, her pores. She could feel the burning in her body and sense the pain dimly through the haze that clouded her mind. Grimly, she hung on. To what, she did not know.

An eternity passed before the E-net came on around them. It hovered outside the sphere of her control, cocooning her and Waon and separating them from the rest of the outpost. And then someone was touching her arm, urging her to let go, to release control. No. She shook her head. They did not understand. He would kill them all . . .

The touch was insistent. Demanding. Let go. Let them take over. She tried to shake her head, but her neck cramped up and her body refused to respond. Waon hummed before her. He pulsed once and solidified, briefly, then more permanently as she sensed—felt—his Change. She could not yet see. Were her eyes closed? No, it was only blood that glued them shut. She raised her hands, forcing her eyes open even though it felt as if she were ripping out her eyelashes. The Hub was almost cleared. No bodies lay scattered under the wreckage. The shards of plastics and metal had been cleaned away. How much time had passed? Around the two of them, Waon and herself, a team of chute guards stood like black statues in their neutral suits. They were safe from Waon; the suits cut the wearers off from all esper bands and almost all electromagnetic and particle fields, as well. Only the medic and her assistants did not wear the suits. The medic was beside her, not touching either of them. An alien was beside the medic, and there were three other med-assistants she did not know.

"Let go now, Kiondili," the medic urged, her pale alien skin tinged white as her hairs stood on end. "You can relax. We've got a neutral zone on around us. He'll be controlled. Let us in."

Let them in? She shook her head. She wondered at what the medic had said until her eyes began to focus and she realized that they could not yet touch her. The field she held herself in was keeping them away. With their neutral suits on, the chute guards could not come near her without disrupting her fields, and she could not release the fields without releasing Waon. Chute guards—if they shocked her, she could lose control and kill herself with her own field fluctuations. It was another eternity to realize this. Then, slowly dimming her fields, she pulled her energies back into herself. As she withdrew, she sensed the neutral zone closing down over her and Waon. Then there was the cold touch of blindness when it passed through her and enclosed Waon in its sphere of safety: a hatchling in an egg of energy.

"Come down, Kiondili," the medic urged gently. "Let me get this into you. You're still generating enough energy to polarize the metals in these fluids, and I can't treat you like this."

Kiondili gave in the best way she knew how. She fainted.

When she woke again, it was to see the familiar holo on

the ceiling of her own quarters. She rolled over gingerly, threw up in the tub someone had conveniently attached to her bunk, and passed out again.

The second time she came to, a robo med-assistant was beside her, watching her with its unblinking eyes. She hated it for staring at her while she still had the vile taste of nausea in her mouth. She did not need it. The only thing wrong with her was that she was still a little queasy from the force of energy she had controlled that afternoon.

"Lie still," the medast ordered in its carefully programmed human voice. "The readings will take another thirty seconds."

Kiondili ignored it and sat up. "I'm fine. You can report to the medic that everything is on the green."

The robo extended its arm and projected a needle from within its hollow palm. "You are to remain at rest for two more days until regeneration is complete. This will relax you so that you can rest. Please lie back so that you do not hurt yourself when you relax."

"Relax, my foot," Kiondili snorted. "Get that thing away from me." She did not even try to reach out, but the robo froze, its appendage paralyzed as Kiondili unconsciously killed its fields. She waited for it to withdraw its arm. And waited. She frowned. "This is not the time to play tricks on me, Poole," she muttered, but the robo gave no answering hum. Finally, becoming frightened, Kiondili tapped the robo and felt for its energy pack.

"I couldn't have—I don't have the power to turn a robo off," she whispered. She stared at it, but the fields were dead as if the robo had never been turned on.

She shuddered and fumbled for the robo's on switch as a thought hit her. "Waon," she said, her voice rising in panic as she sent the energies surging through the medast's circuits before her fingers actually touched it. She had turned it on without touching it.

"Waon?" Her voice was almost a scream. "What have

you done to me?'' The robo medast's needle descended as she cried out. She did not try to stop it from going in. The last thing she remembered was the cold metal of the medast reflecting the holo into her numb eyes.

CHAPTER 14

Kiondili stared at the medic. "What do you mean, I was 'changed'?"

"Calm yourself, Mu. You are still basically the same." The medic's translated voice was soft but not soothing.

"How can you say that?" Kiondili demanded angrily. "Every system I touch fries. Every field I interact with flexes with my biofields. Ayara's eyes, but I might as well turn my own persona adapt back in to supply for all the good it does me."

The medic touched Kiondili on the arm, and she stiffened. "Some of your natural sensitivities are greater than they were," the medic said. "But yes, you have been changed."

"How changed? How sensitive?"

"I do not have much information to give you yet, Kiondili Wae." The medic shrugged with the thick side of her body, leaving the translucent side unmoved. She tapped the flashbook on the desk before her and explained, "This has yet to be completely analyzed. It will take some time before I can give you an accurate answer about the differences you feel."

"Then when will I change back?" Kiondili ignored the medic's discomfort. "Am I going to be getting hit with every field fluctuation a picosecond long? Oh, and can I still breed with my own kind, or will I be doing a little fusion every other month with Waon?"

"It is natural to feel some anger, Kiondili Wae. But you are not as changed as you think. Although it is rare for a race rating to shift, yours has not changed as much as your natural power has grown." She nodded at Kiondili's look. "Your power has increased with the realization of Waon's skills."

But it was other words that had caught Kiondili's attention. She clenched her hands. "So my race rating *has* changed?"

The medic gave a delicate shrug and gestured with her three-fingered hand. "From the base human stock, you were xeno-2. Now? You could be on the borderline between xeno-2 and xeno-3, or you could have shifted completely into the xeno-3 category. I will know for certain once I examine the data. That change is trivial. There are other changes you will feel more than that of a race rating."

Kiondili felt her slow anger grow. "Other changes? Like what? Am I going to start eating proton shakes instead of protein shakes?"

"You must look at this objectively, Kiondili Wae."

"Correct me if I'm wrong, but you're saying that I'm not even done changing yet." Kiondili's voice had become dangerously soft. "You trust me too much to be telling me this when you're not wearing a neutral suit like the chute guards. Look at me—" Her voice broke. "I don't even have to touch something to blow it out." She thrust her hand at the medic's scanner, and its screen flared briefly and died.

"You do not have to fear this change," the medic said softly. "With your natural aptitude for field manipulation, this should—"

"It should be cut out of me." She looked at the medic with horror deep in her eyes. "I can't even touch a field now without disrupting it so badly that it can't be repaired. Look—" She thrust out her forearm. "I couldn't even walk through the force fields around the shower this morning; I singed myself just getting out to dry myself off.''

The medic shrugged. "This is now a part of you.''

"That's great. In the meantime,'' she raged, "every time I turn around, I'm interfering with some system field and screwing up a boost chute or persona adapt. This morning I blew up my node by turning it on. What am I supposed to do now? Become a hermit? Hang out in a forgotten float library till I finish becoming whatever Waon had in mind?''

The medic met her gaze squarely. "Who you blame for this is not my concern. It is true that until you learn to control yourself, you will be dangerous to yourself and those around you. However, my concern is not for your level of control. My concern *is* for the way you treat your body, psyche, and mind. If you cannot accept yourself the way you are, I will be forced to recommend chemical treatment to pacify you until you can make a sane decision about yourself.''

"Chemical treatment? Why not add a personality rebuild on top of that? You might as well tuck some hormone treatments in to help along whatever freak changes I'll be going through. You disappoint me.''

The medic blanched.

Kiondili gripped her fists until her knuckles whitened. "I'm sorry,'' she said tightly. She rose stiffly. "I will come back later.''

"Your feelings are understandable, Kiondili Wae,'' the medic repeated softly, stopping her at the door. "But if you looked at yourself in a different light, you would see that there is also a positive side to this change.''

Kiondili did not answer. Barely waiting till the door shimmered clearly open before her, she walked stiffly out into the corridor and away from the medic's words.

Damn Waon. They would not have fused if he had not Tested her a month before. Everything came back to that. If he had not Tested her, she would not have known his field patterns. If she had not known his patterns, she could not have manipulated them. And if she had not manipulated the fields, he would not have tried to fuse with her during his Change. And now she was not even a normal Mu anymore. An unengineered change? What the hell chance did she have of being on a launch team now? She was somewhere on the borderline between xeno-2 and xeno-3. Where was that? *What* was that?

She did not dare use the free-boost chutes to get back to her quarters. Instead she walked around the outpost, and even that was not enough to keep her out of trouble. Passing a rec room, she reacted uncontrollably to the surges of power that emanated from it. She could not help squashing the field that threatened to rupture the bones in her ears. It was not until she heard shouts of dismay that she realized that she had destroyed the grav field around a free-jump game.

Damn Waon to a black hole, she spit. She could not turn around without disrupting one field or another. And Lan-Lu had not helped her feelings any. "If you had not lost your concentration at the critical moment," the Ixia had snarled at her, "you would have saved yourself the trouble of Changing with Waon." Trust Lan-Lu to make Kiondili feel better. She stalked to her quarters, slamming through the shimmering door and wiping out her messages angrily without reading them. She kicked at the small bookcase she had bought two weeks earlier—a futile attempt to make her quarters warmer—and, gathering her flashbooks, trudged to a float library.

This change—this was not the same as the Test she had survived. Waon's Test had proved her innocent of Effi's charges; the power of the Ruvian that had shafted through her mind had cleared her thoughts and forced her to see the truth of herself. This—this was not a clearing of images but a change of them. It was a shift akin to Waon's own metamorphosis.

Kiondili shivered. Waon. It had taken the Ruvian a full day to become solid again. Even his colors were different: His gray skin tones were now streaked bronze, with lighter gold around his energy gates where the nerves centered close to his skin. Although he looked as humanoid as before, the medic told her that his internal organs were changed. Even his—its—sexuality was male/T'se/female instead of male/male/male. Ruvians had three sexual centers, the medic told her. When they went through a Change, it affected the orientation of their sexual centers, as well.

Lan-Lu's thoughts nagged at her: *You could have saved yourself the trouble of Changing with Waon . . .*

Kiondili flung herself into the float library and bounced around for seconds before she figured out how to stabilize the fields for her mass. It was a small triumph. The flashbooks hung in a neatly rotating stack, clinging to each other by their weak magnetics. She stared at them, unseeing. What if Lan-Lu was right? The Ixia had noticed the strength Kiondili had gained by working with the backup team after the Truth Test. If Lan-Lu was correct, then if Kiondili had not panicked, Waon would not have been able to fuse with her whether he wanted to or not.

Ten minutes later she had not read a single line in the flashbook she had powered up. She flung the book away in frustration. There had been a deeper message in Lan-Lu's words, one that did not deal with Waon but with Kiondili: What if Kiondili panicked during a launch?

She rolled over and stared at the ceiling projection as it rotated by. She would not panic. She could not. The psych, Siln, would know even before Kiondili if she was going to put the team at risk.

Or kill them.

It was that thought which held her. She watched unseeing as the flashbooks sought each other again, their weak magnetic attraction for each other augmented by the float library's fields.

It was a sobered Mu who made her way back to her quarters again. She barely registered the messages gathered again on her com, once more wiping them clear without reading them. She turned up the new E-damp in her quarters and settled on the overstuffed chair with which she had replaced her Soft—and then the tubemail bin toned. Staring at the mail bin, she sat without moving. Finally she got up and removed the box from the slot in the wall.

It was from the medic. Kiondili snorted. The alien could have saved time and given it to Kiondili when she had seen her earlier. But, unwrapping the miniature field damp, Kiondili wondered. A damp that small would have taken time to build. Or had the medic adapted it from something Waon had used at the outpost? She sat down in front of her new node—the old terminal had been removed, and the burn mark on the wall where she had accidentally blasted it that morning had been cleared—and turned the damp over in her hands. As if something this small would help. Even the new, extra-heavy E-damp on her room, which made all her senses feel encased in cotton, gave her only a small measure of relief. Abruptly, before she could change her mind, she jammed the plug of the tiny damp into her persona adapt.

She frowned. The damp's projection was narrow. Curious, she turned off the heavy E-damp she had on in the room and reached toward her terminal. The system was as undisturbed by her presence as if she had not changed at all. Not quite believing, she moved around the walls, touching and running her hands over the areas behind which she knew the circuitry ran. Again, nothing.

She breathed a heavy sigh. Safe, was her first thought.

Fury, her second. It was not enough that she had lost her race rating, but she would have to wear a complete field damp on top of her persona adapt? Even if she could feel other fields through this damp, it still felt like a thin cocoon wrapped tightly around her, dulling her senses and muting her nerves. The rage built until she flung herself at the walls.

"Damn you," she screamed, pounding on the wall. She kicked the terminal stand and sobbed when the jar shivered up through her ankles. Finally she sagged to the floor, the rage leaving her as suddenly as it had come. Empty, exhausted, she huddled against her bed, ignoring the warning on the door that someone wanted her again.

She was tightly under control when she punched the com with Tior's ID. "Tior?" she said shortly as the other assistant came online. "It's Kiwi. I need some company."

She could almost see Tior frowning, but the other woman did not hesitate. "They're still repairing the Hub," Tior said slowly, "but we can try one of the new solo rooms they put up last cycle."

"I do not want to be at the Hub, anyway," Kiondili returned tersely.

"Then let's try Solo Six. They programmed it with a new holo show last quarter cycle, and we can still get the regular dreamer channels, too. I'll meet you there in a few—" Tior paused as she realized that Kiondili could not use the free-boost chutes. "How long will it take you?"

"As much time as it takes you. I've got a field damp on, so I'm certified for the chutes. See you in four." She turned off the com and clenched her arms around herself, her gray eyes closed tightly.

CHAPTER 15

In two days, Kiondili had become used to the muffled feeling of the tiny E-damp. She did not like it, but she wore it. She did not realize how bitter she sounded about the dulling of her senses until Tior, on the way to the Hub with her, snorted in exasperation.

"Stop complaining, Kiwi," Tior said sharply. "All you've done for the last four days is groan about how you can't sense the fields anymore. That's a laugh. You can sense just as much as you ever did. I *know* you. I'm staring at you, and I can tell you right now that your probe is even stronger than it was before. If it doesn't feel as sharp to you, it's probably because you are twice as sensitive as you were before, and the difference is noticeable. The only difference I care about, though," she said angrily, "is that you were a lot more fun to be around when you weren't so goddamn sanctimonious about your martyred mutancy."

Kiondili stopped in the hallway and stared at the other woman. How dare Tior . . . The nerve of that blue-skinned, water-bagged . . .

Tior glared back at her with equal vehemence. "I heard that."

Kiondili flushed.

Tior gave her a sideways look and blew bubbles across her water bags. "And if I can read you this strongly, just think what you've been sending to Argon."

"He isn't esper."

"No one needs to be esper to pick up what you've been broadcasting."

Kiondili was silent.

"Even Poole can read you now, and he's a Dhirrnu." Tior's voice took on a dry tone, and Kiondili glanced at her.

"What did Poole do to you now?"

"You know how I sleep like the dead?" Tior glanced at the door to the Hub. "Yesterday he took a dreamscan from me and broadcast it this morning on one of the regular dreamer channels."

"That doesn't sound bad. There isn't much *ti'kai* in that."

"It was a mating dream with a Biluane in it."

"A Biluane? You mean the ones with the kinky fingers?" Kiondili surprised herself by laughing.

Tior was not smiling. "Just once I'd like to get him back publicly."

Kiondili fingered her E-damp as they stepped through the doorway and made their way to Stilman's table. "Maybe you can."

At the table, Coos extended an arm to wave a greeting at the two. ". . . and the engine master is holding the stakes," he continued without a pause, "so we can wager in fair security."

"Who are you betting on, Dr. Stilman?" Tior asked as she sat down.

Stilman raised an eyebrow. "In analyzing the situation and, limited at this point to the two choices of Prime B and backup, I have put my credits on backup."

"Just as I said." Rae was pleased. The short esper

nodded at Kiondili. "Sensor and navigation skills are better on backup than on Prime B."

"It was not the skills of the individuals that guided my decision," Stilman contradicted her. "Rather, it was the skill of the team as a whole."

Coos frowned. "You old mold brain, why don't you just say that Prime B isn't as good a team as backup?"

Stilman looked surprised. "That is exactly what I did say."

"And on what do you base your wildly unsubstantiated statements?" Effi Ragan challenged, catching the end of the conversation as she sat down by Coos, opposite Kiondili.

But it was Siln, the xenopsychologist, who answered first. Clicking her long, silicon fingers together, Siln said, "Prime B has not progressed as far as backup." Kiondili glanced at Siln from across the table. Her days with the psych had not been pleasant, and the alien's voice wakened memories she would rather forget. Siln did not acknowledge Kiondili as she added, "Circumstances have pulled the backup team together so that they function as a unit and not as individual entities."

Rae Arr, next to Siln, glanced at the xenopsych.

Siln nodded. "The greatest impact came from Waon's Change, in which backup provided the support for Kiondili's control, a situation identical to the projected Lightwing launch." She indicated Kiondili and Tior. "Controlling the Ruvian's Change would not have been possible without such a team already formed, but—" She shrugged. "—that is of little interest to you." She met Effi's eyes with her own unblinking blue ones. "On the other hand, Prime B is in effect a fragmented team with uncertain leadership, occasional cooperation, and little trust." Kiondili shivered. She had too recently sat through just such a brutally honest evaluation of her own self. Siln, continuing, added, "There is friction between team members, Effi. The instruction they receive from you is laced with pressures under which two of the team members have withdrawn."

Effi stared at her. "The team is complete and working

well; none of them have withdrawn. The next blast is scheduled only a day cycle away, and their success is almost guaranteed.''

"Guaranteed by what, Effi?" Coos chittered irritably. "Your will to succeed? I don't think that will push them to light and back. I find myself agreeing with Stilman. My credits are riding with backup.''

Stilman nodded at Coos, and when the Robul's eyes met Kiondili's briefly, he winked in a surprisingly human expression. Caught off guard, Kiondili averted her eyes but found herself looking straight into the filmy blue gaze of the xenopsychologist.

"Which reminds me," Stilman said quietly to his assistant, "Kiet, down in engines, wanted to borrow you to help adjust one of the drives.''

Stilman lending her out so close to a launch? What—or who—had convinced him to do that? "I might be back on the launch teams, but I'm not back on the sensor rolls for any other work," she said flatly.

"You were okayed through Central Control two hours ago," he returned, searching his pockets to pull a credit chit out from under his tunic. "You can drop this off while you're at it.''

She took the chit slowly. Stilman's silent projection of the xenopsychologist was so audible that she could not ignore it. It had not been Kiet, she suddenly knew, but Siln who had suggested Kiondili's help down in engines. Kiondili avoided the psych's eyes but felt Siln reading her even as she stood up. Tior, glancing silently from Kiondili to the psych, blew soft bubbles in her water bags.

Kiondili tucked the credit chit into one of her jumper's pockets, turned to leave, then changed her mind and sat down again suddenly. She flashed a thought at Tior, and the other woman followed her sudden gaze across the room.

"Kiet wanted you down in engineering soon, Wae," Stilman reminded her.

"In a minute, if you don't mind," she said softly. Poole

had just joined two of the other assistants at a table in the Hub, and an idea had just come into her head as she watched him punch his lunch order into the dispenser.

Stilman followed her gaze, rubbing one finger along his hawklike nose. "Having some fun, are you?"

"Just working in a little *ti'kai* for a friend," she said in a low voice. Tior, her eyes suddenly gleaming, hid her grin. Kiondili glanced across the room. Poole was having the green mash again, and she knew there was plenty of iron in that. It would be easy to polarize and explode.

Both Coos and Rae Arr had followed her attention across the room, and the others, curious as well, followed suit. Only Rae caught the subtle movement of Kiondili's hand as the younger Mu turned down her field damp. But everyone heard the startled yelp of the Dhirrnu. His meal had suddenly rearranged itself on his plate and then exploded. His table broke up; the others scrambled as Tior bowed to Poole. Kiondili grinned to herself, though the expression did not quite touch her eyes. She wanted to keep her amusement under blocks. It would not do for Poole to know who had set him up for this one, especially since it was supposed to be Tior's *ti'kai*.

Stilman choked as he held in his chuckle. But Effi Ragan pointed a long, bony finger at Kiondili. "You're a trouble-maker, Wae. If you ever try anything like that on backup—"

"Effi, stuff it up your nostril and pad some of those swollen brain cells from rupturing," Coos retorted before Kiondili had a chance to speak.

The old woman stared at him, sputtering.

"Coos is right, Effi," Stilman added. "The galaxy doesn't spin on your whims. So for once, leave Wae alone."

Siln's unblinking eyes followed Effi, then Kiondili, and Kiondili found herself unable to meet that gaze.

"Don't lose my credits, Wae," Stilman admonished her as she rose again to leave. "Kiet is holding the stakes for the blast, and I don't want to disappoint anyone."

She did not answer, but her shoulders twitched beneath Siln's gaze as she left the Hub. Until she trotted to the nearest free-boost chute and dove in, she felt as if the psych's eyes were still reading her mind. Unnerved, she hit an acceleration pad too fast and barely missed an alien that spit an oath at her for having to change its landing trajectory.

That look in Siln's eyes . . . Kiondili was suddenly curious about the extent of her control. If she turned down her field damp, could she handle more flux in the boost tubes? She could control fields over a distance. What if she applied herself to a limited portion of the chute fields? Granted, the boost-chute fields were more powerful, but it should only take a touch on a few fields here and . . . there.

She grinned fiercely, then *oomphed* as she hit a redirection pad harder than she had intended. Her speed was increasing. She used the damp as a brake, then sent another surge to the chute fields to pick up speed again. As long as she tampered only with the free boost immediately around her launching and redirection, none of the others in the chutes were affected. She found that out as she shot past two H'Mu clinging to the emergency handles. She had sensed them long before she saw them, but the two Mu had not seen her coming until she was almost on them. Gleefully she sped up again.

She bounced off a redirection pad so hard that she almost scraped the edge of the chute. Taking more care, she hit the next one right on center and the one after that even faster. She was getting the hang of it. Apply a little damp at the right time, and she could pick up a couple hundred clicks in speed. She was almost disappointed to slow down when she reached engines, but then, there was always the way back.

She vaulted out of the chute and took two steps before the scene in front of her stopped her in her tracks.

"Kiondili Wae, BZ60449." The cold voice startled her, and she jumped guiltily and smoothed her hair in self-consciousness. The three chute guards were as unemotional as Siln, and their neutral suits made them look like robots, not men. "Kiondili Wae, BZ60449," the center guard repeated.

"I acknowledge you." She forced the formal words out

with difficulty. It was not fear, she told herself, trying to control the sudden jump in her heart and the catch in her breathing. Chute guards—they were for emergencies. What had she done?

The center guard spoke again. "The chute speed limit for Mu of your type is two hundred fifty clicks. You were boosting at four hundred and seventeen clicks at top speed."

The chute guard looked as cold as he sounded, Kiondili thought, and then she stared at him. Four hundred clicks?

"You have demonstrated your ability to go beyond the speed limit; however, your reflexes are not fast enough to compensate for your velocity. Do you understand?"

She nodded, speechless. They were giving her a speeding ticket? A speeding ticket in a free-boost chute?

"Control will monitor your chute manipulation from now on," the guard continued coldly. "You will restrict your velocity to two hundred fifty clicks. If you go beyond that, your chute access will be terminated."

She stared at them. They were serious. She did not breathe till they left, stepping lightly into the chute she had just vacated and disappearing along the empty tubes. She let her breath out. She had not realized how closely the chutes were monitored.

Or was it Kiondili who was being watched?

She shrugged, but the suspicion remained to nag softly. Central Control could have used the chute com to call and stop her, but they had not. Why? Was she listed in Control as unpredictable? And the chute guards had had neutral suits on, too, she remembered. She stopped. It did not matter that the neutral suits had not been activated. No, it was a message that Control wanted her to read. And the message was clear: Kiondili Wae was now an unknown quantity, not to be trusted.

She slapped her damp back on full and stalked down the hall of the engines triad. By the time she reached engines, she was grinding her teeth at the snail's pace of walking, but she could not risk a free jump in the grav corridors. It just was not done. Free-boosting in a grav field, she told herself bitterly, remembering the chute guards.

The door to Kiet's lab shimmered open at her touch, and she stepped through into a cold atmosphere where her breath steamed in the air. Shivering, she turned up the heat on her persona adjust, but the cold had already reached her bones. She glanced at the three slender hulls cradled in the prototype engine area. Three Lightwings. Two chances to make light-speed. She studied the last ship in the cradles, noting the open engine area where part of the drives had been canni-balized to refit the other two.

"Is Kiet here?" she asked the assistant crouched under the blast tubes of the first Lightwing.

"In a moment," it answered without looking. "He is set-ting the polyxeforum concentration. Adjust yourself to com-fort over there." The bulbous creature squatted, unconcerned whether she complied.

Sit, Kiondili translated. Looking around, she found a Soft and collapsed into it, watching as the assistant floated several tools up along a bidirectional grav beam. "He requested some help adjusting one of the drive fields," she called over. "I'm Kiondili Wae—"

"I know who you are," the assistant cut in. "Your E-presence precedes you. You were requested because you have been working with simulation and control. Your expe-rience in knowing what is required for blast will be useful in adjusting the required sensitivities into the drive."

Kiondili raised her eyebrow at the assistant, but the Soft was on its lowest setting and felt like a pool of water, relaxing her with its flowing support. Now that the fright from the chute guards was over, she did not feel like conversation.

"Wae?" Kiet's heavy voice startled her.

She opened her eyes. She had fallen asleep in the Soft. "I beg your pardon," she said quickly, struggling out of the Soft. Where was that control to firm?

The burly man reached down and touched the control, giving her a sudden platform to climb off instead of the marshmallow that had soothed her to sleep. "No offense, Wae." He was glancing around the Soft as if puzzled. "Did your sensors get lost in the Soft? They should have been spit out by now."

"I don't use sensors anymore," she said shortly. "I use a damp." The sensors that augmented others' skills would have burned out within an hour if she had pushed her power through their small amplifiers.

"Hope that won't be a problem."

"It hasn't been so far," she said. "But it may take me a little longer to adjust the drive field."

But Kiet was shaking his head. "I don't want you touching the fields, Wae. I just want you to tell me where it's most comfortable for you to control. I set *Lightwing IV* for Prime A before that launch, and now I've got to set *Lightwing V* for Prime B. The pilot for Prime B is due here in two hours. What I need from you is to verify the setting before I get him up here. He's sensitive enough that I could fry him without knowing it. How's your reading level?"

"I've been tested to R-9."

"That's clear enough for me. You should have no trouble picking me up. Climb up there to control and let me know when you get set."

She obediently climbed up on the slanted craft. The control cabin was small, barely big enough for three Mu, a duplicate of the simulation cabin. Glancing around, Kiondili nodded to herself, then reached out for Kiet's thoughts.

. . . drop down two points, but that's going to set the flux too high . . .

I'm set, she projected.

His thoughts halted fractionally as he received her message, then continued. *. . . bring the bore up to eight and the flux down to five. That'll keep the collapser at a steady two . . .*

Too high, she interrupted. *At two, the fields are jumping too much to control.*

Hmm, I'll have to add a damp on FG3, then bring the collapser into the circuit when surging goes to zero.

Kiet's thoughts splintered as he shifted his body to reach the bore, and his alpha line was inundated with stray thoughts and impressions of physical and mental adjustments. By the time Kiondili had worked within his thoughts for an hour and a half, she was exhausted. She was more than relieved when the pilot for Prime B showed up early. Perceiving her weariness, Kiet said he had adjusted the system enough for the other esper to take over from there.

"Thanks for setting up for me," the other pilot said with genuine appreciation as she crawled out of the Lightwing. "With launch going on tomorrow, I could not afford to get distracted by the setup procedure in the middle of simulation."

"Glad to help."

The pilot gave her a sharp look. "It isn't easy working with Effi, Kiwi."

Kiondili flushed slowly. She had not realized that he was a high-level reader. He must have picked up her envy without her realizing it. "I'm sorry, Arond. I do want *Lightwing V* to be a success."

"I know that. If I was on backup, I'd feel the same way."

She glanced at him, biting back her thoughts. "There's still some surging over the bore," she said, "but it's damped pretty well. The collapser's set just about right, and the disintegrator still needs work."

"Thanks."

She gave him a hand up onto the wing of the craft. He was tired, she realized; his hands shook as he pulled himself up. She said nothing, but she wondered if she should mention it to the psych before Prime B went to blast status.

"He might be one of the ones Siln says is withdrawing emotionally from Prime B," she said later over dinner with the backup team. Jordan, the systems link for Team B, was eating with them, giving Kiondili a buffer between herself and Argon.

Tior gave Jordan a sharp look at Kiondili's words.

Jordan frowned. "If our sensor can't take the pressure of simulation, how is he going to do in the real thing? It is our lives, not just his, if he cannot handle it."

Kiondili looked up. "Siln would not okay him for launch if she did not think he could make it."

"How do you know, Wae?" Argon said snidely. "Did you read Siln's mind, too?"

"Burn dust, Argon." Kiondili swallowed her urge to shock him through his persona adapt. "Everyone knows you can't read Siln's mind unless she projects on a standard wavelength; her brain is too different to make sense. I did not ask her to give her thoughts, and she did not offer."

"I'm surprised she said even that much about it," Jordan said slowly, tucking one of his triple-jointed legs halfway under him. "Siln isn't known for talking. She either thought it was important enough to tell someone, or she was testing your reactions."

Tior swallowed some water into one of her bags. "I think she was influencing the bets for the blast."

"Hah," Argon said. "Siln doesn't bet."

"Want to put credit on that?"

"What do you want to lose?"

"One gourmet meal with suitable beverage of my choice."

"Or mine, if I win." Argon pointed at the flashscreen in the middle of the table. "You're on for the wager, but you have to prove it."

Tior blew bubbles so that water flecked her lips. "This will be easy. Kiet's holding the stakes, and he is a methodical person. He probably has the records on his system instead of in his head." She pulled her temple jacks from her pocket and pressed them against the sides of her head, sighting in some commands on the flashscreen. "I just call up Kiet's files . . ."

Jordan sat up. "Where did you get that kind of access, Tior?"

She shrugged guiltily, her water bags bouncing up tightly

against her chin. "I borrowed one of Poole's programs."
She punched in another sequence. "With a little adjustment," she said, "I found I could access a lot of things I couldn't get to before."

Kiondili frowned. "Be careful, Tior. I don't want Control tracing that back to us and especially back to me."

"This is foolproof. See? Here's his betting records already. I just copy from a backup instead of the monitored files, and we're out. Hardly enough time to slap a trace through the scramble I put on the line. And here is Siln's bet right here . . ." Her voice trailed off. "There must be some kind of mistake."

Argon studied the numbers, which were reflected right side up toward him, as they were toward the others. "I see no mistake. Where are the odds for backup?"

Tior shook her head, still staring at the numbers on the screen. "The odds are correct, that's not what I meant. Look here—" She sequenced the numbers. "Siln bet over five hundred credits on backup."

Kiondili saw her disbelief reflected on Jordan's face. "Five hundred credits is a lot to bet on a team that hasn't even gotten approval to simulate in a real Lightwing." Jordan shook his head.

"Especially when the odds against backup are three to one," Kiondili added.

Argon's look of surprise was giving way to smugness. "Well, Siln seems to think that we'll be the first to go light."

But Kiondili caught the worry in Jordan's tone. "Jordan?" she said, touching his arm.

"It's getting late," he muttered. "I'll see you tomorrow in the labs."

Argon snorted, looking after Jordan. "For a system's link, he hasn't got much nerve."

"Shut up, Argon." Tior did not even bother to project emotion as she cut him off. "He's been spending hours every week with the xenopsych, being trained for the stress of the launch—something we'll have to do when it's our turn. If, after all that, Siln does not think his team has a chance, how do you expect him to react? And how is the rest of his team going to react to the news?''

"Jordan wouldn't tell the others," Argon stated derisively.

"He does not have to." Kiondili watched Jordan move through the Hub doors. "Their pilot's E-level is higher than Rae. If he senses anything wrong, you can bet he'll figure out what it is."

"Zingor's balls." Tior scowled. "That's all we need. If Effi finds out that Jordan's upset because of a stupid bet, we're all in the blast tubes next launch."

"He'll probably sleep it off," Argon said. "The launch is scheduled first thing tomorrow. He won't have time to talk to anyone else."

Kiondili was not so sure. But Jordan would not have been chosen for a prime team if he could not handle it.

The next day there was already tension in the control room when Tior and Kiondili arrived. Kiondili avoided looking at Lan-Lu and Rae as she took her seat in the observation lounge. The knowledge that Siln, the psyche, had bet so much on the backup team frightened her, and she felt as if the information were written like a holo in her eyes.

"You have been avoiding me, Kiondili Wae."

She froze, then wrenched at her E-damp to suppress the surge of fear that threatened to break her persona adapt. It was Waon who had sat down beside her, and the H'Mu's voice was a soft curse in her ears. Look at him, she told herself. Face him.

The body he sustained with his fields still seemed as raw to her as before, and she clamped her mouth shut to keep from whimpering as he reached out his hand to touch her. His hand stopped a finger's width away from her arm. "You have no need to fear me, Mu," he said sharply.

She deliberately turned away from him and stared at the control room. With technicians scurrying to make last-minute connections, talking, yelling over each other, and gesturing across the room, Kiondili could ignore Waon easily. But the

Ruvian was persistent. And he did what Kiondili could never have expected. He projected a sharp thought and turned off her field damp.

"You—you—" she sputtered, floundering in the fields that flooded her senses. "You cut my damp!"

"You will not ignore me, Kiondili Wae. You will listen to what I have to say." His voice took on a deep tinge as his fields swirled and pulsed with his words. "Feel this," he commanded. "You have sensor skills. Feel me." He reached out to immerse her in his feelings.

"No," she spit angrily, but no sound came out. She could almost taste him, drowning in the fluctuations that drove him and clawed her like a digger at a hill. Without the damp, she could not help but sense everything. Waon. The control room. The Greggor by the view screen. Argon, disdainful. Poole, unreadable. Tior, mesmerized in launch preparations. Xia, curiously indifferent. Siln, an emotional blank that watched and waited for—what?

"Do you still turn away from me?" The Ruvian's voice was like a rough-edged saw. "I gave you a gift, Wae—the gift of a merging—and it was not one I meant to give. Use your skills to sense this. You are strong enough now to know what I mean." He checked her involuntary movement. "You began a process that you have not yet finished," he said softly. "You owe me its completion."

"Owe you?" Kiondili was outraged. "You twice-removed Mu—you Tested me! You stripped myself from me. You—you mutated me beyond my own race rating. You turned me into a freak."

"Is that what I have done?"

His voice was a cold shock. Was that what *she* had done to herself? the thought had projected. Kiondili stared at him.

"I may be far removed from your kind of Mu"—Kiondili was not sure if that was an insult—"but I am still of human blood. My feelings are not less worthy than yours. You blame me, yes. But you took from me also. And that theft I cannot recover."

Waon's voice cut off instantly, and Kiondili found her field damp was back on. She sat, shaking, until she realized that her forehead was wet, and she wiped sweat from her brow. Waon? He was leaving. She felt nothing now. Just a cold blackness that receded with him, leaving her to stare blankly at the control room below.

From behind her the xenopsychologist stirred, tapping her long plastic fingers together. Kiondili jumped. Even after several days of examinations by the psych, Kiondili was still not used to the sound of those fingers. She shuddered, wondering if Siln was watching the launch to see how Team B would do. As she looked over her shoulder to make sure Waon was gone, it was Siln's unblinking gaze that she met.

"You are cruel, Kiondili Wae."

"It is none of your business, Siln."

"It is the reason I am here." The psych regarded Kiondili for a moment, then manipulated her own persona adapt until its damp strengthened and isolated their conversation from the rest of the observation room.

Kiondili was startled. She had not realized that Siln was authorized to use a broad damp in her persona adapt. "Who are you to judge me?" she said sharply as the damp enveloped them both. "What do you know of *my* feelings? You dissect me and turn me out for everyone else to see, then tell me I am cruel?"

"For such a strong esper," Siln said, unperturbed, "you are singularly insensitive to others."

"I'm sensitive enough to feel every pulse of your second heart, Siln."

"You can feel physical things, yes, but you have no concept of emotions."

"That's good, coming from you, Siln," she returned sarcastically. "You wouldn't know happy or sad if they bit you."

"That I do not subject myself to the emotions of other species does not mean that I do not understand them. You, however, have no comprehension of the basic emotions that drive Waon or any other creature. You rely completely on your field perceptions—do not interrupt me, Mu—on your sensor skills to read the world around you. You rely on your esper skills to determine how each person feels and reacts to their world, skills which Waon has strengthened in you. You ignore the value of emotions in others. You resent becoming part of the interactions of others. There is very little in you, Kiondili Wae, that ties you to any of us.''

"Thank you for that encouraging bit of psychoanalysis, Siln. And as you so aptly put it, thank Waon for the need for that diagnosis as well as for my new mutancy.''

The psych tapped a silicon finger on Kiondili's arm. "This is not new," she said bluntly. "This has been developing in you since the death of your parents.''

Silence choked Kiondili, and her voice, when she finally answered, was tight. "You have no call to bring that up here.''

"Each citizen here is my responsibility. You are no more or less than others. This includes the Ruvian. You can give back to him some of what that merging stole from him.'' She paused. "If you wish.''

Kiondili flushed, suddenly finding her hands fascinating. "If he wants his fields soothed," she muttered, "why can't he use a variable damp?''

But Siln surprised her. "Waon has gone through three Changes since he's been at Corson. As with the other two Ruvians here, Waon's rooms are equipped with complete neutral fields and damps. The field generators are programmed to respond to his needs. What happened this time was an accident. The Change for Waon was imminent.'' Siln paused. "And uncontrolled. His current need is also uncontrolled, and he must have a human response, not a mechanical one, to help him.'' She met Kiondili's eyes. "Waon was an accident. You were an accident.''

"Oh, that makes me feel even better," Kiondili retorted. "First I'm a Tog knows what kind of a Mu, then I'm totally devoid of emotions, and now I'm an accident. My ego's in fine shape now.''

"Don't expect the galaxy to kiss your skinned knees, Mu." The psych stared at her till Kiondili dropped her eyes. "You have now freely what you once asked of Lan-Lu and were willing to pay for." Siln's voice was cold. "Reconsider your debt." She snapped the persona adjust off, and Kiondili was suddenly aware again of the crowded observation room.

"Stop seething, Kiwi," Tior whispered. "You're going to disturb the Greggor, which is going to disturb the rest of us."

Kiondili slumped in her seat. She could not believe Siln. The nerve of that plasticized psych, telling Kiondili she should pay for what Waon had done. Effi had not had to pay for her accusation except with a paltry fine. Argon had not had to pay except by losing his normal trade privileges. Waon had not had to pay for turning her into a new line of mutant. A plug in their boost tubes, she wished violently. A plague in their hydrogardens. It was not until an audible sigh rose from the room around her that she was finally startled into paying attention.

"Launch at last. Look at that boost!" Poole was leaning eagerly over Kiondili's shoulder.

In the control room Stilman was scribbling notes as fast as he could. "They're at point six already. Point eight. I think they'll make it."

"Jordan should be warming up the disintegrator by now." Lan-Lu flexed her wrist claws.

"It should kick in any second," Coos chittered from beside her. "Point nine . . ."

In spite of herself, Kiondili leaned forward and bit her lip. Point nine five, point nine six—the disintegrator kicked in. Holoimages shimmered, dissolving into energy patterns that had a curious overtone of the pilot's thoughts in them.

"Bring up Tracking Station Number Two."

"What's stress status?"

"On the beam. We're right on the beam." The controllers'

voices jumbled with Effi's orders while Coos chittered happily to the side.

"Look at that—perfect decomposition—" "Point nine nine light—" "They're going to make it—" The voices blurred into a cheer as the silver craft became two beams that spiralled into tachyon spacetime.

"Tracking—we're still tracking . . ." "Acceleration constant—" "We have decomposition. Repeat, we have complete decomposition. We have light! Zingor's balls—we've got trouble with the mass displacement."

The control room seethed suddenly, and the controllers' voices cut in over everyone. "What's beam efficiency?" "Transmission integrity fouling—" "Get that beam efficiency on the screen *now*—"

Effi threw one of the controllers from his seat and punched at the controls, biting out orders like a drill sergeant. "Get the emergency tracking stations online! Cross-check the transmission status from each station—where's that beam efficiency?"

Lan-Lu snarled as one of her claws hooked Coos's fur and spun the Robul around. She correlated calculations with her flashscreen as fast as Coos chittered them at her, matching her hunter's speed with that of a striking snake. His temple jacks glowed, and his four spindly arms rattled the keys in front of him while the images in his holotank twisted.

"Beam integrity fouled fifteen percent." "Tracking Stations Three and Four online—" "Get the flux status up," someone snapped, while another controller reported in. "Primary beam falling apart. Beam integrity fouled thirty-two percent."

Stilman snapped at Lan-Lu, ignoring the predator's fangs as she whirled on him and hissed back.

"—integrity fouled forty-one percent—"

"Beam disruption imminent—"

"Tracking—still tracking—"

"Gravity pull at 02X-B17," the controllers remorselessly intoned. "Transmission disrupted."

"Transmission efficiency at ten point four percent. Six point oh percent. Two point nine percent. Transmission efficiency gone. Repeat, beam disintegration complete."

"Tracking stations are going down. We've lost the launch. Repeat, the Lightwing is lost."

CHAPTER 16

Effi's hands fell to her sides. Up in the observation room there were no sounds but for the heavy breathing of the Greggor and the slow, considering clicks of Siln's hardened fingers. Dugan, the Corson director, left without a word, three others from the observation room going with him. Down in Control, only the chittering of Coos to Lan-Lu and the muted status reports of the controllers broke the heavy stillness.

"No," Effi whispered, staring at the blank screen. "Not now. Not this launch."

One of the controllers, his face pale and strained, cleared his throat. "Efficiency readings are coming in now." He turned and tapped a key on Effi's control board to link her flashscreen to his. "They're on System Two."

Effi stared at the lists of figures that scrolled past her haunted eyes, and Kiondili wondered how she had never noticed that the wrinkles on the old woman's face were dried and crinkly like plastic cracking under a heat lamp.

"Stupid," Effi whispered. "It was a stupid mistake."

Stilman, staring at the holotank, put his hand on Effi's

shoulder, but she shrugged it off. "Look at this," she snapped. "He had both beams online before launch—he had total control over the primary before the secondary beam formed. My God, but he would have made it except that he unbalanced the secondary beam. He lost too much mass too fast . . ."

Stilman stared at her. "For God's sake, Effi, we lost the team. I don't give a flying fancy about the launch. Arond, Jordan, Evissa—they're gone. They're all dead."

She looked at him. Her eyes were narrowed, but she did not hear him. "Too much mass too fast . . ."

Above, in the observation room, even Tior's blue skin was pale. "I don't understand," she whispered to Kiondili. "Arond's control is excellent. The launch was perfect up till then. How could he suddenly lose focus of the secondary beams?"

Kiondili's face was tight. She had felt nothing when they had gone down, and Siln's voice haunted her. She stared at the holotank. That could have been her team. That could have been her . . .

"We don't balance the mass of the secondary like we handle the primary during transmission," she said finally. "Mass loss is a function of the primary beams. If the primaries are focused and balanced properly, everything is fine. If the primaries are even a bit out of focus . . ."

"Kiwi, if Prime B's pilot could not handle the beams—"

Kiondili cut her off. "Arond knew more about the drive mechanics than I did, but I always had better control."

In the room below, Effi stood up and clutched at the control chair. "It was a stupid mistake," she repeated. "It shouldn't have happened. I trained him to concentrate. I trained him—"

"Effi," Stilman cut in, mistaking her outburst. "You are not to blame. This is all experimental. Any number of things could have happened, and," he said heavily, avoiding a glance up at the observation room where Kiondili sat, "they knew the risks."

"You don't understand," Effi snarled, rounding on Stilman. "We have no more time—"

"What has time got to do with it?" Stilman snapped. "A team is down. Dispersed. Dead." Rae, watching Effi closely, murmured to Stilman, and he took a breath. "The research will continue, Effi. We have another team for launch, and we still have another ship. We can make the Federation deadline. If this dispersal was a mistake, it can be fixed." He tried to take the old woman's arm and get her to sit down again, but Effi shook him off.

"Idiot," she snapped. "I *know* what went wrong, and I know how to fix it." She whirled and stalked out of the room.

"That old witch never lets up, does she?" Tior muttered, angry in spite of herself.

Kiondili shrugged. "Forget it, Tior. She's a bitter old woman looking for someone to blame her life on."

"Kind of like you."

Kiondili froze.

Tior flushed. "I'm sorry. I—I must be reacting to the blast."

"Let's go to the Hub," Kiondili said stiffly. "They've got half of it repaired enough to get something to drink."

Xia, the other H'Mu on their backup team, passed them, paused beside Poole, and looked back at the control room. "That beamer sure looked good for a while, didn't it?" she said quietly.

Poole nodded slowly, and even Argon was subdued for once. "Sharp as that Ixia's claws," he muttered. "It's a lousy deal to lose it in hyperlight space."

Xia met Kiondili's eyes squarely. "What do you think our chances are now, Wae?"

Kiondili looked at the other woman. *Too much mass lost too fast*—Effi's words echoed in her head. The focus, the shift and flux of the drive fields . . . Arond, Evissa, Jordan— they were gone, and Kiondili felt nothing. She was as blank as when her parents died. The focus, she thought absently.

The beamer was not the key, or Stilman would have a different expression on his face even now. No, it must be in the control of the sensor lens . . .

". . . chances, Wae?" Xia repeated.

"Arond miscalculated," Kiondili said abruptly, flatly. "He left an opening in the primary beam, and when it focused in the sensor lens, the mass unbalanced and dispersed."

"We know that, Mu," Argon said impatiently. "Xia was asking about your control versus Arond's. Or are you planning on sending us all out in a blast like Arond did Prime B?"

"Put a plug in your boost chute, gas breath," she retorted. "If you don't trust me, back out now before I decide to forget your recombination when we reach sublight—"

"Kiondili," Tior cut in urgently, pointing at the observation window. "Shut up, all three of you. Look at the control screens."

Kiondili followed her finger, then stared. "The launch lights are on."

Poole leaned forward, his yellow eyes gleaming. Beside him, Argon's eyes narrowed. "As if we were supposed to be on the blast and someone forgot to mention it to us."

Xia's eyes were sharp. "Look at the boost rating."

In the room below, one of the controllers had called Lan-Lu's attention to the flashscreens. "We've got a Lightwing on launch," he warned. "*Lightwing VI* is on launch."

"What the hell?" Stilman snapped, spinning around as Lan-Lu, startled, snagged his tunic on her elbow claw before retracting it. She flung her flashbook down and grabbed her temple jacks.

"No," Kiondili whispered. "That's our ship. That's our launch!"

"*Lightwing VI* is primed and ready to go. We have launch in two minutes." The controller punched in the com. "*Lightwing VI*, this is Control. Who's in command there?"

The com remained silent. Stilman grabbed the controls.

"*Lightwing*, this is Control. Who the hell is messing with the launch?"

Kiondili stood up. "That's our launch," she said urgently. "That's our last chance at light."

"Control, this is *Lightwing VI*." There was a shocked pause as they recognized Effi's voice on the com. "I am primed and ready for launch. Do I have a go?"

"No," Kiondili said louder, desperately. She did not notice the hands on her shoulders where Siln dug her long fingers in and forced her back down. "You cannot stop it now, H'Mu," Siln said. Kiondili did not even have time to register the fact that the xenopsychologist was unaffected by the buffers in Kiondili's persona adapt as Siln snapped Kiondili's E-damp on a stronger setting and withdrew to the seat behind her.

In Control, Coos and Rae were arguing fiercely while Stilman punched the com.

"Effi, what the hell are you doing? Cut those drives down now," he commanded. "Get out of that ship and off the launch pad before you get yourself killed."

"Control, this is *Lightwing VI*. Do you have launch status yet?"

"Yes, we have launch status," Stilman raged, "and the status is no go. I repeat, the status is no go. Who the hell is in there with you, Effi? Whoever it is is going to be spaced with you if you don't shut down the systems *now*."

"Sixty seconds and counting," the controller murmured under Stilman's elbow.

Coos chittered irritably as he called up the ship's status. "Stilman," he urged, "she's not giving up on this one. She is going to take it out. Primary drives are engaged, and secondaries are boosting up now."

Lan-Lu exclaimed in disgust, "Get the master controls kicked in fast. She killed the override before she left the control room. If you want to stop her, it's got to be in the next twenty seconds."

"Effi," Stilman shouted, "if your brains haven't dried out

too much to think, you'll shut down those drives right now. We've got a backup team to take that ship out. We don't want an old woman who's lost her senses."

"I'm not half as old as you, fungus brain," Effi snapped back.

"You're jeopardizing the whole damned project," Stilman raged. "Get out of that ship."

"Stilman," the com crackled, "you alien lover, eat your heart out. Control, all systems are on the green. Launch is a go. Repeat, launch is a go."

The com cut out, leaving Stilman speechless.

"She's enjoying this." Coos chittered faintly. "Very clever, our Effi Ragan. It takes time to override the manual controls since they're supposed to be the last level of safety. She did not engage the drives until all other systems were on go status. She made sure she had enough time to take off after we noticed."

"She has enough time to fry what's left of her brains in that piece of junk she's flying. Does she know what this will do to the project? If that Lightwing goes down, we're finished. There isn't a single Shield ship within range we could call up to stop her, and we haven't got a tractor beam on the outpost that could hold a Lightwing against a launch." Stilman flung the com back at the controller and strode to the other data bank. In the holotank, the Lightwing flared, launched, and accelerated away.

"We have launch," the controller intoned. "Repeat, the Lightwing is launched."

"Oh, shut up," Stilman snapped. "We can see that."

The controller ignored him. "Blast status on go. All systems green. Acceleration constant."

"You don't really think she can do it," Tior whispered from beside Kiondili, staring at the screens below.

"She will be able to manage the initial controls," Xia said quietly, "but she won't be able to make the jump. She's only one person; the Lightwing was built for three. She'll have to junk one, maybe two stations and rely completely on the master board.''

''Impossible,'' Kiondili said flatly.

Argon snorted. ''How do you know, Mu? Maybe you can't do it, but that's no reason to assume Effi can't. After all, she's the one who designed the boost controls.''

Tior protested. ''How is she going to kick in the disintegrator and control the mass loss through the lens at the same time?''

Kiondili became still. ''Who set the coordinates for her?'' she asked slowly. ''Team B's Lightwing was the last ship programmed for a launch. *Lightwing VI* wasn't even primed, let alone registered in the tracking stations for transmission. She did not have time to program the new test route into that ship from Control before she left. She must have set her coordinates by hand, from inside the Lightwing.''

Poole began to wheeze until Tior hit him angrily. ''Don't you get it?'' he gasped, ripples surging down his stomach fur. ''The coordinates. She had a breakdown going through a warp gate eighty years ago—she can never travel FTL again. At her age, she's too old to last through another sublight voyage. Effi's on a one-way trip home. The only coordinates she knows well enough—that anyone except a navigator knows well enough—to set at the last minute are those of Earth.''

''Shut up,'' Kiondili snarled. ''She'll never make it to lightspeed, let alone get halfway to Earth. The ship hasn't enough mass to lose.''

In the room below, the tension grew. ''We have point six light,'' the controller chanted. ''Point seven light. Point seven five light. All system are green; blast status is still a go.''

''Get those tracking stations back online,'' Lan-Lu hissed.

''I'm getting no response from Number Three, but One and Two are up and tracking.''

''Keep trying,'' Rae snapped. ''Coos, what's the acceleration factor?''

''Acceleration slowing fractionally; however, she's got

enough momentum built up. She should reach lightspeed in two minutes." Coos chittered excitedly. "Twelve seconds past transmission, her velocity should be one light-year per minute."

"What about target?"

"Her coordinates are for Earth," Stilman said soberly. "That trajectory could not take her anywhere else."

"She cannot make it." Lan-Lu flexed her wrist claws in and out, ignoring the controller, who shuddered. "She will lose too much mass during the crossover."

Stilman growled, sending another set of data to his flash-screen almost savagely. "She needs more than one brain to control the ship from here on out. She's got to change her coordinates to something easier. A path with fewer gravitational masses to get around."

Coos chittered quietly. "She would never do that."

Up in observation, Siln tapped her fingers together. "The ease of the launch does not matter to her," Siln said calmly at the question in Poole's eyes. "You see," the psych added softly, "Effi Ragan is an old woman of human type. Right now she is somewhere between age and the stars."

Kiondili stared at her.

"Between age and the stars," Poole repeated in a low voice. "Yes."

"We have point nine light," one of the controllers reported. "Point nine five light. All systems on green."

"The disintegrator is kicking in," Tior said softly. "She should be starting the energy incline now."

"She's late," Argon breathed.

Behind them, the director of the outpost entered the observation room silently, other aliens and H'Mu entering behind him as they heard the news. Dugan took in the assistants at a glance but said nothing. He simply stood and watched, his arms crossed and his yellow-orange eyes not wavering from the control room screens.

"Point nine six light. Point nine seven light." "Emergency tracking cutting in for Station One.'' ''Point nine eight light.'' ''All stations now tracking.''

''What if she makes it?'' Tior whispered.

''She won't,'' Kiondili whispered back. ''She can't.'' Inside, she found herself wishing the old woman would prove her wrong, but she could not see how even Effi's knowledge of the systems on the ship could make up for the lack of the navigator and the linkman.

''She's on the beam,'' Xia breathed. She hit the chair arm with a fist. Kiondili stared at her. Xia had never shown such emotion before. ''She's on the beam.''

''Acceleration constant.'' ''All stations tracking.'' ''All systems on green.''

''She's late with decomposition,'' Rae snapped as she twisted in her seat and punched a new set of data up. ''Coos, check the trajectories of the beams going through the lens.''

''Come on, Effi, bring her up,'' Stilman muttered.

''Point nine nine light.''

''Disintegration begun. Primary beam transmission kicking in on the mark.'' ''Check that mass transference.'' ''Get tracking up on the screen.'' ''Beam integrity intact. Repeat, primary beam intact.'' ''Secondary beam transmission kicking in on the mark—holy molshet!''

The flashscreens flared and died. The tiny black area in each holotank expanded as the ship dispersed and the tracking stations lost the transmission.

''Secondary overload,'' the controller intoned. ''Transmission rupture and mass dispersal. We have lost the Lightwing.''

There was a moment of complete silence. Then Lan-Lu flexed her wrist claws and said tonelessly, ''Tracking station reports, please.''

''Tracking Station One reports complete dispersal. Station Two reports complete dispersal. Station Three reports—''

''Damn you, shut up!'' Stilman cut in savagely. ''Is that all you can do right now, Lan-Lu? We've lost the Lightwing. We've lost Effi. That's four dead. Four! And the last Lightwing went with them. We don't need any more status reports. The project's finished.''

Lan-Lu hissed. "I can still save much of my research, Stilman."

Coos chittered quietly. "There won't be any more research at Corson, Lan-Lu. Our funding dispersed with that ship." He projected his head and twisted around to face the observation screen.

Dugan seemed to meet the Robul's eyes through the window before turning and leaving once more without a word.

Xia, her face wiped once again of all expression, said, "Damn."

The emotionless curse stuck in Kiondili's throat and choked her as if she had swallowed a fist.

"Damn her to all the hells of all the spacetimes of this and every universe!" Tior blindly stacked her flashbooks and gathered them up.

Before Kiondili, someone murmured, "What a waste. Such a stupid, stupid waste."

"Well," Argon said, wiping his brow and breaking the uneasy quiet of the observation room. "What are your plans now, Wae?"

Kiondili looked up blankly. "Plans?"

"Are you heading for the job pool or have you got something better lined up when Corson goes down? Personally, I've always kept my contacts open," he added, waving at the control room below. "I'll probably land another job within the cycle."

"Shut up, Argon," Kiondili said quietly. Since she said it without anger, he did.

CHAPTER 17

Kiondili was in her quarters when the meeting notice came. It took a few minutes to register; she had been staring at nothing, her mind blank except for the litany that the voice in the observation room had left with her. "Such a waste . . ." The words echoed back on themselves, repeating the blankness that Effi's death had suddenly made in her mind.

She had already transferred her flashbooks into data cubes, the small pile representing the sum of her work at the outpost. Her bookcase and overstuffed chair were marked for supply. Her one precious leather-bound book and wooden dolphin were carefully packed into a small parcel with her other things. She did not bother to smooth down her hair as she trudged to the free-boost chute. There was nothing left for her at Corson.

She had no future. Thanks to Effi, she snarled silently, none of them did. Only Kiondili was worse off than the others: She was still on probation. The recommendations she might be able to get from Stilman and Rae would count for little as soon as anyone checked her probation record.

With a black mark like that on her work history—along with the tangles of her parents' bankruptcy—the best she could hope for was a sixth-class job out of the nearest pool. Menial work, fit more for drones than for H'Mu. She spit after the alien that cut in front of her at a redirectional pad. Her job as an assistant was over: Stilman had said nothing to her about going with him to his next posting. Not even Lan-Lu had offered to help her find another job. She might as well space herself if she did not want to end up picking vegetables under a Tursceon sky.

Xia did not bother to acknowledge Kiondili when she slumped into a chair in the meeting room. Only Argon raised a cynical eyebrow, but Kiondili ignored him. In the front, Dugan did not wait for the room to quiet.

"The Lightwing project has been canceled," he said without preamble. "All research credits forthcoming for Lightwing and any associated projects will be stopped as of three days from today. This will give most of you time to set your notes in order and prepare for leaving the outpost. If you need help setting your credit records straight, the outpost auditors are standing by on a first-come, first-served basis."

He paused.

"You must vacate your quarters in three days. After that, the maintenance drones will be remodeling for new projects. If you have doubts as to whether your project is canceled with the Lightwing project, tap into System Forty-two. The listing of valid projects and cancellations is current as of today." Dugan looked slowly around the room. "Any questions?"

There was a moment of silence, then Kiondili was startled to hear Siln's voice break the depression. "Does this mean the Lightwing project is canceled as of today? Or that the project is canceled as of three days from today?"

Dugan shot the xenopsychologist a sharp look. "Lightwing is canceled, Siln. There are no more ships. There is no more project."

"As of when?" she persisted quietly.

Dugan tapped his flashwriter irritably. "The project is canceled in three days; however, it's best if those of you involved concentrate on clearing out your labs and packing to leave the outpost. You can do no more research without funding, and if you are not gone in three days, you will be kicked out whether you have collected your notes or not."

"Three days," Siln repeated. "What exactly are the terms of the Federation's funding, Dugan?"

"Siln, I see no purpose—"

The psych made a curt gesture. "It is a valid question, Dugan. Please answer: The terms of the funding?"

Dugan glared at her. Siln just waited.

"The terms," he said slowly and clearly, "are that a new method of traveling FTL is developed and validated by Federation authorities. That the new method is appropriate for H'Mu and other class MX1B3 species."

"Dugan," Coos chittered over the angry murmur that rose, "as I recall, the contract also said that while we showed continued and steady progress toward that goal, the lease of Corson for our research was extended as long as our funding allowed. It was only if we stopped showing progress that they could reclaim Corson. No one can fault our progress to date."

Dugan was silent for a moment, then he sighed heavily. "I cannot fault our progress, and neither have the Federation observers. However, there are no Lightwings left, and there is no funding to provide another such prototype. Our resources are exhausted, and the goal is not reached. The Federation does not support inefficient research."

"But resources are not exhausted yet—" "I still have a hundred thousand credits—" "I've ordered my hypercyclotron—how can I cancel now?" "What about *Lightwing VII*?"

The room stilled as the last voice cut through the clamor of other voices. "What about *Lightwing VII*?" one of the engineers repeated, his booming voice now echoing in the chamber. "It was the third and last ship down in the cradles. It is still there."

"*Lightwing VII* was stripped to provide mass stabilizers for *V* and *VI*," Dugan said flatly. "There are no resources to rebuild *VII*. It would be impossible to refit that ship for an FTL blast. The project is canceled," he said firmly over the angry voices of the researchers. "The meeting is adjourned."

"Hey, Kiwi," Tior called as Kiondili straggled after the others. "Wait a minute. What are you doing tonight?"

"Packing," she said sourly. "What else?"

"We're going to have a last get-together in the Hub. Why don't you meet us at half past third quarter."

Kiondili hesitated.

"Come on. Argon's breaking out his private collection of Bist juice—he even said you could have some—and Poole's bringing Dominion wine. We might get to try some of those bip buttons if Xia can swing it."

"I don't really feel like it, Tior."

Tior stared at her. "None of us really feels like it, either," she snapped finally, "but it's better than sitting alone in our quarters. Join us—it won't hurt you to socialize one more time before blasting out to the nearest job pool."

Kiondili stood for a moment, watching as Tior stalked from the room. She might as well hang out with the others. She had nothing else to do but help Stilman pack up the lab.

She started down the hall. She ignored the free-boost chute—making time was no longer important to Kiondili Wae. Not now that she had the rest of her life to work in the fields of some ag planet and contemplate its more bitter aspects.

"Damn that arrogant bitch," she said tightly, leaning suddenly against a wall and pressing her hand to her eyes. "Damn Effi Ragan to a thousand hells." She finally forced her way down the hall to Stilman's lab, her vision blurred.

Home. The word should have a special meaning, she thought as she clenched her fingers around a flashbook. She had not had a home since her parents died and she watched their ship sold at a guild auction. The closest thing she had

had to a home since then was Stilman's lab. Now even that would be gone in another two days. She slammed the stack of flashbooks down on the counter and jerked the top one off the stack. Even if she hurried, it was going to take her a quarter cycle to finish all these notes. She would not be done before Stilman left. If Stilman had any brains outside his precious beamer, she cursed, he would have had some of them transferred a long time ago.

"Wae," Stilman yelled, as if her unwary thoughts had called him. The sound was muffled as if he had his head in a bag. Kiondili, making her way slowly through the precariously piled flashbooks, found that it was true. "Wae," he yelled again.

"I'm right here," she said sharply.

"Oh." He pulled his head out of the huge sack and looked bewildered for a moment. "Wae, hmm, what was I—dammit, these belong to Rae Arr, too. Here, take those flashbooks to Lan-Lu, that cube to Coos, and these things to Rae." He straightened his violently orange tunic and yanked irritably at his white-striped trousers. "And make sure you don't deliver Rae's stuff to anyone but her. And don't leave them in her lab, either—she won't realize they are there, and they won't get packed."

She took the objects without answering. She had been stupid to hope he might want to keep her on as his assistant. He was not one to think of anyone else but himself or his own research, and he often forgot the first because of the second. She clenched her jaws for a moment.

Coos was in his lab, although it took a moment for Kiondili to find him. The Robul had curled up between two lab tables to think, and Kiondili almost tripped on him as she walked slowly through the lab. He did not acknowledge her except to project one of his arms and hold out his hand, so she dropped the data cube in his grip and left.

Rae Arr was harder to find. By the time Kiondili got to Rae's office, it was second bell, and the scientist had already taken off to the Hub for lunch. Kiondili repocketed the items she was to deliver and made her way back to the free-boost chutes. It would take her another twenty minutes to find Rae, and she still had over 130 flashbooks to transfer to cubes. And, she sighed, Stilman would probably take up the whole afternoon having her run errands. He was as disturbed as everyone else, she knew, because he had bothered to match his socks and pants for the first time since she had met him.

Only two of the assistants were in the Hub when she got there, but she ignored their halfhearted wave.

"Just my luck," she muttered, finally spotting Rae Arr, the esper. The short researcher looked even smaller sitting next to one of the large Mu from engines. Kiondili sighed. It took several minutes to squeeze through the throng—too many aliens and H'Mu were saying good-bye to each other. As Kiondili would have to do, too. She did not want to think about it. "Rae?" she asked as she finally reached the researcher's table.

"She's flashing in her last formula before the outpost erases all her notes," one of the others explained, gesturing for Kiondili to sit. "Give her a few minutes and she'll be with you."

Kiondili sat reluctantly.

"At least she's still working," another man said sourly. "I can't even have a minute on the computers since we're shutting down. Everything is back up this and save that. If I'd thought I'd have to do maintenance at this stage of my life, I'd have gone into designing drones."

"There's better credits in it," Poole agreed.

Kiondili ordered a protein drink from the dispenser in place of lunch. She would be lucky to have dinner that day, and she did not have time for a full meal.

"Where's Stilman headed?" Poole asked her quietly.

She shrugged. "I don't know. Probably back to Ogen, from the amount of stuff he's packaged up."

Siln regarded her with a slight frown, but Kiondili ignored the psych.

"He's not leaving till the last day, then?" one of the other researchers asked.

"Not that I know of. It'll take me at least that long to clear out his lab, anyway."

The researcher sucked up his drink, then tossed his glass down the table chute. "You're not booking out till the last day, then. Most of us aren't going till then, but I wasn't sure about Stilman. He forgets to tell us a lot of things."

"He just plain forgets a lot of things," Kiondili corrected sourly. She did not bother to correct that slip about her going with Stilman.

"Which reminds me." The researcher turned and poked the engine master in the shoulder. "Are you going to return those stakes you've been holding?"

The man looked puzzled, then his face cleared. "Oh, yeah. Pass me that temple jack, will you." The engine master called up the list of bets. "Forgot completely about those. Someone would have reminded me sooner or later."

Lan-Lu's fangs were sharp against her slitted lips. "Better sooner than later in this case."

Poole leaned over to tap his code in and wipe his bet from the tab.

The xenopsychologist tapped her fingers on the engine master's arm, stopping the man before he set her code. "Let my bet ride, Kiet."

The man looked up in surprise. "There's nothing for you to bet on, Siln. I can't hold stakes for a nonexistent blast."

"Let it ride," Siln repeated. "There are two and a half days left before Lightwing is canceled. Many things can happen between now and then."

Kiondili frowned, but it was Poole who said curiously, "I do not see your point, Siln. We have no ship, no crew, no computers."

Lan-Lu ran her tongue across her teeth. Her slitted eyes stared at Siln for a long moment. "None of the backup team has left yet," she said softly. "Is that it?" Siln did not answer, and Lan-Lu let her gaze move across the assistants.

"And Poole, you could get around Central Control's priority queue for a launch if you wanted to code in a bypass, something which you often brag you can do."

Poole raised his shaggy eyebrow. "I have no reason to do it. There is no ship to take the backup team out—even if the computers were there to set up the launch."

"There is still *Lightwing VII*," Siln said quietly.

"Dammit, Siln," another researcher said, too sharply, "it does not do any of us any good to fantasize about something that will never happen. And it makes you just plain irritating to boot."

The engine master nodded. "He's right, Siln. There's no way we could rebuild a set of stabilizers for *VII*. We could not even get replacement parts for a quarter cycle—"

The sudden, clear tones of the Moal's voice startled Kiondili. Looking left, she realized that Elim, the Moal, had been cowering by the engine master the whole time she had been drinking her protein shake.

"Elim Qu Ibis sings flux," the Moal sang in dual tones.
"Elim Qu Ibis sings cyclic stress

launch to focus
launch success

Elim Qu Ibis sings mass again."

The table was silent. Rae stopped flashing notes into her book and stared at the Moal with renewed respect. The engine master, sitting next to the alien, frowned. "That's true enough, Elim," he said finally, "but I don't know about the flux stabilizers being easily replaced with transitory beamers."

"You want to repeat that in Basic, Kiet?" one of the other researchers prompted. "I didn't quite catch everything Elim sang."

"We stripped *Lightwing VII* to outfit *V* and *VI* for launch," he said slowly. "But we had already adjusted the engines to compensate for the problems we had had with *IV*. The only thing wrong with *VII* is that there are no mass stabilizers for the disintegrator or stress equalizers for the beam transmission.''

Kiondili could not help snorting. "The only thing wrong? That's like saying the only thing wrong with the ship is that it can't go FTL.''

"Yes," he agreed slowly, a note of excitement creeping into his voice. "But Elim just pointed out that both the mass stabilizers and the stress equalizers could be reprogrammed through the main control banks.''

Rae frowned and flicked on the design pad for the table. "You are saying that here and here"—she outlined the fields—"we would need another set of decomposition buffers.''

The tall man scratched his chin. "Yes, but it would take days to build a set of beams stiff enough to hold through the light barrier.''

Poole slumped back in his seat, and Kiondili found that she had been holding her breath.

"We don't have days," Lan-Lu said softly. Her wrist claws tapped the design slowly.

Rae sighed and switched the table off.

"You might as well take your stakes, Siln," Kiet said. "It's a Tinlig's pipe dream to get that ship off the docks.''

Siln got up. "Let my bet ride. Backup has done things other teams have not. As I said before, many things can happen in three days.''

"Three days?" The engine master scowled. "There's no way we could redesign the beamers in that time.''

"Unless we worked together," Rae suggested softly.

The engine man met Lan-Lu's eyes and shuddered. "Maybe." He hesitated, glancing at the predator again. "Maybe I'll just drop on down and tinker with the engines before I ship out," he said slowly. He did not look at Kiondili. "I guess I can hold on to your stakes for a couple days, Siln.''

Lan-Lu smiled at the man's wary expression. "I will go

with you, Kiet," the Ixia said. "Sometimes two can see what one cannot." She paused, then leaned over to Kiet and tapped a code into his flashbook. "You might as well put my bet back on the books."

"And mine," Rae said. "I may drop by in engines later. I have some notes you might be able to use."

Kiondili stood up quickly. "Rae," she said hurriedly as she thrust the flashcube and other deliveries at the short Mu, "these are from Stilman." She edged out from between the others. "Excuse me, please. I've got some . . . packing to do." She hurried from the Hub, her quick strides becoming a run as the crowds thinned near the doors.

Scant minutes later she was pounding on Tior's door lock. "Tior, let me in—" She almost fell into Tior's arms when the door shimmered open. She did not apologize.

"Unless Lan-Lu's after you," the other Mu snapped, "there's no reason to pop my water bubbles."

"Listen." Kiondili drew the woman across the room. "Is your com offline? What's security here?"

Tior frowned and punched a button. "The com's offline now, but the control link stays on."

Kiondili shook her head. "Let's go to Argon's." She dragged the other woman out and down the hall.

"Since when have you wanted to pay a house call to that bunch of Bolduin's balls?"

"Since we need him for a launch." Kiondili ignored Tior's demand for an explanation. "Later. When we see Argon."

"What the hell do you want, Mu?" Argon answered his com as he saw who had buzzed.

"Let us in, gas brain," she retorted. "We've got news."

The door shimmered open, and Kiondili dragged Tior through before the door completely cleared.

Tior gave a startled yelp as the currents hit her water bags. "Ayara's eyes, Kiwi," she snapped. "You could give me a warning."

Argon did not invite them to sit, but, at Kiondili's expression, he regarded her thoughtfully.

Kiondili gestured to his desk. "The comlink?"

He snapped it off. She motioned toward the control link that still blinked quietly by his terminal. If anyone would have a link bypass, it would be Argon, Kiondili bet, and she was right. He hesitated, then coded in a quick succession of numbers. "All right, we're protected. There's no access here without me knowing. What's this about, Mu?"

"The launch is on," Kiondili said flatly. "We're taking *Lightwing VII* out as soon as—"

"*Lightwing VII* is in no shape to launch, let alone blast FTL," he retorted, cutting her off. "What has she been drinking, Tior?"

Tior was regarding Kiondili with a pitying look. Kiondili suppressed the desire to slap them both. "I've not been drinking, and what I say is true. If you don't believe me, check the engine master's betting stakes. He's still holding them for half the project team."

"He probably forgot to give them back," Argon said disparagingly.

"No, I was there at lunch when he offered. Half the bets are still riding on blast, and Kiet and Lan-Lu are working on the Lightwing right now."

"I think she breathed too much space last timed she went solar surfing," Tior said tersely to Argon. "The engine master would space himself before he worked in an enclosed space with Lan-Lu."

"It's the stress," he agreed. "Maybe we should call the medic before she gets worse."

"Plug it with a bucket of topes. Listen: Elim Qu-Ibis came up with a new way to stabilize the transmission beam. It will be jury-rigged," she admitted, "but it's better than nothing, and it will let us take the Lightwing out on schedule."

"We don't have a schedule," Argon reminded her.

"We do now. If they can get the circuits redesigned and Lan-Lu can build some transitory beamers, Rae will put the computers back online for a launch. And Poole will build a bypass through Central Control."

Argon stared at her for a moment.

"If, if, if," Tior cut in. "There's no certainty in any of that, Kiwi." She gestured at the stack of data cubes sitting on Argon's desk. "The whole outpost is packing to leave, and you want us to help you steal an experimental ship and pilot it away. I'm sorry, Kiwi, but even if I wanted to be part of this, I just don't see it as being possible—not in the two days we have left."

"Two and a half days," Kiondili corrected. "In two and a half days I'll either be shipped out for a sixth-class job on a backwater planet or spaced for stealing a ship worth over a hundred thousand credits. There's not much difference in the sentencing." She looked to Argon, but he said nothing, tipping his head back to think. Kiondili leaned over and turned the comlink back on. "I'm going to call Xia," she said.

"Kiwi, don't get her hopes up."

"Do you think she would rather not know? What if it is possible?"

Tior fell silent.

"Wae might be right," Argon said suddenly. "If she is, and if the ship is refitted in two days, we could set the launch off ourselves."

"By ourselves?" Tior looked shocked. "Without Control?"

"You and Poole have been running simulation Control for a cycle now. Why not go in real time?"

"But we can't do it without Lan-Lu and Stilman and Rae," Tior protested.

"Do you really think they're going to jeopardize their futures to help us steal a Federation ship?" Kiondili snorted. "Rae and Lan-Lu are building the ship for us. It'll be up to us to take it out."

"What about coordinates? And how will we get access to the ship if it's locked up in engines?"

Argon waved his hand. "You read into Kiet's accounts a quarter cycle ago. He'll have a listing for short hops. Hell, he probably has the coordinates for half this quadrant. Xia and I can build a cross-circuit bypass to get us into the ship if the access is cut off. I've done it lots of times to get into Contr—uh, to deliver things to different places," he amended carefully.

Kiondili said nothing.

"How can you be sure Coos will go along with this?" Tior objected, pointing at Argon's pack. "I heard he was shipping out tomorrow."

"Call him," Kiondili told Argon. "And call Xia, too."

"I know what to do, Mu," Argon snapped at her. He turned to the other woman. "But Tior," he warned, "whether Coos or Xia or even you are with us or not, if what Kiondili says is true, I'm on for the launch."

Tior was silent again and finally raised her head. "If you're on for the launch," she said quietly, "you need someone to keep Central Control out of your hair till you hit light."

Kiondili began to grin. "Light." She looked from Argon to Tior. "We're going light."

CHAPTER 18

"Is it on?" Xia asked as Kiondili slipped through the door.

Kiondili nodded and dropped the flashbook on Xia's desk. "Your boss left this out for us."

"Coordinates?"

"Control instructions. I've already copied them. Give them to Tior when you're done. Navigation will be different, and the monitors that feed directly through Central Control will be disabled, but this should give you enough information to compensate." She turned to leave.

"Argon is with Poole. He said for you to meet them when you were ready."

Kiondili did not reply. She was already down the hall and diving into the free-boost chute. Reaching beyond her E-damp and speeding up to just under 250 clicks, she wondered briefly, If a launch of *Lightwing VII* had never been brought up, would she have cared whether the chute guards caught her speeding? She passed a pair of side tunnels and caught a glimpse of dark hair as another H'Mu made his way through the chutes. If it was not for a Lightwing launch, would she take a chance and change a few settings on Argon's persona adapt? He had been almost tolerable lately; maybe he was beginning to forget about his grudge against her. She hit the next pad off center, slicing awkwardly along the wall field until she regained her line. Argon. If she did not have to work with him . . .

Just as she did not have to work with Effi Ragan anymore.

She dove silently, frozen in a straight line as she speared through the center of the chute. Effi was dead. The pale lines of the boost tube flashed by like light on a launch as she skimmed a wall and shifted into the next chute without hitting the redirection pad. She noted the color shift absently. What made her think this launch would be successful where the others were not? The other teams had had more advanced studies, more training. And they were now dead or still in recovery. A strange reaction twisted in Kiondili's gut, and she recognized it as fear. What if she did not set the beams correctly? What if the refitted stabilizers did not work? Her team was just the backup. Even Argon admitted that they could use more time on the simulator—as if she would sit in another simulation session with that Mu if she did not have to. She would not have to if she were dead, the thought came unbidden. Prime Team A . . . fragmented. Prime Team B . . . dead. Effi Ragan . . . dead. Stop it, she told herself harshly. She straightened out her line along the chute and steadied her breathing.

At least, she told herself with a twisted smile, if they were caught launching the Lightwing, they would all be spaced without suits before anyone asked why—Argon included. She tumbled lightly along the wall, hitting the redirection pad on her thigh and breaking off into a new tube. If she could not go with Stilman or get another job at the outpost, she would rather disperse with a blast in hyperlight space, anyway.

Space—she would be challenging spacetime itself in four hours.

She stopped at the door to Poole's lab and tapped the access lock, but before she could step through, Siln's lanky frame stretched out of the shimmering surface and startled her.

"Mu," Siln said quietly, stepping into the hall.

"Siln," she acknowledged, waiting for the psych to move aside. But the xenopsychologist remained in front of the door, barring her way. "What do you want, Siln?"

Siln tapped her long fingers together and regarded her thoughtfully. "You have left two things undone, Kiondili Wae."

"What are you talking about?"

"Two things, which must be done before you launch."

Kiondili looked over her shoulder guiltily. "Ayara's eyes, Siln, the corridor comlinks are on."

"Two things, Mu," the psychologist repeated. "Speak with Stilman before you go, and see Waon."

Kiondili pursed her lips. "I see Stilman every hour," she said, adding flatly, "and I have nothing to say to Waon."

"You owe both of them that much."

Kiondili stared after the psych as Siln walked away in her strange, gracefully stiff gait.

"Hurry up, Wae," Poole said, poking his head out the door and noticing her. "Check out the coordinates. We set them for Northase. We should have enough fuel for that, plus a little extra. Tior's going to program them into the computer if they look all right to you."

"Yeah, sure." She paused and stared after the psychologist before Poole drew her inside. Why the hell did she have to speak to Stilman? All he had done for the last two days was yell for this and that. He had not even bothered to ask her what she was going to do after he left. Why did he not want her to go with him? It was bad enough Siln wanted her to go through some sort of teary good-bye with her boss, but then she had to make up with Waon, the fusion plant?

She glared after the psych. "Damn it," she said finally. "Tior, how late can you set the coordinates?"

Tior frowned. "Just before launch, I guess, but that is pushing it, Kiwi. I'm not sure how long it will take me under the blind we're running.'' Her skin was tight, and Kiondili wondered if Tior had the fear of the launch in her guts that Kiondili had. "We still have to install Rae's circuits,'' the blue-skinned Mu added, "and the beamer—which you haven't gotten out of Stilman yet.''

Kiondili nodded impatiently. "I'll be back as soon as I can.''

"Wait a minute. Where are you going?''

"I have to get the beamer and talk to—someone.'' She added sourly, "Since I'm burning all my bridges, it would be nice to know which side of the river I'll end up on when the smoke clears.''

"Kiondili—'' Tior turned to Poole in exasperation as Kiondili turned and ran down the corridor. "What the hell is she talking about?''

He shrugged. "If she gets back in time with those parts, I don't care how she thinks or what she talks about.''

Kiondili jogged toward the nearest free-boost chute. She did not have much time.

At Rae's lab, the short esper did not look up from her packing crate when Kiondili entered. Rae was examining the box with a frown but waved a silent greeting.

Kiondili glanced at the crate. "We're ready to put the boards in, Rae.''

"One moment, Mu,'' Rae muttered. She scowled and thrust the packing list in her pocket, then strode to a shielded box on the counter. "There are eight boards in here,'' she said, handing them to Kiondili. "Six for the control patterns, two for the decomposition. Don't get them mixed up.''

Kiondili nodded.

"Are you going straight to engines, or do I need to wrap these first?''

"I have to get the beamer from Stilman before I go on down.''

Rae studied her, and Kiondili felt the feather touch of the researcher's probe. "I am surprised that he is letting you take his beamer out of the lab. I would have expected Stilman to insist on installing it in the ship himself.''

Kiondili flushed slowly. ''He doesn't know that I'm taking it, so he does not know it has to be installed.''

''Stilman is scheduled for outbound passage at noon today, Kiondili Wae. What is he going to think when he shows up at the loading dock and you are not there? Or when he realizes you have the beamer that cost him the last twenty years of his life?''

''What do you mean, when I'm not there?'' Kiondili could not hide her sudden projection of resentfulness, and Rae's eyebrows rose. Kiondili muttered, ''Stilman's only use for me in the last two days has been to make sure all his precious flashbooks and data cubes were packed. He's not going to miss me at the docks.''

''So you're not going with him,'' Rae returned bluntly. Her probe sharpened, and Kiondili stiffened. ''Who gave you a better offer?''

''Nobody offered me anything. When Stilman leaves, I'm out of a job and a future.''

''Did Stilman fire you?''

Kiondili opened her mouth to reply, then paused. ''No,'' she said slowly.

''You were not hired by the Corson outpost, Mu,'' the scientist said sharply. ''You were hired by Stilman. This Federation research post, in the person of Director Dugan, merely approved the hire.''

''But if Stilman—if you all lost your funding—''

''Unless Stilman fired you, for which he would have to give you a termination review in front of the board, you still have a job, Mu. Your contract could not have expired. You have been here only five cycles.'' The derision in Rae's words was pale compared to that of the woman's esper voice.

Kiondili felt suddenly small and insignificant.

''Where Stilman works should not make any difference to you, Kiondili Wae. You were hired to do a job for him, not for Corson. I suggest you speak with him. He may be able

to get a later berthing on one of the other traders out of here."
The scientist turned back to her lab work.

Kiondili stared at Rae's back. Stilman was taking her with
him? She did not have to go into the job pool? Why the hell
had he not told her? Why had she not picked that out of her
contract? Ayara's eyes, she realized suddenly, but she had
only a half hour to catch him. Stilman had been planning on
boarding early in case he was bumped from the flight by
others crowding off Corson, an idea she had encouraged so
that he would be out of the way in time for her to launch the
Lightwing with the others.

"Thanks," she said slowly. "Thanks, Rae."

The woman did not turn around, but a flash of empathy
surprised Kiondili, and she backed out of the lab, clutching
the box of circuits in her hand. She tucked the box into her
jumper thoughtfully before sliding into the free-boost chute.
Hanging on to the acceleration pad before boosting down the
chute, she realized that she had a choice of her future. Down
in engines the Lightwing was waiting, silent in its cradle and
dead without her. But up in the labs she still had a job—a
future and a life out of the pool. She shoved off the pad
slowly, changed her mind at a branch tube, then changed her
mind again, speeding faster with new decisiveness.

Waon's quarters were in a cold, dim part of the complex.
By the look of the corridor IDs, the entire triad was reserved
for the alien, and she hesitated before approaching the central
door. There was a curious numbness around the halls that
signaled strong field damps. Kiondili hesitated, then tapped
the com before she could change her mind again. But she
almost turned and ran when the door shimmered open and
she heard Waon's cold voice say "Come."

She stepped through, then stopped. One entire wall of the
Ruvian's quarters was open to space, the clear crystal of the
window barely marred by dust. She caught her breath. Bil-
lions of stars streaked across the sky in the galaxy's outer
arm, and one of the nebulas was as clear to Kiondili's eye as
if a patch of lint were stuck to the window. She barely noticed

the thick carpet of living grass that climbed up the other walls and grew into a series of vines. With the wall's shadowy colors and the flat black of space, the room looked as cool as night on Northase. Against the window Waon stood, unmoving, staring at the stars. Kiondili paused awkwardly as she realized he was holding a holo in his hands.

"Waon—" She cleared her throat. "Waon, Siln told me that I've caused some problems in your Change."

The Ruvian said nothing for a moment. When he turned, she took an involuntary step back.

"I don't pretend to understand what you are or—" She swallowed. "what you need from me, but I want to set things right between us."

"You come to assuage your guilt?" The nerve centers close to the Ruvian's skin glowed with a golden pulse.

She stiffened. "I am not apologizing for my feelings."

He met her gaze, then nodded curtly.

She suddenly realized that he had read her. Instinctively she hardened her blocks, then forced them to relax. As she met Waon's depthless eyes again, she thought she saw his appreciation of the effort. "What happened to you?" she asked quietly. "What did I do to you?"

Waon glanced instead at the holo in his hands. "Inryia has Changed by now," he said slowly. "But she is female/S'ki/male now, and I—" He looked directly at Kiondili. "I am male/T'se/female."

Kiondili shook her head in puzzlement.

"I was not scheduled for this type of Change for another hundred and twelve years," he said shortly. Sensing her consternation, the Ruvian passed his hand over his eyes. The dim fields he generated hugged his body, and as his hand crossed his cheeks, it looked as if a warp were crawling across his bronze-streaked skin.

"I was not male as you know it, Kiondili Wae." His voice was subtle in the field-damped room, and the cottoned deafness that filled Kiondili's ears did not hide his words. "I was male/male/male, waiting to Change to male/T'se/male." He paused. "You have only two sexes, Kiondili Wae, and you do not understand others, so I will try to explain. Like you, we Ruvians are human-Mu, but we have three sexual centers in our bodies. Each center can have one of four sexual orientations. We go through metamorphosis several times in our lives until we reach a sexuality compatible with our mate's sexuality. We mate young, Kiondili Wae, and we mate for life, and Inryia and I have already waited two hundred and forty-three years to merge."

"I—changed you to something incompatible?" she said uncertainly.

"Being human, you did not understand the sexuality I needed to shift into. You Changed me to male/T'se/female." He paused, his gaze burning blacker. "It will be another one hundred ninety years before Inryia and I are compatible again."

She stared at him. "I'm sorry," she said in a low voice.

"You did not just Change me to something you understood, Kiondili Wae," he said flatly, his hidden anger flaring in golden pulses across his streaked skin. "You left the Change unfinished so that now I must be in a constant state of flux until the next cycle begins. And I cannot ask another Ruvian to adjust me out of such a flux. It would force the other into the same state."

"Gods, Waon, I'm sorry—truly, I am—it's just that you were out of control."

He raised an eyebrow. "As this," he gestured down at his body, "I will be out of control for the next fifty-four years."

"Can you—can't you precipitate a Change?"

"It would throw the cycles off permanently. Inryia and I would never merge. We would never be able to live together or make our child." He sensed Kiondili's confusion. "Think what would happen if two of me were in one room together, Wae. The fields would be uncontrollable even with heavier damps than are on here now."

Kiondili hunched her shoulders. "I'm sorry, Waon. I—I

would like to help.'' She looked at Waon, then, with her hands clenched at her sides, deliberately lowered her blocks.

The Ruvian stared at her for several minutes.

Read me, she forced the thought out.

There is no need.

She nodded abruptly, withdrawing herself behind her blocks in shaky relief.

Waon watched her. ''You have not been hurt by your Change, Kiondili Wae, except in your own thoughts. Had you asked to merge with me as Lan-Lu encouraged you to, it would have been the same as what happened in the Hub.''

She stared at him in surprise.

''Yes, the guild trains its espers the same way. But few espers merge with Ruvians. The experience is not always . . . pleasant.''

Realizing the question she had projected, Kiondili flushed, but the memory of the guild did not taste as bitter as it once had. ''May I help?''

He hesitated, then nodded.

''What do you want me to do?'' she asked quietly.

An hour later Kiondili walked out of Waon's quarters feeling slightly stunned. Working with Waon had forced her to stretch inside her own mind. She reached again with her field sense and let the strength of the damps ripple across her arms. The truth no longer burned. Now a vastness seemed to fill the corners of her mind, as if adjusting Waon's fields had expanded her own senses. She trailed a finger along the wall, then turned suddenly and, with a sob, slipped down until she was sitting on the floor. It was not until her chronometer beeped that she raised her head and stared at it blankly.

Third bell. She leapt to her feet. It was less than two hours before launch! The circuits and the beamer had been due in engines fifteen minutes before. And if Stilman was gone from the lab before she got there, the time lock would already be set and she would not be able to get in to get the beamer.

And worse, there would be no way for her to ask Stilman if he was really going to take her with him.

She ran down the corridor and dove into the free-boost chute with careless haste, hitting the redirection pads hard even for her. It took less than a minute to traverse the outpost to Stilman's triad, and she emerged from the chute just as another Mu was diving in.

"Watch it."

"Sorry."

Stilman's lab was around the corner. If he was not there, it would be her own fault. She was the one who had hinted that he would be bumped from his flight if he did not show up early. She loped down the corridor, not noticing this time the way the indirect lights played across the walls like a faint, ever-moving mural.

A future . . . She could stay with Stilman and work on hyperlight drives for the rest of her life. She did not have to chance the Lightwing. It was jury-rigged at best, and if it did not work, she would not be able to do anything about it but die in the dispersal. Her lips tightened, and she forced herself to relax.

But it was a chance to make it work.

Around the corner, a maintenance drone was already at the lab door, and Kiondili brought herself up short. Her choice might already have been made for her. She swallowed.

But she pushed past the drone and triggered the door, barely waiting the scant second for it to shimmer clearly open.

"Where the hell have you been, Wae?" Stilman snapped irritably. "I can't find some of the equipment anywhere. Did you pack the adjusters for the beamers and beam recorders?"

"Are you—am I going with you to Omisis?" she demanded.

Stilman yanked at his tunic as it caught on a box. "Of course. I can't very well send you ahead with the equipment to Foxglove while I settle the terms of my new proposal. You know nothing about setting up a lab. Which gets back to the subject. Where are the adjusters for the beamer? I can't figure out which boxes you packed them in and whether they're already on board.''

"That's probably because I didn't pack them yet," she returned. She could not hide her grin.

"Dammit, Wae, sometimes I wonder why I hired you. I can't afford to lose those components; the cost of the parts alone was half the last grant. Get that stuff packed now and get it down to the docks.''

"It's going to take me a while to pack everything that's left," she said slowly.

Stilman gave her a sharp look. "Explain, Wae, and be quick. Our ship leaves in two hours.''

"There's three more ships leaving at third quarter tonight that stop at Omisis. Why don't we take one of those instead? I must have made a mistake earlier. All of the later ships still have open berths.''

Stilman regarded her curiously. "If there's one thing I've noticed about you, Wae," he said slowly, "it's that you don't make that kind of mistake." He nodded to himself. "All right, get that beamer out and let me see it.''

She opened a cupboard and pulled out the carefully padded box. "It's still assembled," she muttered, handing the box out to Stilman. At his sharp look, she added, "I guess I thought there was time to take it apart and pack it later.''

"There's time, but not for that," Stilman ran his hand through his white hair. "Let's get going.''

"But I—" She closed her mouth. "To the docks?" she asked finally.

"To engines." He grinned in turn at her surprise. "I can't have you installing this thing at the wrong angle.''

Kiondili stared. "You know about the launch?''

He snorted. "Why else would you want to hide the beamer and adjusters in a cupboard under a sink—intact? And you would not have suggested a later flight unless there was something left undone, which you assured me this morning was not the case. Which means that there would be no reason for you to carry a package of Lightwing chips in your pocket unless you were planning on stealing a very experimental ship for a launch.''

Kiondili looked down at the telltale circuits in her hand and flushed. ''This seems to be my day to be caught out in everything,'' she muttered.

''The best laid plans of mice and Mu . . .'' Stilman said. ''Never mind,'' he said at her blank look. ''If you're planning on a launch, how did you work around the missing field fluctuation controllers?''

''Lan-Lu came up with an equation for a dispersion that will hold through the light-barrier singularity. It's like an instant of complete decomposition, then we're through, and we recombine in hyperlight.''

''Hmm. Sounds interesting. Who's on control? Backup?''

She nodded. ''We'll lock out access and run the launch through the Lightwing control room. With the new controls, it would be a first time for anyone, so we're as qualified as anyone else. Besides,'' she said wryly, ''no one else volunteered.''

The older man carefully set the beamer back in its packing material and closed the stuffing around it. ''Well, then,'' he said, tacking the box top back down, ''we'd better get going.''

''You're still coming?''

''If you really pull this off, Wae, I wouldn't miss it for the original world.''

They hurried to the free-boost chute and dove in, Kiondili finding it hard to hold herself back to Stilman's speed while they slowly floated through the tubes that laced the outpost's triads. Scant minutes later they emerged on the engines deck. There was no one in sight, and Kiondili looked around, worried.

''I was supposed to meet them here twenty-five minutes ago,'' she explained in a low voice.

Stilman glanced up and down the hall. "Was their access shut off?"

"We all still have access to the halls, just not the rooms themselves."

"If they had a bypass, they're probably already inside."

She shook her head. "They can't get in without this." She held up a tiny piece of plastic and steel that looked like a dispenser card. "They need it to bridge the bypass code in the door circuitry."

Stilman raised one of his heavy eyebrows till it looked as if his whole face were tilting and would slide off his head.

"Wae," a voice snapped, stifled but clearly angry.

Kiondili jumped, but Stilman just glanced over his shoulder as Xia slid out of a maintenance drone cubby.

"Where the hell have you been?" she demanded, her eyes tight. So, thought Kiondili, the tension was getting to Xia, too. Xia looked her up and down. "Do you know what we've been through waiting for you?"

Argon eased out of the cubby after Xia. "Is he—" He nodded toward Stilman. "—in or out?"

"He's in," Kiondili answered, surprising herself with the note of pride in her voice. "He's going to adjust the beamer for us."

Xia gave her a sharp look. "I thought you said you could do that."

Poole uncurled and dropped to the floor without a sound, following Argon and Xia to the door of the engines room. "What she can do and what she should do are two different things." He pulled a circuit board, sensors, and set of temple jacks from his marsupial pouch. "Nice to see you again, Dr. Stilman."

Stilman raised his other eyebrow. "Nice to join the party, even if I was invited at the last minute."

"Give me that bridge, Kiwi," Poole directed, kneeling by the door's panel. "Argon, take these sensors and find the circuit that unlocks access. Xia, watch the corridor map for company; we need five minutes."

Argon gave Kiondili a dark look. "I kept expecting to see a squad of chute guards every minute we waited, Wae. Ever since Effi walked in and took off with the last Lightwing, Central changed the access codes on all the doors to the engine rooms. Only the engine masters and their design crews have access now. You even have to apply through Central to go in without one of the crew as an escort. It's like an obsession."

Stilman peered over Poole's shoulder. "It's not an obsession if it's necessary." He harrumphed, then handed the beamer to Kiondili. "You've got the access circuit crossed with the timing mechanism, Poole. It's the second set of data cubes farther in that you want."

Poole glanced over his shoulder, his fur rippling as he met Stilman's gaze. "Excuse the impertinence, Dr. Stilman, but how would you know?"

Stilman chuckled. "My first posting was at an installation so poor, we only had one maintenance drone. We had to service our own equipment if we wanted it to work."

Xia hissed. "Someone's coming. The free-boost chute just flashed."

Kiondili exchanged a long look with Argon, but Poole did not look up. "I need another minute," he said over his shoulder. "Stall them."

"It's Lan-Lu," Kiondili said in relief as the Ixia's body dove lightly out of the free-boost chute and landed in the corridor. Lan-Lu strode toward them, her wrist claws half-extended and her muscles rippling across her arms.

"Close that panel access quickly or get that door open now," the predator snapped. "You tripped an access warning. Control's sending the chute guards to investigate."

"I need another minute," Poole said calmly. "Dr. Stilman, hold the bridge for three seconds while I set this trigger into the circuit. There, got it. All right, it should open— now."

The door shimmered from solid into the semishape of a large mouth before dissipating into its invisible gas as it opened, and Kiondili recognized Argon's irregular teeth as she dodged through. Argon, on her heels, grimaced at Poole's joke but grabbed the two bags the Dhirrnu tossed at him.

"The guards," Xia said urgently. She took two steps down the hall. "I'll stall them."

"No." Lan-Lu caught her arm. "You're the pilot."

"There's no time. The bypass is shutting down," Stilman said sharply, shoving the nearest assistant through the still-open door. But it was Poole, not Xia he grabbed. As he released the Dhirrnu's furry arm in sudden dismay, he could recover only enough to think clearly of the precise install-ment angle of the transmission beamer. He caught Kiondili's startled look as the bypass cut out and the door fused shut, cutting him off from the precious beamer still clutched in her arms.

Xia, flinging herself at the door, stopped short and stared at the fused and ruined area.

Stilman glanced down the corridor. "The guards," he said urgently.

"We need an accident," Lan-Lu hissed. "Trust me," she said softly to Xia.

CHAPTER 19

Kiondili, holding the beamer as if it would bite her, stared at the ruined door. Stilman's last thought echoed in her head among the images and instructions for installing it. He had wondered if she had picked up his instructions. He would be irritated if she dispersed herself like his other assistant. She laughed, but the sound was almost hysterical, and she cut herself off abruptly.

"Well," Argon said flatly. "Now what?"

Yes, now what? Kiondili realized. Xia was their pilot, and she was on the other side of that ruined door. They could not bypass another entrance to the engine room, and if the guards were already on their way, Xia would be in their custody before Poole and Argon could cook up another way to get her in.

Poole wheezed, and the other two turned to stare at him. "Ayara's eyes, Poole," Kiondili said. "What are you laughing about?"

The Dhirrnu broke into a new set of fur ripples. "Stilman," he wheezed. "Much *ti'kai* to him again, Kiondili Wae."

"Poole," she returned slowly, "this isn't a joke."

Argon snorted. "It will be if he doesn't stop wheezing and help us figure out what to do now. Otherwise, Central will lock us out of the ship before we can get the access open. Cut it out, Poole."

"Xia is the pilot." The Dhirrnu gasped as another ripple loosed itself down his stomach fur. "Stilman pushed me in here with you. I am no pilot."

He began wheezing again, and Kiondili turned away, setting the beamer down carefully on the cold floor and squatting beside it. "Yes, sure, Poole. Lots of *ti'kai* to him."

Argon spit, his spittle forming a perfect sphere in the low-grav room before the fluid hit the meta-plas of the hardening door. "So now what?"

Poole shrugged. "We launch."

Kiondili stared at Poole's calm assurance. "Launch? Just like that? We launch? We're missing our pilot, or didn't you realize that?"

The Dhirrnu just grinned, his sharp teeth hanging over the edge of his lower lip. "You have training to be a pilot, Kiondili Wae; the record of your history with the traders is clear." He acknowledged her expression with a shrug. "And I have learned a great deal by watching Xia and the other pilots on the simulator. I have even run some simulations myself. Look around. We have access. We have tools and equipment. We have the control sequences. Why not put the beamer in the Lightwing and see if it will fire up."

"And when the chute guards figure out we got through?" Argon retorted.

"We launch," Poole returned.

"A Dhirrnu pilot, one sensor, and one linker . . ." Kiondili muttered.

Argon looked around and shivered. "At least it will be warmer in the Lightwing than here on the dock. We might as well get to work."

* * *

Up in the lab triad, Tior slipped into the Lightwing control room. She was late. She had waited for Poole as long as she could, but neither he nor any of the other assistants had shown. She could only hope they were in the ship already. As it was, there was only half an hour left to load the dummy program and get the tracking stations online. She crossed to her console, then turned and traced her steps back to the door. Popping the door panel, she reached down, pulled a cable from one of the unused machines, and gave it a wrench. Then she jammed it into the panel and watched dispassionately while the shimmering door slowly coalesced into a blank shade of solidity.

Kiondili peered into the recess that held the drive's control cubes. "Argon, hand me a light."

"Just don't change the wrong cube," Argon warned from below. "I have no desire to be shot all over hyperspace because you cannot read the labels."

"I do not see what you are worrying about," she retorted, her voice muffled from inside the recess. "We have only half a pilot to get us near the light barrier in the first place. The chances of your getting dispersed are about nil."

"Don't remind me," he returned sourly. "I'm trying to think of this as an exercise in maintenance, which is probably what my new career will be when the chute guards come back and break in to get us."

She did not answer. "Take the old ones," she said, holding them out blindly behind her. "Give me the new ones."

"Yes, mighty Wae," Argon intoned sarcastically. "Here. Don't drop them."

She bit back her comment, wondering what Poole was doing in the control cabin. He had said he was programming their coordinates, but he should have been done by now. "What time is it?" she called over her shoulder. She shifted, touched the frozen wall of the cubby, and shuddered visibly.

"Fifteen minutes to blast."

She backed out of the circuit recess and turned off the

pencil free-grav beam she had used to set the cubes into the slots. "We are ready, then." She shivered again, pulling her jumper close. "I hope Poole found some of those thermal jumpers." She popped the recess cover back on, jamming her hands back in her pockets to warm them as soon as she was done. "We don't have time to test the settings. I hope Rae is as good as always, or we really will be dispersed on the boost."

"If we boost."

She followed him silently up the ladder and climbed through the narrow cabin port. "Did you forget something?" she said irritably as the man remained standing. "Like moving out of the way?"

He moved so she could get by him. "Where's Poole?"

Kiondili shrugged. "Give him a yell. We're supposed to be on transmission to Control in five minutes. We should at least let them know we're here."

"Even if we don't launch." Argon stuck his head out the port. "Poole, hurry up."

Kiondili jumped as Poole emerged from a tiny closet behind the control chairs. "I was reading the pilot's manual," he explained.

Argon snorted. "In the closet?"

"I was looking for thermal jumpers. Even for me it is cold in here. I read as I looked."

"And?" Kiondili could have bitten her tongue as Poole grinned toothily at her.

"My great-to-the-seventh grandmother was a test pilot for the Federation during the third Quadrant War," he said, his yellow eyes unblinking. "As I thought more on the idea of using the pilot's controls here, I found that those memories were passed down more clearly than I thought. It is fortunate. I did not have to read the manual from front to back."

Argon snorted, then asked, curious in spite of himself, "How much did you have to read?"

"One thousand five hundred and six pages."

Argon laughed, then faltered. "You can't be serious."

The Dhirrnu did not answer. His fur was already rippling across his chest, doubling him over.

"Of course they'll go through with it," Stilman said irritably. "I would not have gone to the trouble of setting the beamer for that piece of tin if they were going to pfitz out at the last minute."

Waon nodded silently, and Rae leaned back in her observation chair, rubbing the back of one hand as she tried to knead the tension from her fingers. "It will be good enough for a simple transmission from here to Northase," she murmured.

Lan-Lu swung around sharply, her left elbow claw flexing. "Northase? The coordinates were for Emrisen. Space curves less over that path, and the Lightwing has enough fuel for only a jump of sixty light-years."

Behind them the Moal stirred, and they fell silent.

"Elim Qu-Ibis sings topes
Elim Qu-Ibis sings light   boost to point
                                    blast beyond
Elim Qu-Ibis sings beam on, beam off."

"What do you mean, they don't have enough fuel?" Coos chittered. He projected two of his arms until they lined up with his head. "Since when did the fuel bins go down in size?"

The Moal trilled a single triple note and cowered down in her chair till she was nearly invisible against the dark cushion.

Lan-Lu tapped her wrist claws against her persona adapt. "It's not the fuel bins. We had to go to a more stable mix, and it has more mass."

Rae leaned forward with a frown. "I did not know about the topes, Lan-Lu," she said slowly. "I set the control coordinates for Northase."

Coos chittered. "As Elim pointed out, if they run out of fuel halfway through the transmission, their beam will play out like a stream running through a Martian desert."

Waon's face was expressionless, but the nerve centers near his skin pulsed slowly. Stilman ran his hand through his hair. "There's still time to let them know," he said in protest.

Rae shook her head. She motioned sharply at the observation window. "They cut off the access to Control. The dummy program activated five minutes ago. There is no way to reach them without blasting the door or cutting through one of the walls. They're on a closed circuit."

Stilman got to his feet, pacing between the chairs. "Then send someone down to engines."

"Can't do it," Coos retracted his legs as Stilman strode past. "You were there when the door was fused. It won't be released just because someone rings the com."

"The application of a field of appropriate oscillation will soften the molecular bonding of the forming crystals and re-create the partially static superfluid of a normal port," Stilman retorted testily.

Coos snorted. "Even for a scientist you're damn stuffy, Stilman."

But Stilman was not listening. He stared at the Ruvian who sat so silently behind them. "Waon?"

The Ruvian met Stilman's eyes, then nodded briefly.

Lan-Lu glanced at the chronometer and then at the launch clock in the room below. "You've got six point eight minutes, Waon." She flexed her knuckle claws and glanced at the Ruvian.

But he was already gone.

"Drive engines all go. Tracers all go. Control lines all go." Kiondili checked off the items on the list one by one as Poole and Argon read their status into the computers.

Argon nodded. "Let's check the field controllers."

"Controller One, all go. Flux backup all go . . ."

* * *

Tior ran the last test, watching the play of lights across her terminal. She belched in one of her water bags. "Come on, Kiwi," she muttered. "Give me the signal."

She switched on the com. "Lightwing," she said, "this is Control. What is your launch status?"

"Control, this is Lightwing. We're still on checkout for launch."

Tior frowned. "Who the hell is that?" she snapped into the com.

"Poole. Xia had an accident stalling the chute guards. We traded places. I'll be piloting this launch."

Tior belched again, losing water. "Control on standby." Her voice shook slightly, and she steadied it. "Take your time, Lightwing. The situation is all go here."

Kiondili switched the panel to green. "Clear status across all primary boards."

Argon nodded. "Let's go to thruster fluids."

"Core sealant all go. Coolant all go. Tope bin—" She broke off in consternation. "I hope this reading is wrong," she said slowly, "but the tope bin is definitely not a go. It reads completely full, but the ratios are all wrong. If I understand this, we haven't nearly enough fuel to reach Northase."

Argon stared at her. "We're out of fuel before we even start? Ever get the feeling we're on the Federation's joke hit list?"

Kiondili reached along the line with her field senses. She shook her head. "The bins are full. The readings are right. We have to change coordinates."

Poole frowned. "We can't change coordinates; it would take an hour to reprogram the parameters."

"And we can't use the drones to change the tope ratios; Central would read the power drain." Argon slammed his fist against the inside of the ship. "Damn it, where are you going, Wae?" He grabbed her arm as she unstrapped herself from her seat.

She shook him loose. "We don't need Central. I can work the activation fields for the drones myself."

"They'll still read that the drones are active. The power has to come from somewhere."

Wrenching at the port handle, Kiondili gritted her teeth. "Power can be shunted," she retorted. "Finish with the checkoffs. I'll get the right ratio in the bins."

She switched her boots on full so she could walk, if awkwardly, down the sides of the ship—it was faster than using the ladder—and dropped to the dock with a soft clang. The maintenance drones were lined up like chute guards, except their blocky shapes made them look more like trolls. Kiondili glanced around. The maintenance unit—that ought to do it. It would look like a malfunction for it to kick on. And she could channel the field surges back into the unit. The drones should not even show up in Central's holotank.

She set the ratios on the engine room tanks to flood the Lightwing bins with the right isotopes, then hurriedly turned on a drone and shunted its telltale fields back through the maintenance unit. The drone, senseless, purred as it shambled across the dock to the fuel bins. She let it work, flooding a new mixture into the bins on the ship, bleeding off excess fuel, concentrating on stray lines of power. She felt the expanse of her mind and wondered if she could control two drones.

She turned her E-damp down another notch and turned on another drone, ignoring the background static that surged against her senses. Then she froze. Something was happening to the door as she watched. Ayara's eyes—the chute guards . . . Her breath caught in her throat. She watched, frozen, stubbornly urging the drones to hurry as the doors dissolved into a shimmering white.

The door cleared abruptly as if water had suddenly washed over it, and Kiondili clenched her hands. The drones had another five or six minutes to go to change the fuel mixture completely, and Kiondili needed another half minute beyond that to reach the comparative safety of the Lightwing cabin.

And then the door shimmered open and a dark figure stepped inside, and Kiondili, poised to run, stared.

"Waon?" She turned and clutched frantically at the drones' fields as they came near to crossing from her inattention. They ground to a stop.

The Ruvian glanced at the drones. "Your coordinates are for Northase or Emrisen?"

"Northase," she answered shortly.

He crossed to the tope bins. "Central knows what is happening. You do not have time to fill the bins yourself." He read the dial settings, tapping his finger absently on one of the knobs. "You are mixing the topes in the bins *and* changing coordinates?"

She shook her head. "We've already set the jump. We have to go to Northase now. We can wait for the topes."

"Mixing the topes will add stress to the flux."

"I can handle the stress," she said quietly.

"So." He nodded briefly. He set his temple jacks, then ran his hands at blinding speed over the dials, resetting the bins to an even tighter mixture. The hum of the drones increased in pitch and frequency.

Kiondili struggled with the sudden surge of power in the drone lines. Bars of energy whipped in the air before her as she visualized the drones' directions. Even the simple fields of the maintenance programs appeared as auras around each machine. She almost staggered as Waon pointed at the Lightwing's still-open port.

"Go," he ordered simply.

"The topes?"

"I will finish."

She waited no longer. With her boots on half strength, the soles rattled as she hauled herself up on the wing and loped awkwardly up the side of the ship.

Argon dragged her inside and locked the port.

"Just a minute, gas brain." She looked back. Waon was directing the drones out of the Lightwing's exhaust path. He had put a surge on the drones deliberately, she realized, to give her a preview of what the transmission fields would be like. "Thanks, Waon," she whispered.

Likewise, Kiondili Wae.

She dropped into the launch chair while the port's vacuum seal sucked itself shut.

"Primaries are ready to go," Argon snapped. He flicked on his com. "Control, this is *Lightwing VII*. We are sealed and ready for initial launch."

Poole checked the tope meter and frowned, his fur gathering into small ridges over his eyes. "We're already getting stress in the bins, Kiwi," he warned.

Kiondili strapped herself in. "I'll handle it, Poole." She jammed her temple jacks on and reached along the lines of the sensors.

"*Lightwing*, this is Control. You have launch status." Tior's voice was urgent. "And if you're going to launch, do it now. Central's tracing your call."

Poole brought the primaries up to boost. "Take us out with another ship so we don't catch so much attention. That should get us a couple minutes."

"That's a go if you blast in one point six minutes."

"Can do."

"See you in the brig when you get back," Tior returned. "This is Control, on launch in fifty seconds at the mark."

Kiondili forcibly relaxed her fingers in the sensors.

"We have standby tracking on Stations Two, Three, and Four," Tior reported, her voice tinny and strained. "Tracking on Station One will kick in after boost."

"Transmission frequency?"

"HC2, red sigma, one point four five nine."

"Frequency set. We'll open transmission at point eight light."

"Roger that. We have launch in twenty seconds."

"Open the bay," Poole ordered Argon.

Argon flicked on his holotank. "Launch chute clear. I've set the launch path parallel to the drones."

"Launch in fifteen seconds," Tior reported.

"Sure you can handle the topes, Mu?" Argon questioned Kiondili sharply.

"You could still make it out the port and maybe even out of engines before the blast," she suggested nastily.

"I'd rather be dispersed than irradiated," he retorted.

"Then shut up. We have launch in three seconds."

The power blast was unfelt by Argon and Poole. Only Kiondili sensed the backthrust of energy that dissolved in the afterfield and clogged her senses as she slipped her control over the ship's lines. Darting out into the clump of drones, the ship ignored the nagging trace that followed them from the docks. The outpost's Central Control banks had found them and wanted them back.

"Cut over to Line Fifty-eight," she muttered as Argon snapped across comlinks to the channel. "Now Twelve. Jump back to Two, then cut off for five seconds." She waited the scant ticks and then breathed a sigh of relief. "Call Control in on two point six, and we should be set."

"Since when can you transmit on a half com?" Argon demanded as he obeyed.

"We're using two links over drones to transmit half signals. The Lightwing picks them up, combines them, and gives us the whole signal. It will take Central another couple minutes to figure it out. By then we'll be out of range."

"Clever." The Dhirrnu glanced at his flashscreen. "We're accelerating beyond the asteroids—"

"Lightwing," Tior's voice cut in, "this is control. The drones are falling away. You are clear for blast. What's your status?"

"We have blast in ten seconds," Poole returned calmly. "We estimate light in one minute."

Kiondili's hands were tense. The tendrils of the engines were feeding up her arms and into her brain, and the energies began to tickle her mind.

"Point six light. Point eight two light. Go, Kiwi." Poole's voice was intense. "Point nine five light. Keep the pressure on."

"Control the topes, Mu," Argon snarled as a green light went into the red.

Kiondili did not answer. Her mind was locked into the twisted threads of energy that flared and burned in the engines. Breathe, relax. Breathe, control. Breathe and feel. She was one with the engines, one with the ship. Its skin was hers, and its fields were a shirt that enclosed her with invisible paleness. The topes jumped, gained energy, stabilized, and then blasted away. Point nine eight light. Point nine nine light. Did the tracking stations read them clearly? A tope flared, and she damped it hard. *Think* Northase. Five gravity wells and countless dust, but the path was curved and clear. Empty lanes. Empty space. Watch the topes . . . Energy built like pressure behind a dam. Her body glowed. Energy, not matter. The ship surged. Speed—not slowness, not space. The beamer caught, and—

There was a flash, a burning flare, a last burst of direction, and then inertia caught and hurtled them beyond the boundaries of light.

"They've gone light!" Tior leapt to her feet, losing water across the flashscreen. She flushed, glancing over her shoulder at the blank observation window—she could not see the researchers behind it—and sat back down abruptly. She stared at the screens. "Tracking Station One reports they're on the beam," she muttered. "Tracking Stations Two and Three kicking in now . . . Beam integrity is ninety-eight percent and holding," she crowed. "Oh, shits—"

She lunged across her panel and threw a black switch down. The dummy program had been terminated. Her fingers raced over the bank of keys. She had to cut herself off from Lightwing or Central would take control away. She ejected the data cubes from the control slots and threw them in the bin under the holotank. The white flare at the edges of the jammed door told her that she had only a few minutes before security melted the door open. "The tracking stations—" She scanned and dumped entire blocks of memory. The Lightwing had four minutes left before sublight recombination, and Central could read their status through the stations. "One is down." She belched. "Two and Four are down. Dammit, where's Three?"

Outside the control room, Dugan, the Corson director, waited impassively while the chute guards took turns melting the door. Had every H'Mu and alien in the outpost gone crazy? Three ships in three days? And he had already contracted that last Lightwing to another group of researchers. "You—" He caught a guard, ignoring the radiant heat from the guard's suit. "Get Stilman and the others in here."

He turned irritably back to the door. It would take another two or three minutes to burn through that fusing. The Ruvian, Waon, could have done it in seconds if he had been predisposed to help.

Inside the control room Tior clenched her hands and sat, the holotank dying into blankness before her. One point six minutes to the sublight drop, she told herself.

As if a melting point had suddenly been reached, the off-white dullness of the door grew brighter, and then a slow wave washed over the portal and left it shimmering.

"See you in the brig," Tior whispered to the blank screens.

"Get those control lines shut down," Dugan snapped at the chute guards who had burst through the door in front of him. "Get that Mu away from the panels and trace that com." One of the guards obediently snagged Tior and thrust her away from the console, slamming her against the wall so that she spit fluid across its smooth surface. She wiped her mouth silently.

"Is that communications line open yet?" Dugan paced the room, stopping in front of Tior and glaring at her until she shivered.

"Just a minute, sir. They've got it rerouted through some drones. We'll have normal channels opened in a few seconds and hyperlight radio back in a minute."

Tior bit her tongue. How long before Poole tried to contact

Control again? They should have dropped out of hyperlight seconds before, right onto the Northase docks.

"Nice day cycle for a launch, eh, Dugan?" Stilman beamed at the director as he was herded with the other scientists into the control room.

"Go to hell, Stilman." He turned to Rae. "And don't look so smug, Rae. We caught your assistant down at the door to engines, trying to make a bypass. And this one," he snarled, pointing at Tior, "ties up one-tenth the compute power of the entire outpost." His voice dropped menacingly. "And then Central informs me that the last Lightwing left the outpost ten minutes ago and blasted into nothing."

Stilman frowned reflectively, and Coos projected one of his arms to scratch his face.

"I must disagree," Stilman protested mildly. "That the Lightwing disintegrated is obvious, but that it has dispersed into nothing is an unsupported projection."

"I'll have your story in a minute, Stilman. Siln, for God's sake, stop tapping your fingers together. It's driving me nuts."

It was a burning that blinded every cell. A wash of fiery acid that clung to every synapse and scalded every coalescing thought. And then her soul was seared back into reality, and matter grabbed her back from light. Circuits flared and died; panels blazed and drowned in the antifire foam that welled up from the meta-plas banks. Poole's fur rippled, and Argon's heart began to beat hard. Kiondili Wae sat motionless, the energies of the ship still racing through her body and mind until the gravity brake took hold and slammed them to a near halt at point one lightspeed.

"Status," Poole croaked.

Argon, wild-eyed, shook himself and reached an unsteady hand toward the control panel. "All main systems go," he said a second later as he read the flickering lines of data. "There's a breach in the inner wall of the emergency tope bin, but it's not critical yet. Secondaries are gone. Sublight engines are still shaking.''

Poole nodded. ''We're on a direct float line to Northase.''

Argon paused, reading a new screen with a shake of his head. ''Recombination efficiency was worse than lousy. We lost almost forty percent of our heat shielding and a third of memory where one of the data banks fried on the transference. The ship's hull mass is down by twenty percent.''

''Stop complaining,'' Kiondili said in a hoarse voice. ''The recorders caught it all, and you lived to tell of it. Raise Northase so we can pass the word.''

''Goddamn,'' Poole said. ''We made it.'' His stomach, then his chest, rippled. He wheezed, grinning, and flicked the comlines on. ''Northase docks, this is the Lightwing, Q3-2-10-HMU Experimental, requesting emergency service. Please have Federation authorities on standby.''

A flashscreen crackled, and Rae glanced at her watch. Stilman, who caught her look, fumbled his own watch out from under his scarlet sleeve and tried to catch the director's attention. ''Dugan,'' he broke in, ''you might want to wait a few moments before you send them to sentencing.''

Dugan ignored him. ''Get Central on the tank.''

''Can't, sir. Priority message coming through. Federation authorities.''

''What the hell do they want?''

''It's urgent, sir.''

''Well, pipe it through this link, then, and get that trace started on the Lightwing.''

Lan-Lu caught his shoulder with her wrist claws. ''Don't waste your time,'' she hissed. ''The Lightwing—''

Dugan rounded on her. ''Back off, Lan-Lu.'' The Ixia froze, then forced her claws to retract. Dugan punched the button viciously on the com. ''This is Dugan,'' he snapped.

''Northase port authorities request authorization for maintenance bill for—''

"What maintenance bill?" Dugan snapped. "We have no programs out at Northase."

"—Q3-2-10-HMU for forty-three thousand two hundred eight-nine credits."

"Get these bill collectors offline and get Central back on. I'll deal with Northase later," Dugan said in a too-calm voice, his orange-rimmed eyes almost black against the flaring yellow of his irises.

"But sir," one of the chute guards said hesitantly, "Q3-2-10-HMU is the Li—"

"—for shield and beamer repairs and replacement data bank," the message continued. "Personnel transmission as follows."

"I don't care what Q3-2-10 is," Dugan snapped coldly. "Trace that Lightwing. Get that idiot offline. Respond tomorrow day cycle if you have to."

But Waon thrust his hand between the chute guard's fingers and the comline control. The guard stepped involuntarily back.

"Keep the lines open," Waon said.

"Shut up, all of you," Stilman yelled. "They're coming through."

"Repeat, transmission efficiency ninety-six point four-one percent. Sublight recombination—"

Dugan froze.

"—successful, though we lost almost half the shielding, fried the beamer, and toasted a third of the data banks along with the auxiliary control. Hyperlight transmission time: eight point one minutes."

Dugan stared at the com.

"Repeat, hyperlight transmission eight minutes. Calculated transmission rate: seven point five light-years per minute."

"We did it!" Stilman yelled. He grabbed Lan-Lu and swung the startled Ixia around, kicking Coos across the floor. The Robul slammed into one of the consoles. Dugan, regarding the comlink as if it would bite like Lan-Lu, did not notice when Coos clamped onto his leg to help himself up.

"—still need about forty-four thousand credits, and we would appreciate it if you would send them as fast as possible." Kiondili's voice, having replaced Poole's at the com, went almost unheard in the din. "Northase already wants us out of here. Poole got a hold of some radioactive tracing dye and painted Argon's drawers, so he glows when he walks."

"Wire the credits," Dugan commanded. "Wire them—now!"

The guard jammed the temple jacks on and flashed the message out of the comlink.

Dugan looked at Stilman, then back at the com. "And add this," he said to the guard. "For the theft of an experimental ship, for the break-in at engines and Control, and for the unauthorized use of excessive compute power, all those involved in this launch are docked half pay for a year and are on probation for the next two years." Someone thumped him on the shoulder, and he brushed them off absently. "Any infringements of any regulations by any of those involved in this fiasco will result in being spaced without a suit." He paused as he caught Waon's golden eye. "Suspensions are in effect immediately, and—" He hesitated and finally added softly, "Congratulations."

Siln, at the back of the room, tapped her long silicon fingers together and smiled.

EPILOGUE

Six hours after the maintenance drones finished with the ship, a Federation tug pulled the Lightwing rather ignominiously from the maintenance and landing docks to the repair docks. The slender ship, looking like a burned and pocked survivor of a battle, hung at the edge of a narrow repair cradle. The ship's engines were stilled—until its shielding was replaced, the Lightwing could not fire up again. The risk of it spewing radiation was too great.

Inside the engine housing, the beamer was a broken lump. Cracked and twisted by the stresses of the blast fields, it was as dead as debris from a full-impact crash. Most of its data cubes were melted, and several banks below the auxiliary console were fried, as well. On the outside of the ship, the spiral beam of the primary had worn a distinct pattern into the once gleaming sides of the vessel, and it seemed as if the ship itself had been twisted by the heat of a searing flame.

Kiondili shut down her sensors as the repair cradle accepted the nose of the ship. She did not need them to tell her that the tug's tractor beam had been shut off. Her own senses, abused by the recombination, were too acutely raw to miss that. Her hands were shaking, too, and she flexed her weary fingers until the cramping left them enough for her to take the temple jacks from her head without fumbling.

"I've linked us with the repair drones," Argon reported. "So if Dugan's credit chit is worth anything, in four days we should be ready for our ride back to Corson."

Kiondili winced at the sound of his voice and jacked her persona-damp up as high as possible. "Much as the port authorities want us out of here quickly"—she shot an exasperated look at Poole—"we can't leave for Corson until we have approval from the Federation."

"And they," Poole said, with a frowning ripple of fur across his forehead, "have not yet found the time to review our logs. According to the assistant to the underling to the subordinate clerk of the Federation representative's office—" He paused for breath. "—they will schedule a review of our logs as soon as we fill out the appropriate forms and file them with Central Control. A task which will take longer than normal, since a third of our data banks are fried, and we will have to recreate much of the data they want filed."

Kiondili twisted in her chair to look at him. "Surely we can get some of that from the tracking stations?"

"Some. Corson would have more, but Tior shut down the control consoles when Dugan's men cut into the control room."

Argon snorted. "We're heroes, and we're getting the hero's welcome we've always wanted. Our assigned bunks are in the lowest-status housing on the other side of this asteroid, we've been appropriately greeted by the lowest-status gofer in the Federation offices—a H'Mu who probably has to ask permission to use the dispenser for water—and we've been showered with the gifts befitting heros of our time: flashbook forms."

Kiondili, looking at the list of information they would have to fill in by hand, cast him a sour look. "At least your boss hasn't gotten on your case yet about the work you would be doing were you not lounging in your luxury accommodations on the resort asteroid of Northase.''

Poole raised one of his eyebrows. "Stilman's last com message?''

She nodded shortly. "He already wants to know when he can expect the lab crates back at Corson—as if I should already be tracing those shipments from here—and can I reconstruct the beamer enough to demonstrate it to the H'Mu Guardian, and did I remember to run a sequencer during the blast, and what did I pack his favorite tunics in, and when can I get a copy of the beamer log back to Corson? Hells, but he's already moved back into the lab and patched a pulse-comlink through to the Northase data banks—there's no way I can ignore him now.''

Argon chuckled nastily, and she rounded on him. "It's all fine for you," she snapped, rubbing her aching temples. "No one cares if you work across the com, and with that rad-paint making your shorts glow like that, no one here will want to get close to you, either.'' She chuckled slyly at his instinctive gesture to cover his nether region.

Poole rippled his stomach fur. "Then we will go waste our time meeting with the underling to the assistant to the gofer to the Federation representative," he told her as Argon opened the hatch. "It will easily take a few hours, but it will give you time to answer Stilman's queries.'' He grinned at her, his sharp, carnivorous teeth gleaming.

She nodded sourly, and they swung out. As Poole's head disappeared below the hatch, the door swung shut again, resealing the ship. Kiondili's lips twitched in amusement. She jammed her temple jacks back on and leaned over, tapping her console quickly. Within seconds, her holotank was powered up and the two figures it reflected were sharp and clear. Kiondili leaned back and grinned. She flicked a command to the console. In the holotank, a tiny rectangular box on Poole's persona-adapt lit up. Yes, she thought with satisfaction, her holographic generator was on, and he had not noticed it. Poole's back shifted colors in the tank, then expanded suddenly sideways in the artificial field. Should she turn his visual projection into an apple? Or maybe a Denusian lime? Wait—what about a peach? A nice, soft, Terran peach for a Dhirrnu's sharp carnivorous teeth . . .

Behind Poole, some of the dock workers were staring at the giant, peach-colored fruit that moved unconcernedly beside Argon on its furry legs. Argon turned a puzzled look at his companion, then, as his eyes caught the projection superimposed on Poole's back, he smothered a laugh that turned into a choking sound. Let Poole try to earn *ti'kai* at Northase after this, Kiondili thought smugly. She wondered if he would notice before they got to the Federation clerk's office. With a grin, she turned to Stilman's list of computations. In the holotank, the last view of Poole was that of a giant peach rolling into a free-boost shute.

About the Author

Tara K. Harper lives in Northwest Oregon. She graduated from the University of Oregon in 1983 with a Bachelor of Science. After serving an internship on a newspaper, she worked several years as technical editor for a Fortune-500 company in the electronics and computer test-and-measurement field. Currently, she works as a documentation specialist in the state-of-the-art microwave (that is, electronics, communications, and wafers—not kitchen appliances) testing industry. Continuing with her education, Tara K. Harper takes classes in both sciences and arts. To keep up with the advances in genetics, biophysics, physics, and space exploration, she reads constantly and discusses current and futuristic ideas as often as possible with peers and friends in research-and-development fields. When asked where she gets the inspiration for her books, she admits to tapping her nightmares for ideas. Her hobbies include camping, hiking, white-water rafting, costume design, music, and martial arts.

Science Fiction

at its best
from
Tara K. Harper